I0618653

HARMONY

Laurie Winter

www.BOROUGHSPUBLISHINGGROUP.com

PUBLISHER'S NOTE: This is a work of fiction. Names, characters, places and incidents either are the product of the author's imagination or are used fictitiously. Any resemblance to actual events, locales, business establishments or persons, living or dead, is coincidental. Boroughs Publishing Group does not have any control over and does not assume responsibility for author or third-party websites, blogs or critiques or their content.

HARMONY
Copyright © 2019 Laurie Winter

All rights reserved. Unless specifically noted, no part of this publication may be reproduced, scanned, stored in a retrieval system or transmitted in any form or by any means, electronic, mechanical, photocopying, recording, or otherwise, known or hereinafter invented, without the express written permission of Boroughs Publishing Group. The scanning, uploading and distribution of this book via the Internet or by any other means without the permission of Boroughs Publishing Group is illegal and punishable by law. Participation in the piracy of copyrighted materials violates the author's rights.

ISBN 978-1-948029-75-9

To my family—the ones who fill my life with love

ACKNOWLEDGMENTS

A huge thank you to Boroughs Publishing and my editor Adi for helping give a voice to Jordan and Eli's love story. Thanks to my mom, Sharon, who was one of my early readers and provided helpful feedback. Lester's Place is dedicated to you.

Thank you Tim and Liza Korry for your guidance while writing the original lyrics found in *Harmony*.

Thank you to Paul and Jenna, my family at home who often is neglected while I'm writing. I appreciate you allowing me to live part-time in my fantasy worlds!

And finally a shout out to Taylor Swift, Brett Eldridge, and Dustin Lynch, whose music served as inspiration for the story.

HARMONY

Chapter One

"Five minutes, Ms. Spencer." The voice of Jordan's concert producer, who was tucked away in the control booth, sounded through her earpiece.

Jordan adjusted the clip over her ear until it felt secure. "Got it," she said into the tiny microphone hovering by her mouth.

Five more minutes. She needed to pull herself together and get in position. Soon, the spotlights would power on, her band would begin to play the first song in the set, and the backup dancers would follow her onto the stage.

It had been her routine for the last four months. Night after night, she'd sung the same songs, heard the same shouts coming from the crowd, and felt the same rush.

She'd made it to the final concert of her tour, and tonight, she wanted to celebrate by skipping all the theatrics and singing straight from the heart, with only an acoustic guitar for backup.

"Like that's going to happen," Jordan mumbled to herself as she pulled on her tiny gold-sequined top. Every concert tour, her wardrobe continued to shrink. Next tour, she'd only have a Band-Aid-sized patch of fabric covering her chest.

"What?" Lacy muttered. Most of her attention was directed at the electronic tablet she had clutched in her hand. "I'm messaging the sound guy to make sure he remembers to turn down the volume of the bass guitar for the third song in the second set."

Jordan wouldn't be surprised if someday her dear sister would wake up with that device fused to her hand. "Where are we again?"

Lacy looked up and sighed. "Milwaukee. Like in, 'You're looking good tonight, Milwaukee. Go Bucks. Go Brewers. Go Packers.'" She tucked her tablet under her arm and waved her hands, shaking pretend pom poms. "You're in Wisconsin, Jordan."

"Oh, that's right." Now she remembered. For lunch, a local restaurant had catered in brats and fried cheese curds—staples of a

Wisconsin diet. They were yummy but she'd eaten only a little. As her dietitian had drilled into her, that kind of food was very bad for her waistline.

Her cell, which she'd placed on the makeup table under a lighted mirror, gave a chirp. *Don't you dare look.*

Cole, her personal bodyguard, entered the dressing room. "You don't have time to text back your jerk of an ex. You need to get to the stage. Now." He resembled a professional wrestler: tall, wide, and usually scowling. On the job, he was all business. But his gruffness disguised a big, caring heart. Cole Dufour was one of Jordan's best friends.

After a few seconds of indecision, curiosity won. Jordan picked up her phone. Trust Cole to know it was Henry texting. His message was short and straight to the point.

...You're crazy. Soon the whole world will know just how crazy you are.

Wait. Had Henry just called her *crazy*? She read the text again.

Anger simmered. Hadn't he been the one who'd pushed her to act up for media attention? All the nights he'd kept her out way too late at his favorite nightclub ordering drinks until she couldn't see straight would never have happened if it weren't for him. "I'm *not* crazy." She launched her cell across the room. Too late, she noticed it sailed straight at Cole's head.

Using his highly tuned military reflexes, Cole ducked out of the line of fire.

Her phone hit the wall with a thud before falling onto the tile ground. The poor thing didn't stand a chance. The sound of cracking glass made her cringe. That was the third phone she'd broken that month.

"Not again." Lacy grasped the phone in between two fingers and picked it up. "Why?"

Heat flooded Jordan's body. Her vision blurred. Not a panic attack. Not now. She placed the palms of her hands over her eyes. The slight pressure helped ease the sharp pain in her forehead.

"Henry is nothing," Lacy said. "He's just another name at the bottom of your list of ex-boyfriends."

Why did she always pick men she knew would break her heart? Each one of her relationships had been a media circus that ended in disaster. *Kind of hard to get to know someone when you're stalked by cameras every time you step outside.*

Henry's game had been different from the start. She should have caught on earlier that he'd only been interested in the publicity of dating Jordan Spencer, not the woman herself.

"Good riddance." Lacy gingerly set the phone back on the makeup table. "I'll have another phone brought here before the end of the concert. Now, shake it off, girl. You have a show to do."

Jordan pictured the last time she'd been with Henry. They'd been in Paris, where he'd been shooting a movie. He'd told her he loved her. And she'd been stupid enough to believe him.

"Sixty seconds." The voice in her earpiece now sounded perturbed.

"We need to get in position, Jordan." Cole pulled at her arm. "Don't waste another second on that loser." He stopped walking long enough to put a finger under her chin and lift her head so his gaze met hers. "You are not crazy. You hear me?"

Jordan nodded her head. She couldn't talk. What she needed to do was sit and collect her emotions, which were now scattered on the floor like a ripped bag of marbles. "Tell them to hold on. Give me a few more minutes—"

Lacy didn't let her finish her sentence. "Don't forget that they changed the order of songs in the second set. 'Falling for You' comes first, followed by 'My Love Can.' Oh… and there's a little girl in the front row in a wheelchair. Make a point of paying special attention to her. She'll be holding a pink sign with a glitter heart."

As they continued down the hall, Jordan struggled to breathe. Her chest squeezed until her lungs refused to fill with air. The stage came into view. Her band was set. The noise from the crowd rumbled like thunder from an approaching storm.

A lady from wardrobe came over to smooth out her skirt. "You look divine, Ms. Spencer. Knock 'em dead."

I can't sing. I can't even breathe.

Over the past months, Jordan's nerves had been coiling tighter and tighter. Standing at the side of the stage, she felt a small snap of release.

She needed to calm down, so she closed her eyes and pictured a peaceful, country scene. Kids playing on green grass, their laughter carried with the breeze. A beautiful farmhouse sat behind them. A man stood on the front porch, waving at her to come join him. Jordan could almost feel the warmth of sunshine on her face.

A small smile formed on her lips. After this concert, she planned on escaping the madness of her life for a few weeks. She hoped a small break would be enough to rid her body of the toxic stress and anxiety currently running through her veins.

Jim, her guitarist, began the set with the strumming of the opening cords.

"Have fun out there," Lacy said over the sound of the music. She gave Jordan a kiss on the cheek before lightly pushing her forward. "Last one. You got this."

The stage was lit by a few spotlights that shone on her band. Using the available darkness as cover, Jordan walked to the center of the stage and waited. On cue, they turned the spotlights onto her. The sudden bright light caused Jordan temporarily blindness. She blinked a few times to help her eyes adjust.

First, she smiled at the crowd, and then she opened her mouth and did what she did best—sing. The opening song, "Hot Summer," was one of her favorites. She'd written it during a vacation in St. Thomas, which had ended up as an escape to mend another broken heart.

At the halfway point in the concert, she started feeling dizzy. The crowd before her seemed to move like a boat rocking over big waves. Her stomach lurched. No way would she throw up on stage. She imagined what those photographs would look like on the internet tabloid sites.

During a long electric guitar solo, she stepped offstage to close her eyes and refocus. Everything spun around her. The sounds of music and screaming all blended together into a high-pitched hum.

"Jordan, are you okay?" Lacy stood next to her, a hand resting on the small of her back.

She brushed away her concern. "I'm fine. Got mixed up and thought it was time for a costume change." No use upsetting her sister when there wasn't anything she could do to help.

"You look like you're going to be sick." Lacy's eyes widened, and she took a step back.

"I'm fine." Jordan straightened her back. That's what she'd keep telling herself until one day it would really be true. "Tell Wardrobe to double-check the straps on the red dress. They felt loose last night, and I don't want anything flying out while I'm dancing on stage."

After taking a few deep breaths, she reclaimed her spot on center stage. One of the road crew handed her an acoustic guitar, and she sat on a stool placed behind her. Calm blanketed her as she wrapped her fingers around the neck of her guitar.

"I wrote 'Home' when I was thirteen years old. It was my first song, and that day, I finally knew my purpose in life was to share my vision of a world full of love and potential through country music."

Cheers went up from the crowd.

Jordan strummed the beginning chord. The melody came to her without thinking, and she got lost in the lyrics. After the last note faded from her lips, the crowd exploded with applause. Which proved to her that the audience didn't need a bunch of smoke and laser lights. They had come to see her and hear her true voice. The validation boosted her too-often unsteady confidence.

A few songs later she handed her guitar to one of the stagehands and exited the stage. Behind her, the noise of the crowd lowered from loud cheers to an eager buzz as they began to file out of the amphitheater.

The show was finally over. She'd finished the final concert of her tour. But at what cost? Every day her anxiety grew, not unlike a rumor in a tabloid.

Jordan returned to her dressing room to change back into jeans and a T-shirt. Her wide array of tour outfits hung neatly on the rack. Soon, they'd be rolled onto a truck and taken back to some warehouse in Nashville, never to be seen or worn by her again.

Citing a headache, she insisted on being left alone in her dressing room. When she finally exited, the only people left in the amphitheater were the cleaning staff and her road crew, who were tirelessly working to tear down the set. Jordan found a quiet, out-of-the-way corner, and watched them work.

"That was a great show." Lacy approached with a bottle of water in her outstretched hand. "I tear up every time you sing 'Home.'"

Jordan took the water bottle and pulled a long drink. Her throat rejoiced from the cool moisture. "I was thinking about how much things have changed. What I wouldn't give to sing at a local rinky-dink fair for a dozen people, like when Phil discovered me. Back then, all I wanted was to write music and sing. All this... is too much." Around her, bangs and shouts sounded from the stage crew. "Everything in my life is spinning out of control."

"So, this hideaway will be perfect," Lacy said. "Henry's not in the picture anymore. No one will even know you've snuck away."

"You sure this is going to work? What if someone recognizes me? Once my cover is blown, I'll be in the middle of a paparazzi storm again. And then there's the record label. They want to start on the next album ASAP."

"Don't worry about your record label or the media. Phil and I will handle all that. The house I rented for you in Door County is very private and rented under the name Ann Dufour. Cole's excited you're using his last name for your cover."

Jordan smirked. "I don't think I'm the Spencer sister he wants to give his last name to."

A crimson blush colored Lacy's cheeks. "Stop teasing. Both of us know Cole will never get married." She took a deep breath. "Plus, we work together, and I know he doesn't see me as anything other than a good friend."

True, Cole had sworn off commitment and marriage, but Jordan knew for a fact that his feelings for Lacy were more significant than friendly. Someday, they'd stop ignoring the obvious and get together. Until then, Jordan would keep her opinions about their love lives to herself.

"What about my hair?" Jordan ran her fingers through her long, blonde hair—her pride and joy.

"Cole went out to buy the hair dye and is waiting for us back in your dressing room. We'll change your appearance just enough so you can sneak out of here unrecognized. Then it's a couple hours' drive up north. The house is all stocked."

Honestly, the thought of spending two weeks alone, hiding out in northern Wisconsin was unsettling. Her life was so busy, and so full of people who *always* wanted something from her. But she knew she needed this break, or she was going to break.

"I want to cut my hair, too." She was a natural brunette, but hadn't seen that color in the mirror in years. Enrique, her personal hairstylist, didn't let her roots show a hint of brown.

"You sure? Enrique's going to have a fit when he finds out."

"I'm sure. But tell Cole he's not getting near my hair with a pair of scissors. While I trust him to guard my life, I don't think he learned cosmetology in the Marines." Wearing a wide smile, Jordan stood. "If I'm going to jump off this hot plate, I need a clean escape. All the craziness surrounding Jordan Spencer has to stay away. Even if it's only for two weeks. I can't risk anyone finding out who I really am."

***

Three hours later, Jordan sat in the driver's seat of her rental car. Lacy's plan had worked. Dressed in shorts and a baggy T-shirt, and sporting a short, brunette hairstyle, Jordan had walked out to the car without being recognized. As she drove away, pounds of stress lifted off her shoulders.

Now she was driving along I-43 on her way up to Door County, Wisconsin. Her GPS told her she had about two more hours to her destination. The house Lacy had rented was in a small town called Bailey's Harbor, situated on Kangaroo Lake.

Her eyes strained to stay focused on the dark road. The rain had started as a light pitter patter on the windshield, but now came down like it was propelled from a fire hose. She lifted her foot off the accelerator, coasting along while several big rigs zipped by her. Their spray made a bad situation worse.

Her hands gripped the steering wheel. Sweat soaked the back of her shirt. All the extra adrenaline coursing through her helped keep her tired body on high alert. Jordan's driving skills were rusty, being that she hadn't sat in the driver's seat of a car for the entire four months of her tour.

A loud *ding ding* sounded, causing her heart and stomach to lurch.

Shoot. The gas gauge was hovering on E. She had to find a gas station soon, and this midnight rainstorm was not helping.

A sign for an exit came into view. There was a gas station advertised. Hopefully it was still open.

The station was located farther away than she expected. Once she arrived, she parked by a pump, sat in the car, and prayed the rain would slow down for just five minutes. No such luck. With a speed known only to superheroes, she darted inside to pay with cash. The station attendant might have looked at her like she was crazy for being out this late in a storm, but she didn't seem to recognize Jordan as anyone famous.

Giddy at her success, she ran to the car and filled the tank.

Back to sitting in the safety of her car, her hair dripping fat water droplets onto her thighs, she turned out of the gas station lot as a bolt of lightning lit up the sky. For a second, the landscape was bathed in a strange, bright glow.

She had to find the way back to the freeway. Peace and relaxation waited for her in Bailey's Harbor.

But the entrance sign to the freeway seemed to have disappeared—maybe blown away by the strong wind. Either that or she'd taken a wrong turn. If I-43 didn't materialize in the next mile, she'd turn around and head the other direction.

Another flash of lightning broke through the darkness, immediately followed by a crack of thunder. *What did I get myself into?*

She mentally kicked herself for not waiting until morning to leave, like Cole and Lacy had suggested.

Another mile passed with no freeway entrance. She pulled off onto the shoulder of the road before making a U-turn. Everything around her was bathed in darkness, until lightning acted like a lighthouse, guiding her along, one flash at a time.

Jordan was intensely focused on the road, and she startled when she saw several pairs of large eyes shining in the headlight beams. Three cows stood in the middle of the road. Before her she could think what to do, she slammed on her brakes skidding on the wet surface. She screamed as the car whipped around and around while holding on to the steering wheel for dear life. After what seemed like an eternity, the car tipped before finally coming to a shuddering stop.

When she touched her forehead, she felt the warm, sticky texture of blood. She couldn't tell up from down. Everything continued to spin even though the car had stopped. Jordan tried the door handle, but the door wouldn't budge. Weariness took over and she lost the battle with the creeping darkness.

***

Eli Hintz hated storms. They always meant more work. He already had enough to do without adding on. Shrugging on a jacket, he left the comfort of his house and headed out into the rain. The wind whipped through the passage between the old farmhouse and the livestock barn. He pressed his hand to the top of his head, preventing his baseball cap from blowing away.

He hadn't made it two steps inside the barn when he noticed the door on the other side had blown wide open. As the wind continued its barrage, the incessant banging of the door against the wall echoed through the barn. Although all the calves were still inside their pens, there were only three heifers left congregating in the corner of the paddock. Where were the other thirty? Looking at the open barn door, his stomach dropped.

Eli sent up a quick prayer hoping that they were still in the enclosed field. Wrangling them back inside would be a chore, but not as bad as if they were running wild all over the county.

Walking through the barn and back outside, he shielded his face from the pelting rain. Up ahead, he saw part of the fencing had been blown over.

He yelled back at Mother Nature for her sick sense of humor. This was going to be a long night.

Time to call in some backup. He strode over to the ranch-style house built next to the main farmhouse and entered without knocking. "Heidi, wake up." Standing by the door inside the kitchen, he wiped rain droplets away from his eyes with his coat sleeve. "I need your help. The heifers escaped."

As he waited, he made an effort not to glance around the interior of the house. Now was not the time for bitter reflection.

When Heidi shuffled down the hall, she did not look happy to see him. The scowl on her face had him retreating a step.

"What the heck, Eli? It's one o'clock in the morning." She rubbed the sleep out of her eyes. Her curly blonde hair stuck out in gravity-defying tufts.

"The door blew open and most of the heifers took off." He remained standing on the doormat, careful not to get mud and water all over the kitchen's tile floor. Tile he'd installed himself. "Part of the fencing in the pasture blew over, so I need help getting the livestock back inside."

Heidi tipped up her chin to the ceiling and groaned. "Are the kids still asleep?"

"I woke Lita to let her know I'd be outside. And Elliot was sound asleep. I don't think he'll be stirring anytime soon."

"Fine. Let me change out of my PJs, and I'll be right out." Heidi disappeared down the hall.

"Thanks," he hollered after her. "You're my favorite sister."

"I'm your only sister," she yelled back through the closed door of her bedroom.

Eli couldn't fight the urge to look around the kitchen. He hated remembering the time he'd lived here with his wife and kids. But those memories were like a toothache. Every once in a while he had to touch them to see if they still hurt.

After the divorce, when Eli and the kids had moved out, and his sister, Heidi, had moved in, the house had undergone a few changes. Heidi had painted the walls a sunny yellow and hung up some of her photography. But overall, the house he'd built to please his now ex-wife looked the same.

Heidi came out of her bedroom wearing jeans and a long-sleeve shirt. She'd put on a hat to protect her face from the rain. "How many do you think are out there?"

"I counted fifteen still loitering in the barn and field, so that leaves about eighteen. I hope they enjoy their stolen moments of freedom because I plan on having them all rounded up before sunrise."

She tied the laces of her work boots. "You call the sheriff's office?"

"No. I'd like to try and handle this on our own."

Eli followed his sister back outside. By now, the worst part of the storm had passed. The rain was no more than a light sprinkle. He even saw a few stars peeking out from behind the drifting clouds.

The air still held an electric charge, which made the hair on his arms stand on end. Nothing beat the scent of the farm after a good rain. Everything smelled refreshed. Even the ever-present odor of manure wasn't as strong.

He walked down the gravel driveway with Heidi at his side. Besides the illumination from the floodlights on the house and barn, the world around them was cast in dark shadows. They both held bright flashlights and scanned the beams from side to side. Up ahead, he saw the glow of eyes.

"They haven't gone far. Let's see if we can drive them back up the driveway and into the barn." Before he could take another step, he noticed headlight beams glowing in the distance. Was another car coming their way? If so, he needed to hurry and clear the road of his roving bovines.

The light was not moving toward them but remained stationary. He left Heidi and went to get the ATV.

After a short drive, he found the source of the light—a car had slid down into the ditch. The driver's side was pushed into the soft ground.

He shone the beam of his flashlight inside the car. A woman sat in the driver's seat, still buckled in. She appeared knocked out, with a few spots of blood marking the side of her face.

Several feet away, a heifer munched on a mouthful of grass, not seeming the least bit troubled.

Eli shot the heifer a dirty look. "I hope you're proud of yourself," he said. "This is coming out of your paycheck."

He carefully stepped down the embankment. As he reached for the door handle, the woman inside gave a moan.

After stirring a moment, she blinked her eyes open and stared back at him, squinting into the beam of his flashlight.

A jolt of attraction hit his chest, though he quickly wrote it off as leftover energy from the storm.

His night was going from bad to worse. Finding his herd of heifers missing was one thing. But discovering a beautiful woman trapped inside a car—that was another level of trouble. And his livestock was at fault for causing her to skid off the road. He had a responsibility to make sure she was unhurt and kept safe.

The woman began to sob. He opened the passenger-side door and reached a hand down to help her climb out.

Eli Hintz really hated storms.

Chapter Two

"Take my hand." The man reached down into the car.

Jordan wiggled toward the open passenger door. She raised her arm, and the instant the man's callous hand touched hers, she felt safe.

He pulled her up and out. Once her feet touched the somewhat solid ground, she breathed a sigh of relief. Her tears had stopped, but her hands still trembled. She glanced up at her savior. Another shock. The man standing before her was as handsome as a Hollywood movie star. Unfortunately, his mouth was turned down in a frown.

"Thanks for your help." Now standing, she fought dizziness while her head pounded like someone had driven a nail into her temple. Despite the discomfort, she fluffed out her newly shortened hair. "I swear there were cows standing in the road."

"Heifers," he said. "My heifers escaped when the storm blew down part of the fence. I'm sorry for the damage to your car. Someone from the sheriff's department should be here soon. You can file a report. I'll give you my insurance information so you can put in a claim."

She waved the worry away. "This is a rental car... at least I'm pretty sure it is." Where had Lacy gotten this car anyway? Didn't really matter. Jordan had enough money to buy hundreds of cars. "Things happen. My name's... Ann. Ann Dufour."

"Elijah Hintz." He shook her hand.

A firm handshake from a strong man. Little pulses of heat skittered across her skin from their brief contact. *Oh no you don't.* Jordan slammed the brakes on her runaway hormones. *No flirting with the farmer.*

In the distance, she saw a pretty woman with a flashlight approach. Here comes Elijah's wife. *So much for runaway hormones.*

"Hi, I'm Heidi." She looked Jordan up and down. "Are you okay? You have some blood on your forehead."

"I'm fine." Jordan went to touch her face but stopped her hand. If there was blood, she didn't want to smear it across her forehead. Best wait until she had a towel to clean herself up. "I'm more shaken up than anything, I think."

"Eli." The woman turned her attention to the man next to her. "Do you want me to call the sheriff's department?"

"Yes. And take Ms. Dufour back to the house. She can wait there while you call. I need to take care of the heifers before they cause any more trouble."

Jordan looked from Eli to Heidi. "I don't want to impose. It's the middle of the night."

"Your other option is to stay out here in the rain, but it's your choice." Eli shrugged, turned on his heel, and walked away.

Jordan followed Heidi down the road and up a long gravel driveway. Ahead were two houses. On the right was an old, two-story farmhouse. Set kitty-corner to the farmhouse was a modern ranch. That was the direction Heidi was headed.

Stepping inside through the back door, she was happy to be out of the wind and rain. Jordan slipped off her shoes.

"Sorry about my brother. Eli can be kind of blunt, especially when he's dealing with a problem. And half the herd of heifers escaping is a big problem."

Not a wife, but a sister. Huh. Regardless, Jordan would never date a farmer. She needed a man who was more polished, and on the same level as her, either in fame or money. Preferably both. Otherwise, the men tended to be gold diggers.

"I'm going to start a pot of coffee. I think it's going to be a long night." Heidi went to pull out a can of coffee grounds from the cupboard. "You want some?"

Jordan tried to keep her expression neutral. Blech to store-bought coffee from a can. She doubted there was a French press hidden in this country kitchen. "No, thanks. I don't want to impose."

"You wouldn't be here if it wasn't for our heifers. Where were you going, anyways? Our roads don't see much traffic, let alone at this time of night."

Jordan lowered herself onto one of the kitchen chairs. "Actually, I'm on my way to Door County. I got turned around after I stopped for gas."

Laughing, Heidi poured the water from the pot into the back of the coffee maker. "You really were turned around. The freeway is ten miles away."

Jordan wasn't above laughing at herself. "I don't drive often. Add a storm and unfamiliar country roads to the mix, and you've got a recipe for disaster." The brewing coffee filled the room with an aroma that reminded her of her favorite coffee shop in Nashville. As she second-guessed her decision to skip the offered cup of coffee, her eyelids began growing heavy. The adrenaline was leaving her body with each calm breath, and she was left with a strong desire to take a nap.

They chatted until the coffee pot was full. After Heidi poured a tall travel mug, she turned toward Jordan. "I'm going to run this out to Eli. Feel free to go crash on the sofa. I'll call the sheriff's department when I get back. But I don't know when they'll be able to get out here or get a tow truck for your car. You might be stuck here until morning. I could drive you into town, if you'd rather get a hotel."

Nothing about Heidi's words or actions gave Jordan any hint that she recognized her as Jordan Spencer. Maybe her crazy plan of going undercover as Ann Dufour was working. Plus, no one expected a superstar singer to be driving around Wisconsin's dairyland in the middle of the night. She wouldn't inconvenience her hosts by asking to be driven into town. Jordan would stay here until the tow truck arrived.

"I'm not filing an accident report, so don't call the sheriff. And I can wait until morning to get the car towed out of the ditch. Then, hopefully, I'll be out of your hair. Thanks for helping me out." If she talked to the law, she'd have to give her real name. Her cover would be blown. So much for her two weeks of peace and quiet.

Heidi's brows rose over her eyes. "You don't need to thank me. I'm just glad you weren't hurt." She bent over to tie her boots. "Get comfortable. Sleep if you can. There're a couple blankets on the sofa." After picking up the travel mug filled with coffee, she smiled and waved before disappearing out the door.

Sleep sounded wonderful. Coming up with a plan to get her out of her current predicament could wait until morning. She'd simply call Lacy and ask her to secure a new car.

An awful realization sank to the pit of her stomach. Lacy was leaving for Europe. She had gone straight to the airport from the concert venue. What if she couldn't get a hold of her sister? Then what?

The last thing she needed was for the media to discover what had happened. They'd descend on this quiet little farm like locusts in a biblical plague.

***

Eli checked the time on his phone—6:00 a.m. The last heifer was back in the security of the barn. Each one accounted for.

His eyelids grew heavier with each step. As he walked into the mudroom of his house, he saw Heidi in the kitchen. The wonderful scent of grilled sausage greeted him. His lifesaver of a sister had started breakfast.

"Lita and Elliott are both awake and getting ready. I thought you'd appreciate a good breakfast this morning, so I made scrambled eggs, sausage, and pancakes."

He honestly didn't know what he'd do without her. When they'd moved back to the farm, his wife, Nikki, had refused to live in the farm's original house. After Nikki had walked out on them, Eli couldn't bear living in the new house anymore. So, he'd packed up and moved into the farmhouse. The home he'd grown up in. He'd offered the new build to Heidi. Now, she lived there and helped him out with the kids and the farm.

There might come a day when Heidi would not want to be tied down by Eli, Lita, and Elliot. She'd want her own life. Her own children. So, every day with her help he'd take as a gift.

Elliot came skidding into the kitchen, still dressed in his superhero pajamas. "Did you get all the heifers, Dad?"

"Every last one." He bent to kiss the top of his nine-year-old son's head. "Why aren't you dressed yet? Aunt Heidi made breakfast."

"It only takes two minutes for me to get dressed. I'm not like Lita. She has to try on everything in her closet. *Girls*." Elliot shook his head before running back up the stairs.

Heidi laughed from her spot by the stove. "We girls make the world go 'round, don't you forget," she yelled after Elliot, waving a spatula in the air.

Eli poured himself another cup of coffee then added a dash of cream. "One of the morning crew called in sick, so I need to head over to the milking house and help out." He took a sip of liquid energy before remembering the car still in the ditch. Great, one more problem he still had to deal with. Add it to the pile. "Where's the lady from the car?"

In all the chaos, he'd forgotten about Ann. The memory of her pretty face woke up his body more than ten cups of coffee.

"She's at my house, sound asleep on the sofa." Heidi flipped the pancakes on the griddle. "There's something familiar about her. I just can't put my finger on it. Do you think she's someone we know?"

"She doesn't seem familiar to me." Eli would have remembered a woman who looked that good. "When do you need to leave for work?"

"I have the day off. Don't you remember? I'm going to Milwaukee for the weekend."

Eli now remembered her saying something about Milwaukee a while back. "You're going this weekend?" He couldn't be expected to remember everybody's schedule. There were too many other things fighting for the few brain cells not devoted to running the farm.

"I can feed the calves with the kids before I leave." She motioned her hand toward the stove.

Eli went over and removed the skillet of scrambled eggs off the burner. Over the years since Nikki left, he and Heidi had learned to communicate without words. Sometimes just a simple look could convey more than a ten-minute oration.

"Thanks." He scooped up a forkful of eggs and slid the food in his mouth, causing his empty stomach to rejoice. The wonderful aroma of warm pancakes dialed up his appetite even further. "That's one thing off my plate."

Elliot came back downstairs, now fully dressed, followed by Lita. Eli's little girl was not so little anymore. Ten going on twenty. Somehow, she always looked like she was heading to a fashion show instead of going to do her chores in the barn.

"Dad, can we go into town?" Lita sat next to her brother at the table. "Hailey said a bunch of kids from school are meeting at the park to hang out."

"After last night, there's too much to do. I need your help."

Crossing her arms over her chest, Lita moaned. "I'm so sick of being stuck on this stupid farm. I hate it here."

He'd heard those sentiments before. Lita's mother had expressed her detest for the Hintz Dairy Farm plenty of times before she finally up and left. His biggest fear was Lita would follow in Nikki's footsteps when she was old enough.

But if he was completely honest with himself, he'd said those same words to his own dad when he was young. And ten years ago, when he'd learned the family needed him, he'd sickened at the thought of leaving LA and his budding music career to come home and run the farm.

"Don't say that to your dad," Heidi intervened. "He works hard to take care of you. All he asks is for you to help out."

"You're the only one who ever does stuff with us, Aunt Heidi. All dad cares about is those dumb cows."

"The cows aren't dumb." Elliot poked his sister's arm with his fork. "You're dumb."

"*Ow*," Lita howled. She shoved Elliot, who almost tipped out of his chair. "You're dumber."

Eli had little patience for arguing under the best of circumstances. Throw in little sleep and a full work day ahead, and his temper started to rise. "Enough, you two." he yelled. "Hurry up and eat your breakfast or I'm going to feed the food to the animals."

"Go ahead and feed it to the animals." Lita shoved off from the table and stood. "I'm not hungry anymore."

"Get back here now, young lady," Eli growled. "For your sassiness, you've just earned the privilege of mowing the lawn this afternoon."

"Ugh," Lita shouted, and stomped back to her chair. "Someone save me from this house."

"Hello?" a small voice sounded from the direction of the door.

Eli swallowed back what he was about to yell at his daughter. There stood Ann, looking back at them with blinking eyes. Her pretty mouth opened in the shape of an O.

"I'm sorry," she said. "I saw the note Heidi left and... I can see I'm interrupting your family breakfast." She took a step backward. "I'll just go."

The kids froze, gaping open-mouthed at their visitor. As did he. At least Heidi had enough sense to reply.

"No, please join us." She walked over to where Ann stood. "We were only discussing chores for the day." Heidi turned to glare at them through narrowed eyes. "Lita and Elliot, this is Ann Dufour. Our heifers ran her off the road last night. And Ann, these two little munchkins belong to Eli."

Ann glanced at Eli, and then quickly looked away. She stepped into the kitchen. "Nice to meet you all. I'd love to join you for breakfast."

Eli sighed. No one would ever accuse his life of being boring.

***

Jordan didn't know what she'd walked into, but it wasn't a Walton's Christmas Special. She'd heard the yelling while still outside but had decided to venture in anyway. The note Heidi had left her said to come on over to the big house for breakfast.

Come in through the back door. Don't bother to knock.

Now, she wished she had knocked. At least give the family some time to prepare for company. Instead, she was in their kitchen, wishing she could come up with a polite excuse to leave.

She was surprised the kids were awake, since they must be on summer break. Neither looked tired, though. Quite the opposite, they had too much energy.

"Do you like pancakes?" the little girl asked. Jordan thought the child's name was Lita. Or was it Lena? "Come sit by me." The girl latched onto her hand and guided her to the table. She sat in the only empty chair, which happened to be next to Eli.

"Scrambled eggs, please. Thank you." A plate of food piled too high was set in front of her. She'd never be able to eat all that.

The kitchen looked like it hadn't been updated since the seventies. With its avocado-colored countertop and yellow linoleum floor, the farmhouse kitchen was a stark contrast to the modern one at Heidi's house. The room was clean, but besides a school picture of each child hanging on the refrigerator, it held no personal touches.

Daring to take a peek at Eli, Jordan took a moment to appreciate his muscular arms. She noticed there was no wedding ring or tan line to show he sometimes wore one. He looked tired, had dark circles under his eyes, and seemed angry. When he caught her stare, the scowl on his face went from grumpy to mean.

"You talk funny." The little boy stuffed a forkful of eggs into his mouth.

"Elliot John," Eli scolded. "That's no way to talk to anyone, let alone a guest."

Jordan laughed. "It's okay. My Southern accent might sound odd to Yankees."

"What's a Yankee?" Lita asked.

"Someone who lives in the north, like y'all. I was born down south, in Mississippi, so I have a Southern accent." Which usually was more pronounced when she was under stress. Like now.

"I like your shirt." Lita reached over to run her fingers over the soft fabric. "Was it expensive?"

Eli shook his head but didn't reprimand his daughter.

How to answer that question? To her, the designer T-shirt's cost was an insignificant, but a farmer's family might have a different point of view. "Not really. I bought it on sale."

"I love shopping, but my dad never takes me, and Aunt Heidi is always so busy." The little girl narrowed her eyes at the other two adults at the table.

Jordan had to stifle a laugh. This girl kind of reminded her of Lacy when she was that age. She and Lacy were two years apart, with Jordan the older of the pair. When Jordan had left their dysfunctional family to start her country music career, Lacy had been devastated over being left behind. Jordan had done everything she could for her sister, even send her money in secret so that their parents wouldn't steal it. The day Lacy turned eighteen, Jordan had come to pick her up from the trailer she lived in with their parents. Lacy was now her personal assistant, but she'd always been Jordan's best friend.

"I'm sure your dad and Heidi are very busy, with two kids to take care of and a whole farm." Jordan finished the scrambled eggs on her plate. Her stomach felt full to the point of exploding. "If you don't mind, I'm going to grab my stuff out of the car before the tow truck gets here."

"Shoot," Eli grumbled. "I forgot to call the towing company. I'll do it right now." He stood and went over to the green phone hanging on the wall. After paging through the phone book, he picked up the receiver to call.

Elliot, now done with his meal, set his plate on the counter. "I'm going to the barn to check on the heifers."

"Can I help Ann get her stuff out of the car?" Lita stood and looked at Jordan, pleading with her eyes.

"You need to help with morning chores." Heidi scraped food off the plates before loading them in the dishwasher. "Don't go running off to avoid them or mowing the lawn will be the easy punishment."

Lita set her hands on her little hips and cocked her head. "Pretty soon, I'm going to be too old for you or Dad to boss around. I'm going to leave and never come back, just like Mom." She spun on her heels and ran upstairs.

Jordan stood frozen by the table. She understood the pain and frustration she saw in Lita's eyes, but she couldn't condone where the girl directed her anger. Lita didn't know how lucky she had it, with a dad and aunt who obviously loved her. But a missing mother was a big deal, especially to a preteen girl.

Eli, who was still talking on the phone, appeared not to notice his daughter's latest tantrum. Poor guy. He probably did the best he could as a single parent. And little girls weren't easy to raise under the best circumstances.

"I'm sorry about that." Heidi closed the dishwasher and hit the start button. "Eli's wife left several years ago. Lita lashes out at her dad. She blames him for bringing Nikki here and subsequently, breaking up the family."

"You don't have to explain. I know families can be complicated." Jordan opened the screen door. "I'll go grab my stuff out of the car and wait on the porch for the tow truck, if that's all right with you."

Heidi nodded her head. "Sure. But if you get bored, I'll be in the red barn over there." She pointed out the window to the large structure, which sat beside four tall, blue silos. "You could help feed the calves if you'd like. They're really cute."

Eli hung up the phone and turned to face her. His gaze caused a shiver to run across her skin. He sure had the smolder look mastered, unintentional as it may be.

"Tow truck can't get out here until noon." His attention focused on Heidi. "I need to get over to the milking house. Give me a call in the barn once they get here. I want to talk to Hank and make sure Ann's car gets priority at the shop." With that, he gave Jordan a quick nod before walking into the mud room.

Sounded like she had some time to kill. Maybe helping with the calves would be fun.

As crazy as breakfast at the Hintz's house had been, she had enjoyed the rambunctious family atmosphere. It was something sorely lacking in her own house. There she had people to run errands for her, buy her groceries, clean her house, and cook her food. Some days, she wished she could go out to a store and not be mobbed. Just an average girl, checking out melon in the produce aisle.

No chance of that happening, unless she managed these next few weeks without blowing her cover. Otherwise, she'd be once again mobbed by photographers and fans. Nowhere to go. Nowhere to hide.

As Jordan made the short hike over to her car, she saw Eli come down the driveway in an ATV. He barely looked her way as he passed. What to make of this man? Handsome, a loving father, but not very talkative. Maybe he didn't like unexpected company. She couldn't blame him.

Hopefully, the tow truck would come soon and give her a ride into town. But then what? She had cash but couldn't use her credit cards. And what about a new car?

Jordan needed her cell phone to call Lacy. Her sister always had an answer for every problem.

Chapter Three

Jordan practically tore the rental car apart searching for her cell phone. Finally, after looking in every nook and cranny, she found it wedged underneath the backseat.

Luckily, the phone still had a little battery left. She saw three voicemails and five text messages. The texts were all from Henry. In the first two, he pleaded to get back together. Numbers three through five were various threats. Jordan considered for a moment what potential dirt Henry could use to humiliate her.

Swipe and delete. She didn't have the energy to play games.

Next came the voicemails. Two were from Lacy.

"Hey, Jordan. Looks like there's some crazy weather moving through. Call me when you get this so I know you're all right."

Jordan played the second message. *"Why haven't you called me back yet? I'm at my layover in LaGuardia, waiting for my plane to board. I hope you get back to me soon because I'm really starting to worry. Bridgette, the owner of the Door County rental house, called me. She said a tree branch fell on the house."* Lacy took a breath. *"Honey, I'm sorry but you won't be able to stay there anymore. So, call me as soon as you get this message. My plane's scheduled to leave in one hour. Otherwise, the flight to Munich takes over seven hours and I won't get your call until after I land."*

A beep sounded, ending the message.

The rental house was damaged? What was she supposed to do? No car. No place to stay. Maybe she should just call a car service and catch the first flight back to Nashville. She could be in her soft, comfy bed by dinner time.

She did the math in her head. Lacy's plane should have landed in Munich by now. After hitting her sister's photo icon to place the call, Jordan listened to five rings. Then, the call got kicked to voicemail. *Darn.* She tried again.

Lacy picked up on the second ring. "Are you trying to give me a stroke? Where are you?"

"Calm down. I'm fine. I got into an accident last night."

A squeak sounded from the other end. "I knew something was wrong. Are you hurt?"

"No, I'm fine. The car, not so much. And now the rental house is damaged."

"Don't even bother going up there. The house is a mess. And Bridgette said it's impossible to get another rental with this short a notice, not during the summer tourist season."

"I guess our plan was a bust. I'll just head home." Jordan kicked a rock, sending it bouncing down the road. Defeat hung over her like gravity, holding her down each time she wanted to fly away.

"Where are you now?"

Jordan raised her hand to shield her eyes from the sun and glanced around at the farm fields surrounding her. "Somewhere around Manitowoc, Wisconsin. It's about halfway to Door County."

"Why not rent around there? Use your alias, Ann Dufour, and pay cash."

"This place isn't exactly what I had in mind when I pictured my retreat. Right now, I'm standing by a road between two corn fields. And here comes a tractor." She waved at the old man slowly driving down the road. "And then there's the smell. Each time the wind picks up, I get a wonderful whiff of manure."

Static sounded through the line. "Honey—" Lacy's voice cut in and out. "I need to go catch my ride to the hotel. I have faith you'll be able to figure things out by yourself."

Figure things out for myself? Lacy has lost her mind. "Very funny. I've spent the past eight years being totally dependent on you, my little Fart-Face, and now you're ripping the rug out from under me?"

"Time to grow up, Butt-Breath. I'll call you later."

"I hate when you call me that." Jordan laughed. "Have a good trip. Love you."

"Love you, too."

The call ended, leaving a deep longing to have her little sister by her side. Lacy was her best friend. The one person Jordan could always count on. As the older sibling, she should be the one taking care of Lacy, but with the Spencer sisters, Lacy was definitely the one who kept everything together.

Standing by her car, which still rested in the ditch, Jordan realized that she was totally on her own. No manager. No personal assistant. No dietitian. No music producer. No one to tell her what to do, and where and when to do it.

She waited for the anxiety to wrap around her body like a python, squeezing until she could barely breathe… but nothing happened. Looking around at the acres of green farmland that surrounded her, she actually relaxed. She could do whatever she wanted. These next few weeks were totally her own.

For the first time in years, Jordan was free.

***

Eli was used to being sleep deprived. Between running a dairy farm and being a single father of two, there wasn't much time to lie around in bed. And when one of his helpers called in sick, like today, he had to pick up the extra work. The cows were ultimately his responsibility.

He opened the gate to let the next group of cows into the milking parlor and patted the rump of an ambling bovine. If his eighteen-year-old self could see him now, he'd be totally disgusted. Eli had been a rebellious teenager, with big rock-n-roll dreams. After graduating high school, Eli and Nikki had taken off for LA. They'd gotten married on their way through Las Vegas.

Those had been some of the best years of his life. Eli, Nikki, and the rest of their little band had lived the dream. They'd played in dumpy bars and street fairs. Their record deal had seemed so close, yet so far away.

Then he'd gotten the phone call that his parents had been killed in a car accident. The farm needed him. His brother and sister were too young to manage things without him. Nikki had fought to stay in LA but ultimately followed him, and in the process, put aside her dreams.

So here he was, ten years later, lining up cows for milking. Without his wife. Without music.

With the passing of time, his dreams seemed very far away.

He watched as his farm hands attached the milking machine to each cow in the parlor. The whole process still amazed him. His dad, Frank, had spent a lot of time and money updating their milking process. Their cows, heifers, and calves were so well taken care of, Eli sometimes envied their life.

His thoughts drifted to Lita and her obvious dislike for farm life. Where had his sweet girl gone? In her place was a sassy young lady who was growing up way too fast.

Though, his little Lita had sure taken a quick liking to their guest this morning.

Ann. The woman was beautiful. He remembered how his body had reacted when she'd sat down next to him at the table for breakfast. Eli could easily take a liking to her as well, but he still had some common sense left.

He did not date. He'd sworn off romance. The last thing he needed in his life right now was another complication.

The cell phone in his back pocket started to ring. He took it out and looked at the name on the screen—Nikki James. No longer Nikki Hintz. She'd remarried two years ago.

"Hello." His greeting was as cold as her heart.

"Hey, Eli. You busy?"

"I'm always busy. What do you need?"

There was a brief silence. "The band just got a great opportunity to open for Sons of Chaos. I'm leaving to go on a two-month tour." Another pause. "So… I won't be able to come out to see the kids this summer."

He wasn't surprised by her news. But the thought of telling the kids their mother had once again chosen her music career over them sent his blood pressure soaring. "How can you do this? You haven't seen them in over a year."

"I know," she whined. "I'm sorry. This tour is a once in a lifetime opportunity. Maybe Lita and Elliot can come on the road with me for a while."

Eli pinched the bridge of his nose in hopes of stemming his rising headache. "Absolutely not. They have a home. If you want to spend time with them, you come here."

"Lita tells me every time we talk that she's so miserable. At least let her come. It's summer. She's not in school. What harm would it do?"

"No." His voice rose in anger. "The last thing Lita needs is to be dragged around the country with a rock band. You're the one who abandoned them. Don't you dare put this on me."

There was a moment of silence on the other end. "I didn't abandon my kids."

"You moved across the country. You left them—and me." He felt a momentary pinch in his heart. "I'll tell the kids you're not coming this summer. Goodbye." Eli ended the call.

How could he have ever loved her?

Whenever he looked at his wonderful kids, he felt pity for his ex-wife. Faraway dreams or not, he still knew she was the one who was missing out on the best part of life.

***

Jordan changed into the old pair of blue jeans and T-shirt Heidi had left out for her. When she entered the barn, she was surprised by its size and organization. There were various stalls, some small enough for one, and others built for larger groups.

High-powered fans hung from the ceiling on each end, providing cool, fresh air.

Farm animals and their scents weren't anything new to Jordan. Her mom and dad—though she used those titles loosely—had been carnival workers. The Spencer family had traveled from festival to fair, all year long. The county fairs in late summer were always her favorite. She'd walk around the livestock barns for hours, wishing she could be like the farmer kids who had a loving family to go home to at the end of the day.

When Phil, her manager, had given her the opportunity to leave and start a singing career, she'd run fast and hard in order to slip out of her parents' greedy claws.

"Over here." Lita yelled from the corner of the barn. Her smile lit up her little, oval face and Jordan couldn't help but smile back.

Jordan walked over to join her.

Heidi stood in a stall across the aisle from Lita, stroking the head of a small calf. "The kids' job is to fill up the feed bucket in each hutch. Would you like to help them?"

"Sure." She didn't mind helping out since she had a few hours to kill before the tow truck arrived. Filling feed buckets couldn't be that hard.

Elliot came stomping down the main aisle. "Calves are on this side." He pointed to the row of small pens lined up along the long wall of the barn. "And the heifers are there. They have a door to go outside and graze." Elliot took Jordan's hand and pulled her along. They stopped by a group of large, individual pens. "These girls are going to have babies. This one here I named Henrietta."

Jordan gasped at the round, distended belly of the cow in front of them. "Will she have her baby soon?"

After reading the little sign by the pen door, Elliot nodded his head. "Yeah. It's so cool. They just lay down and grunt and moan, and out pops a slimy calf."

"Have you seen many births?" Jordan asked, fascinated.

"Elliot is always in here," Lita piped in. "Because he doesn't have any real friends."

"Take that back." Elliot approached his sister with raised fists.

"Lita, be nice to your brother." Heidi came up behind Elliot and put a hand on his shoulder. "We have company, don't forget."

"Come on, Ann." Lita took Jordan's hand. "You can help me with the feed."

Jordan needed to get used to being called Ann. She followed Lita to a huge container of feed.

The girl picked up a bucket and handed one to Jordan. "A full bucket is enough to do four stalls. Only do the ones with blue buckets. The young calves are bottle fed."

"Your dad is lucky to have such good helpers."

Lita rolled her eyes. "Elliot loves the farm. Aunt Heidi grew up here. But I'm forced to work against my will. You know, there are such things as child labor laws."

Jordan couldn't stop the laughter that bubbled up. How old was Lita anyway? By the looks of her, ten or eleven. But going off her attitude, she seemed to be about sixteen. *Good luck, Eli.*

Out of the corner of her eye, she watched the little girl go to work. As much as Lita complained, the smile on her face showed her true feelings. She was a petite thing, with long blonde hair that held a hint of a wave. Jordan wondered about Lita's mom. How on earth did a woman leave her own flesh and blood? If she were ever blessed with children—of course, first she'd have to find a man worthy of being the father—Jordan wouldn't leave them, not even for a day.

She thought about being a mother as a touring singer. There were many people in the music industry, both men and women, who made it all work. And it *was* work. She'd also seen marriages fall apart because of opposing career goals. The pressures of fame could cause even the strongest relationships to implode.

Personally, Jordan had never gotten close to having a strong relationship. Once a guy really got to know her, they discovered her sparkle faded fast. They were left with the real Jordan Spencer. A girl with insecurities and anxiety. A woman who wanted to be loved for the person she was on the inside, not the image her publicist promoted.

She went back to the feed bin to refill her bucket. The sounds of mooing, munching, and Elliot's singing echoed through the barn. He had a good voice. Nice and clear, and held the pitch well. *Wonder if he's ever had voice lessons?*

Everyone, including the animals, seemed to be in a good mood. Even Lita, who hummed what sounded like "Kiss Me Deadly." Had she been named after Lita Ford? If so, her attitude was a good match for her famous rocker namesake.

"Do you like to sing?" Jordan asked Lita.

When she looked over at Jordan, her mask of indifference slipped back into place. "I like to sing when I'm bored... like whenever I have to do these stupid chores. Mom's a singer. She has her own band and everything."

"Really? That's neat." Was Eli's ex-wife anyone Jordan knew?

"She's not famous." Lita unknowingly answered the question. "But she wants to be. That's all she cares about."

"Oh." Jordan was at a loss for words. Her brain scrambled to think of something profound to say—but really, what words could make abandonment feel better?

Lita's blue eyes welled up with tears, and she wiped them away with the back of her hand.

"I can tell that your dad loves you," Jordan said, trying to sooth Lita's pain. The true love of one parent was better than the combined neglect of two.

"How would you know?" Lita flicked her blonde hair over her shoulder. "No offense, but you don't know my dad."

Jordan got ready to stand toe to toe with this little dragon disguised as a sprite. "I know what love looks like. Love is sacrifice. And love is doing things you don't like for the good of others. And there are times when a parent has to say and do things that kids don't like, but it's only because they love them and know it's what's best for them." She took a breath. "My parents let my sister and me do whatever we wanted because they didn't care. They didn't live in a spot long enough to call home, and we never got a chance to go to a real school. I'm not saying you don't have a right to complain sometimes, but Lita, you are a lucky girl."

Lita's eyes narrowed, most likely sizing up the competition. Then, her face relaxed. "My dad should take you out on a date."

"I don't think so." She laughed. "Once the tow truck gets here, I need to find another house to rent. And then I can finally start my vacation. Plus, I'm sure your dad doesn't go around dating strange women who crash into the ditch."

"Dad doesn't date anyone." Lita huffed, and then went back to bottle feeding a calf.

Sexy Eli didn't date? Surely, that wasn't the case. He was way too hot to be single. Most likely he didn't talk about his love life with his kids.

She was definitely not interested, no matter how attracted she was to his manual-labor-hardened body. Just thinking about those muscles made her skin flush with heat. And his eyes—deep set, with gold-colored irises and outer corners that were slightly upturned. Back at the farmhouse, when he'd shifted his gaze to her, his eyes had resembled those of a wolf.

Good thing Jordan would be long gone before her attraction caused any trouble. She had to be.

Chapter Four

Eli stood next to Hank, the tow truck driver, on the side of the road. They both looked down at the banged-up car in the ditch.

Hank lifted his ball cap and wiped his brow with the small towel he kept stuffed in his back pocket. "What a doozy. The insurance company's not going to like the cost of fixing the damage."

Ann's face paled. "There won't be an insurance claim. Just fix it, and I'll pay the bill."

Beads of sweat dripped off big Hank's face. "Once we get it to the shop I'll have Trevor look it over. Most likely, we'll need to order parts. We don't stock parts for these fancy foreign cars. It may take over a week to fix."

"Ms. Dufour was on her way to Door County," Eli said. "She'll need a rental car."

Ann had only been here a few hours and her presence had already disrupted his strict schedule. The kids were moving in slow motion. They'd taken all morning to do their chores. Lita's discontent about farm life had seemed to double, if not triple.

Having a stranger here, especially a very pretty one, was affecting Eli as well. Her large gray eyes, framed by thick lashes, weakened his defenses. He was a man, after all.

"I can't rent a car." Ann took a step back, off the gravel shoulder and onto the road. A beep sounded from an approaching tractor. She jumped out of the way, and then overcorrected, almost sliding down into the ditch.

Eli took hold of her arm to steady her. He felt her muscles stiffen in response.

"I don't know what's the matter with me." She set her feet back on the gravel safe zone, between the road pavement and the grass ditch, and went to stand over by Heidi. "Anyway, do you know of any houses for rent in the area? If so, then I'll just stay in town until the car's repaired."

Heidi tilted her head to look at Ann. "Don't you have a place rented in Bailey's Harbor?"

"The house was damaged in the storm, so I can't stay there. Since I have to find a new rental, I thought maybe there was something in this area. This seems like a nice place to vacation."

Both Heidi and Hank laughed.

"This area is not a huge vacation destination," Eli said. "There are a couple of nice hotels by Lake Michigan, though."

"No hotels. I need privacy."

Only pays with cash, needs privacy, and doesn't want the insurance company to find out about the car damage. Was Ann hiding from something, or someone?

Heidi must have had the same thought. As Hank worked on securing the hooks to the bumper of Ann's car, she pulled Eli aside. "I think she's running away. Maybe she's been abused. Why else wouldn't she want to use a credit card and stay in a public place? Have you noticed how she keeps her head down? And did you see the bruise on her cheek? We have to help her."

"That bruise was probably from the accident." Eli crossed his arms over his chest, knowing exactly where his sister's mind was headed.

"Or she could have been hit by her abuser. What if there never was a rental house in Door County? She just packed up and left, without anywhere to go. Poor thing. Ann's so skinny. She looks malnourished."

"We are not getting involved." He had enough problems of his own without adding a stranger's troubles. "If there is some crazy husband or boyfriend chasing her then she needs to get far away from here." His gazed flickered over to Ann.

She fidgeted while focusing on her wreck of a car. Was she really running away from an abusive relationship? Now Heidi had put her own crazy ideas into his head. Yes, Ann did act skittish, but that could be for any number of reasons. Most likely she wanted to get the heck out of here.

"Where is your conscience?" Heidi poked him in the bicep with a pointy fingernail. "How can you turn your back on someone in need? It's our fault she landed in the ditch last night."

"Her accident was the storm's fault—and a few wandering heifers." Eli scowled. He knew how to play this game. All three

Hintz siblings were notoriously stubborn. "So, what do you want me to do? Be her bodyguard while she lives under my roof?"

Heidi's eyes brightened. "That's a great idea. I'll be down in Milwaukee for the weekend, so she doesn't have to stay in your house. Ann can stay in the spare room at my house. It's the least we can do."

"No." He didn't owe her any more explanation than that.

"Why not?"

He sighed. "First, we don't know her. She could be a criminal running from the police. Second." He stopped to think. What was his second point?

"You can be a real blockhead. I'm offering her a room at my house. She can hang out there until she figures out a new plan. Maybe she won't want to stay on a dairy farm, but I have to offer."

Eli grabbed his sister's arm. "This is my farm, and I forbid you to invite that woman to stay here."

Heidi had the nerve to laugh in his face. "I was wrong. You're not a blockhead. You're a jackass."

He released his hold on her arm and watched her approach Ann.

There was no point in arguing with her. And Eli owed Heidi this small favor. For his painfully shy sister to have taken a liking to Ann, a stranger, was unusual. Could be that Heidi sensed Ann needed help. Heidi did have a huge, caring heart. So, he'd let her go do her good deed. He just hoped Ann would decline. Their family's life needed to go back to normal.

Normal.

What was normal, anyway? And did his normal make him happy? Or was he only working day after day, trying to keep everything from falling apart?

***

"I couldn't impose." Jordan had to break eye contact with Heidi. She looked concerned. Too concerned.

"You wouldn't, though. I'll be gone. Staying here for a few days means you can take your time to find someplace else. I know my house isn't fancy or doesn't have a good view of the water, but it's private."

Well, yes. Although this kind of privacy came with the smell of cow manure wafting through the open window, and a sexy man living next door. "Your house is very nice. And I do want privacy, but the farm isn't exactly private."

"You mean Eli and the kids? Eli's so busy you'll probably never see him. And Lita and Elliot will be given strict instructions to leave you alone. I can guarantee you won't have to talk to anyone if you don't want to." She pointed a finger down the road. "You see the closest house down there? It's over a mile away."

"You are very kind to offer." Jordan smiled. She rarely met someone so pure hearted as Heidi Hintz.

Heidi leaned in close. "If you're in danger, we can help," she whispered. "Are you hiding from someone?" Her face held so much kindness.

An abused spouse. That would be a good story. A valid reason why she couldn't risk using any identifying information. It could work. But at what cost? She'd be lying to good people.

Although, Heidi had drawn her own conclusions. So, Jordan didn't dispute her. Kind of a lie of omission. That wasn't as bad, right?

"I can't say." Guilt twitched in her gut. If she was to remain undercover, she had to play fast and loose with the truth. So far, no one had recognized her.

And the freedom felt wonderful.

Heidi drew her into a hug. "Please stay. You'll be safe here. No one drives on these roads but locals, and the rare lost tourist." She laughed and stepped back. "Neither Eli or I could live with ourselves if we just sent you away with nowhere to go."

Glancing over at Eli, who stood by the tow truck, Jordan concluded that Eli most definitely *would* be okay if she left. The scowl he wore on his face seemed permanent. No wonder he and Lita butted heads. Would it kill the guy to smile every once in a while?

"Okay, but I'll pay you." Jordan surrendered, but still wasn't one hundred percent confident she made the right choice. She wasn't used to making decisions on her own. Everything else in her life was micromanaged by her handlers—from what she ate to "keep that skinny waist," to the sheets she used on her bed because "a silk pillowcase helps prevent premature wrinkles."

"Payment is totally unnecessary," Heidi said. "We should be paying you for the damage to your car."

"We'll settle up later, then. You can use the money for something for the kids. Maybe Eli can take them on a vacation."

Laughing, Heidi shook her head. "Eli take a vacation. That's funny." She took Jordan's hand and pulled her along toward Eli.

"Ann has taken us up on our offer." Heidi put extra emphasis on the words *us* and *our*.

Eli remained stoically silent.

"Give Hank my home phone number, since she'll be staying there," Heidi said. "He can call her with an update."

"Heidi, I'm not sure—"

"Just tell Hank." The frown on her face was a twin to her brother's, but then she turned to Jordan and smiled. "Come on, Ann. Let me show you to your new room. Then I need to get going. I'm meeting a friend at Summerfest." Heidi motioned for her to follow and began walking.

"I was just at Summerfest." Jordan snapped her lips shut. She'd been at Summerfest as a headliner at the amphitheater the night before. Couldn't tell them that. "Um, I heard some really good bands."

"Yeah, the bands are my favorite part. Did you know Eli was in a band?" Heidi asked as they strolled down the country road, back to the driveway.

"Lita mentioned that."

"Our little brother Sam and I were too young to run the farm. Eli didn't want to see it bought by one of the big dairy corporations, so he left his band and moved home. Some days, I feel bad for him. The farm's a heavy weight." She sighed.

Heidi opened the front door to the little ranch, and Jordan stepped inside. Her suitcases and guitar still sat next to the sofa, right where she'd left them. They each grabbed a suitcase and Heidi led her through a cheerfully decorated family room filled with brightly colored paintings and overstuffed, comfortable furniture. The walls of the short hallway were lined with family photographs, both formal and candid. Jordan stopped to study a black and white photo of what appeared to be a teenage Eli sitting on the hood of an old pickup truck. His wide smile, which she'd never witnessed in person, warmed her heart.

Her decision to stay felt right. She'd have plenty of privacy. And she could start writing some new music. The song currently running around her head was one about rebuilding after a broken heart. Something she knew a lot about.

"I'll do my best not to get in Eli's way. I know he's busy." Jordan entered a cute guestroom. It looked like it had been a little girl's room at one time, with pink walls and lacy curtains. A brass bed was placed next to a dresser and mirror combination.

Setting a suitcase down in front of the closet, Heidi chuckled. "Don't worry about Eli. Personally, I think he'd benefit from an attractive woman getting in his way once in a while."

Her cheeks warmed. "No playing matchmaker. I just got out of a bad relationship." That wasn't a lie. "I need some time to figure out who I am without a man."

"I get that. I've tried to get Eli to date for years, even signed him up for an online dating site. He threatened to kill me when he started getting date requests."

She'd bet a lot of women responded simply on his looks alone. "He must be okay with being single. That way, he can focus on raising his kids."

"Eli wasn't made to stay single, but Nikki broke part of him. The reason he doesn't date has nothing to do with not wanting a relationship. He's just scared to get hurt again."

Jordan sank onto the bed. "Totally understandable."

"Okay." Heidi spun around the little room. "I think you're all set. If you need something, please call my cell or ask Eli. Otherwise, I need to run."

Five seconds after she left the room, she reappeared. "Oh— food."

"Yeah. Food is good."

"Help yourself to anything in the fridge and pantry. I'll ask Eli if you can borrow his car. Sterling's about five miles away. The town has one small grocery store. Or you could go to Manitowoc."

"Thanks, Heidi." She sniffled back tears, grateful to have crashed in front of the home of good people.

"And if you get bored, you can take a drive to Lake Michigan. There are some nice beaches and hiking trails along the shore." Heidi paused to take a breath. "Oh, since you're from the South, you might be interested in seeing this old, plantation-style house that's nearby. It's about two miles down the road, heading west. You'll see an overgrown driveway. Take that for about a half a mile until you see the weeping willow trees. Technically, you're trespassing on private property, but no one has lived there for more than fifty years, so you'll be fine. The house is really cool looking."

An old, Southern-style house did sound cool. Since she'd never had a permanent home growing up, she was fascinated with architecture, especially historical. Someday, she wanted to build a house that looked like the large mansions she'd seen scattered throughout the South.

Jordan initiated a hug. "Have fun in Milwaukee. See you in a few days."

The sound of a closing door told Jordan she was alone. She opened her guitar case and gently pulled out her baby.

Time to get to work.

***

With Heidi gone, dinner was all on Eli. He knew how to cook and thought he did it quite well. And secretly, he liked having control of his own kitchen. Most days, by the time Eli got home from the fields or barn, Heidi had already set the meal on the table.

But today, he'd made sure to be back home by five. After a quick shower, he went into the kitchen and started pulling out the ingredients for chicken cacciatore.

As he placed the last chicken breast very carefully into the skillet, Lita entered the kitchen with a pretty smile on her face.

"I love your special chicken, Dad." She walked over to stand next to him by the old oven and sniffed the cooking food. "Can I ask Ann if she wants to have dinner with us?"

"No." The crackle of frying chicken grew louder. "Didn't Aunt Heidi tell you to leave her alone while she's here?"

"Well, sure… but Ann would love to eat with us."

"Ann asked for privacy, and we need to respect that. She doesn't want to be bothered."

Lita let out a long, suffering sigh. "Can't I at least ask?"

"No." Eli tried to rein in his frustration. He needed to tread lightly. Once they sat down to dinner, he would break the news that their mother wasn't coming for her planned visit. No doubt that would be as well received as if he canceled Christmas. Especially with Lita, who idolized her mom.

"You're so unfair." She turned to leave. "I can't wait 'til Mom comes. She isn't mean like you."

Eli flinched like she'd punched him in the gut. No matter how many times he heard those words coming out of his daughter's mouth, they never landed softly. "Lita. Come here."

Standing in the doorway to the family room, she faced him. "What? I promise not to go ask Ann to dinner."

Better to deliver the bad news now, while they were alone. He'd talk to Elliot in private as well. Each kid had their own way of dealing with disappointment. Best not to mix the two reactions or he might get an explosion.

"Sit down." He pointed to one of the chairs surrounding their kitchen table. Eli sat next to her. "I talked to your mom today."

"Really?" Her big, blue eyes brightened. "What day is she going to be here? Is she bringing Rick? Is she going to take us somewhere fun?"

He laid a hand on her arm. "Your mom can't visit this summer." His chest squeezed, knowing the pain his words inflicted. "She said that maybe she'll come in October, for your birthday."

Tears welled up in Lita's formerly happy eyes. "You're lying. Mom told me she was coming. She promised."

"I know." He gently stroked her arm. "How about I take a few days off, and we can go for a little trip?"

She turned her head away and began to cry. "Did she say why?"

"Mom's band got offered a tour."

"Why does she love her band more than us?" she asked in between sobs.

Eli pulled her close and wrapped her small body up in his arms. He'd stayed awake many nights asking himself that same question, never arriving at a good answer. "I don't know. But your mom does love you."

"Then why can't I go live with her? She can take me along." Lita's head rose off his chest to peer up at him. "Please, Dad? Ask Mom if I can go with her, just for the rest of the summer?"

"A rock-n-roll tour is no place for a child."

Lita jumped to her feet. "How do you know? You won't even talk to her about it."

"I do know." How could he explain to a ten-year-old about the drinking and drug use? All the nights right after their divorce that Nikki would call him at four in the morning, drunk out of her mind and professing her undying love? He'd led that lifestyle, too. Not the drugs, but he'd partied after shows. There was no way in heaven he'd expose either of his children to life on a rock-n-roll tour. "You're not going with your mom, Lita. That's the end of it."

"I hate you," she shouted before running out of the kitchen.

Resentment boiled in his gut. How many more times would he have to be the bad guy and break his children's hearts? He'd made a commitment to them which he'd kept every day of their lives.

So why was he the one left feeling smothered in failure?

The smell of smoke reminded him of his neglected cooking. He hustled over to the oven. Luckily, nothing was too overcooked. Removing the chicken from the skillet, he added the rest of the ingredients. So much for his nice family dinner.

Lita would probably hide in her room for the rest of the night. He still had to break the news to Elliot. His son's reaction would be more tempered. Nikki was practically a stranger to him. While Lita held on to many good memories of her mom, Elliot rarely mentioned her.

His memories of his marriage were bittersweet, and they served as a reminder of the expense of love.

Chapter Five

Jordan sat on the swinging bench that hung from the front porch. The sun had dipped into the horizon and blanketed the sky with bright orange and purple clouds. Before her lay a farm field filled with knee-high corn plants spread as far as she could see. Crickets chirped hello, birds squawked good night calls to each other, and she answered both with her guitar.

The melody that had been stuck in her head for the past weeks was finally set free. Earlier, she'd written the first draft of the lyrics. Now, she strummed out chords on her guitar and hummed along. This song might be her next big hit if she could get all the elements to blend together.

The sounds of shouting interrupted her musings. Jordan stood and set down her guitar, and then walked the length of the porch to peer around the corner.

There was a long patch of grass between Heidi's ranch and the old farmhouse, with the corner on the farmhouse's front yard blending together with the ranch's backyard.

There was enough daylight left for her to see Eli and Elliot running across the green grass in front of the farm house. Eli caught up to his son, and with another shout, they both went down. Laughter followed.

Elliot stood and tossed a football in the air. They must be playing a little before bed.

Stepping off the porch, she walked around to get a better view. They were now both up on their feet, with Elliot running as fast as his little legs could carry him. Eli cocked his arm back and threw the ball to his son. A perfect arch that landed right in the boy's outstretched arms.

"Impressive catch," she yelled across the yard.

Both guys looked over. Elliot waved his hands in the air, while his dad crossed his arms over his broad chest.

Elliot ran straight toward her. "Hey, Ann, did you see that? Dad says if I'm going to play football this fall, I need all the practice I can get."

"Oh, really?" Jordan laughed. "What position do you want to play?"

Elliot halted right before her and shrugged. Sweat dripped from his curly, brown hair. "I don't know. Dad said that will be up to the coaches."

She almost let it slip that she knew several professional football players who ran camps for kids. A few here in Wisconsin. But she bit her tongue. "You look like you're having fun. I'll let you get back to your game."

Waving at Elliot, she lifted her gaze to Eli. He walked toward her at a slow pace.

"I heard you playing the guitar." He stopped, leaving about ten feet between them.

"Uh, sorry. I can go play inside if it bothers you. I forgot how far sound travels in the country."

"No, it doesn't bother me. I used to play guitar. It's nice to hear the sound again." He stuffed his hands in the front pockets of his shorts.

Standing side by side, Jordan could see how closely Elliot resembled his father. Elliot's brown hair held the same curly rebellion. Both pairs of eyes were a striking gold color. Elliot's boyish body held the promise of growing into Eli's strong frame, with wide shoulders and long legs.

"You don't play anymore?" Jordan imagined how sexy Eli would look holding an electric guitar. Suddenly, she felt very warm.

"I don't have time. Maybe someday, when the kids are grown and the farm runs itself." He ran his fingers through his thick hair.

"I was just working on a song. Maybe I can play it for you once it's done, and you can tell me what you think." What a dumb move—to ask for his opinion. Eli didn't seem interested in her, so why would he care about her music?

A shadow passed over his handsome face. "Have a good evening. I'll leave the keys for the car on the front porch tomorrow morning. Feel free to use it anytime you want." He turned to leave.

"Eli," she dared to call out. When he turned to face her, her heart thumped in her chest—*boom, boom, boom*—like a bass drum in a marching band. "Thanks for your hospitality."

He tipped his head to her before walking back to the discarded football.

Jordan went back to her guitar, which waited on the front porch. The sun had almost completely set. Several fireflies flickered in the approaching twilight. The crickets had ramped up their song, and she was content to simply look and listen to the world around her.

***

Given the lack of food in Heidi's pantry, Jordan decided to venture to the grocery store. She'd go to the one in Sterling. The area was home to more bovines than people, so it seemed to be a safe place to shop.

Over the past two days, she'd grown more comfortable with her disguise. But a new hair color and style didn't exactly make her unrecognizable. Kind of like Clark Kent with his glasses.

She'd stopped wearing makeup and looked vastly different without her signature red lipstick and smoky eye shadow. Hopefully, she looked like an average girl.

On the front porch lay a key fob, and she picked it up. A nervous flutter beat inside her stomach at the thought of getting behind the wheel again.

You can do this. Her new mantra.

Jordan walked up the driveway toward the farmhouse. Up in one of the second-story windows, she saw Lita. She gave a wave, and Lita waved back.

Last night, her little interruption from songwriting had been welcome. And seeing Eli again had given her sweet dreams.

She had to remind herself that she could look-y but no touch-y.

Up by the garage sat a shiny, black pickup truck, which must be Eli's. Parked on the other side was a silver, beat-up car. The one she'd been trusted to drive.

Her hand shook as she went to unlock the driver's side door.

"We don't lock our cars out here." The sound of Eli's deep voice enfolded her.

Her heart jumped in her chest. Even his voice was sexy. She twisted around to face him. "Where I come from, unlocked doors are not an option."

"One of the many benefits of country living."

The way he smiled at her turned every muscle in her body to pudding.

I'm only looking. She took a deep breath and unclenched her hands at her sides. "You sure you trust me with your car?"

"You're not planning to rob a bank, are you?" Another heart-stopping smile.

"No bank robbery on today's agenda." She chuckled.

"Then stay out of the ditch and we're good."

They stood in silence for a few seconds. Jordan dared to meet his gaze, and what she saw in his eyes made her knees knock together.

Eli was pure, unapologetically male. His body advertised his strength, from his jawline to his hands. Everything about him was solid and well-built.

She'd been around enough guys who pumped iron in a gym to recognize the difference in Eli. His brute-like muscles came from hard, manual work.

"See you later." She opened the door to escape into the car before she started drooling. *Stay cool, Spencer. Stop acting like an idiot.*

The drive to Sterling lasted all of five minutes. An intersection with a stop light marked the center of town. She easily found the grocery store situated on the main road. The little building was a miniature, more inviting version of the large stores taking up city blocks back home.

As she walked inside, a lady at the checkout greeted her with just a normal "hello." So far, so good.

First stop, the produce section. She picked up a bunch of bananas, three oranges, five apples, a bag of prepackaged salad mix, and a bulging, red tomato. Pushing her cart, she traveled over to the meat counter. What did she want to cook for dinners? She couldn't remember the last time she'd used an oven.

She considered making dinner for Eli and the kids. She could drop dinner off at their house as a surprise. Hopefully, Eli would appreciate the help, since his sister was gone.

While the man worked to get her order together, Jordan opened up the web browser on her cell and searched how to bake chocolate chip cookies. Couldn't bring dinner without dessert.

***

Eli strode through one of his hay fields, every so often bending over to pull up a plant. The most mature stalks were ready to flower, which meant he needed to cut the hay within the next few days. There was no rain in the immediate weather forecast. Tomorrow, he wanted to do something fun with Lita and Elliot. Heidi would be back on Sunday. Once she was home, he'd work non-stop until all the fields were cut.

His cell rang. The call was from the house phone.

"What's up?"

"Hey, Dad," Elliot said. "Where are you?"

"I told you I was going out to check on the hay fields."

"Oh."

Eli waited for his son to continue. After several seconds, he cleared his throat. "What do you need, slugger?"

"Well... I see smoke."

"Where do you see smoke?" Eli hustled back to the ATV. Smoke meant fire, and on a farm, a fire could devastate.

"Over at Aunt Heidi's house."

"Stay away. I'll be right there." He hit the gas, did a quick U-turn, and then rocketed back to the houses.

When he crested the last hill, he saw a plume of black smoke coming from the kitchen window. His panicked heart kicked down a notch. At least the entire house wasn't in flames—yet.

He didn't bother knocking before he entered through the back door. There was Ann, waving a towel at the smoke streaming out the oven.

She had tears streaking down her face.

As he opened another window, he noticed a tray of black disks sitting on the stovetop. "Were you trying to bake?"

Ann sniffled. "I'm sorry. I wanted to make cookies and I forgot to set the timer. When I saw the smoke, I panicked."

He stepped around her to turn off the oven. "I think they're done."

She hiccupped out a laugh. When she opened the oven door, another cloud of smoke emerged. "What a mess."

"Let's open all the windows in the kitchen and living room to air this place out."

"I should have just bought the ones from the bakery." She picked up a burnt cookie, and it crumbled between her fingertips. "I was going to surprise you by making dinner tonight. I know you're busy. Guess I shouldn't even bother trying to grill the brats."

He was surprised by her gesture. "How about we save Heidi's kitchen from further abuse, and you bring everything up to my house, say around six. I'll grill the brats, and the kids can help you prepare anything else you got. You can join us for dinner."

A pink blush stained her cheeks. "This is so embarrassing. You must think I'm an idiot."

Eli wanted to reach over and take her hand in an effort to reassure. He didn't trust himself to touch her. From the moment he'd entered this kitchen, he hadn't stopped thinking about wrapping her up in his arms and kissing her tears away.

She had the most striking gray eyes, like two polished granite stones. And he liked the cute, little cleft in her chin. Every time he saw her, his attraction grew. But he wasn't concerned. Ann would only be here for another day or two, and then he'd never see her again.

On the day Nikki left, he'd sworn to always put his children's needs first. With his busy schedule, that meant no dating. He'd quickly shut down Heidi's efforts when she'd set up his profile on one of those online matchmaking sites.

And here, for the first time in a long time, a woman had gotten under his skin. Whenever he was around Ann, he felt hot sparks of desire. With her, he didn't feel like just a dad or a brother; he felt like a man.

"So, what do you say, want to do it together?" Listening to the way he worded that question, he could have slapped himself across the head. *Do it together?* It sounded like an indecent proposition. "Do dinner, I mean. Together. With the kids."

Her smile brightened up the smoky kitchen. "Sure. I'll bring everything up around six. And maybe I can learn a thing or two to save my next attempt."

"I can give you the names of several good takeout places." Eli couldn't stop the stupid grin growing on his face. "See you later."

Walking back to his ATV, that goofy grin stayed fixed in place. *Stop acting like you've never been around a pretty girl before.*

He'd been in a rock band in LA. Granted, his wife had been the lead singer, but still, he knew a thing or two about gorgeous women.

But that had been ten years ago. Eli's life was very different now than those high-flying days when he only cared about chasing the dream of being a famous musician.

Now milk prices and growing seasons dominated his thoughts.

Some nights, he'd dream he was back on stage, the crowd screaming his name. He'd wake up filled with longing for a taste of that life again. He still craved the rush of performing. Sometimes, he was envious of Nikki. Not that he'd ever admit that to anyone. He barely admitted it to himself.

Glancing back over his shoulder, he caught a glimpse of Ann, standing in front of an opened window. The breeze blew the curtains around her. Then like a ghost, she was gone.

Chapter Six

Since she'd banned herself from cooking, and the weather was near perfection, Jordan decided to take a walk. She put on a pair of her favorite aviator sunglasses and went outside. She headed west, walking on the shoulder of the road. After about forty minutes, she found the driveway Heidi had told her about, heading into a thick grove of trees. The screech of a blue jay heralded her presence. A rabbit darted across the path ahead of her, scurrying underneath the thick brush.

Embraced in the peace of nature, Jordan's mind wandered back in time to the day that changed the course of her life: the day after her thirteenth birthday. Of course, there had been no cake or presents. Only a few of the other carnival people had wished her a happy birthday. Otherwise, a birthday in the Spencer family was like any other miserable day.

The fair they'd come to work at had started that day. Jordan always loved the first day of any fair or festival. The games, rides, and grounds were clean and ready for customers. Excitement filled the air as people began walking through the gates. After all the hard work of setting up, she and Lacy had spent the morning sitting on a bench by the entrance. They'd watched the crowd while munching on ears of buttery corn.

In the afternoon, Jordan had gone over to the funnel cake stand. The owner gave her all the funnel cakes she could eat in exchange for performing by his stand. He knew from seeing her at previous fairs that she drew a large crowd.

The fair had been busy that day, she remembered, which in turn had made her mom happy. More people meant more money. She'd been using Jordan's voice to line her own pockets since Jordan was five years old.

But Jordan had always loved to sing, especially back then, and the size of the audience made no difference to her. When she stood on her little stage, she felt free, like a bird flying in the sky.

She'd taken her place in the center of their makeshift stage and Lacy pressed play on the cassette tape player. The melody started, one Jordan had recorded on a dusty piano she'd found at some fairground years before. As she sang her first song, a small crowd started to gather. Soon, the group clapped along while she performed a rowdy country song. They quieted during the love song in the middle of the set. Jordan had had them eating out of her hand. She loved the control—even as nothing more than a child.

The last song ended with a long ovation. She'd curtsied in appreciation.

As people started to depart, they walked past Jordan's mom, who held a plastic bucket. One by one, they tossed bills into the bucket. Jordan could remember that awful feeling of knowing she was only a chicken on a hot skillet, made to perform for someone else's profit.

"That was extraordinary." The man who had stood before her held a wide-brimmed hat in his hand and wore an easy smile. "Have you had voice lessons?"

Despite all the other people around her, he had managed to draw her attention instantly. Her instincts had warned her to be careful. Strange men meant danger. "No. I just sing."

"Phil Hampton," he'd said, reaching out his hand. The guy was of medium height and build. His clothing, hair, and demeanor were nothing noteworthy. The man had the brightest blue eyes she'd ever seen, along with a full head of black and silver hair.

"Jordan Spencer." She shook his hand.

"I work in Nashville as a talent manager. I secure record deals for singers and help them build their careers. Your voice, Jordan, is amazing."

In her naïve, childlike imagination, Phil Hampton didn't seem like a Nashville big shot. But in his outstretched hand he held a hundred-dollar bill. "This is for you. Don't give it to your mother."

She had desperately wanted that money. She could remember the burning *want* of being deemed worthy, the fleeting pride it brought along. But the hesitation had lasted for only a second, for not only had she not trusted the man who stood before her, but if her mom found out, she would beat her. "I don't want it. If you want to help me, put it in the bucket." She turned to leave.

"Jordan." There had been a tone in his voice that made her stop. "I'm surrounded by the world's best county singers. What I just heard from your untrained voice was better than most on the radio today. Take the money and my business card. I'd like you to come to my studio and record a demo."

She wanted to both laugh and cry as she thought back to that moment. Phil hadn't seemed real. She had never had that kind of luck. Jordan had carnies for parents. She didn't go to school. Most nights she went to bed hungry. Her only friend was her sister, Lacy.

"My mom would never allow it."

Phil clasped his hands behind his back and rocked back on his heels. "Don't you want to sing on a real stage, Jordan, for your own money?"

"I'm not a farm animal that can be put up for auction," she'd spat back. "You want to use me, too. You're no better than she is."

He'd set the money and card in her hand, gentle and sincere in a way so very few people in her life had ever been. "I apologize for the offense. Take it, please. Allow me to talk to your mom. Your talent is way beyond singing at small-town fairs. Please, Jordan, give me a chance."

Jordan remembered Phil pleading with her mom, who bristled at the idea of someone else hoarding in on her little money maker. Phil paid Jane Spencer a lot of money to bring Jordan for a recording session the next day.

During the whole drive to Nashville she'd been sick with nerves. But Phil had a way of calming her down. His kindness and encouragement helped her to focus only on the music. He'd treated her differently than she'd ever been treated before—with respect. That day in the music studio, she'd realized that she had value, and her dreams would come true.

Where would she be now if Phil had never gone to the fair that day? Years later, he'd told her that back then he and his wife had been on the verge of divorce. He'd been on his way to the lawyers when he'd driven past the fair. Even though he was running late for his appointment, he'd stopped to walk around and clear his head. Fate had brought Jordan's savior to her that day.

She halted by a patch of dark green ferns and closed her eyes for a moment, letting her memories settle back to the quiet place in her mind they belonged. Her attention had been so engrossed in the past, she'd lost track of time and distance. How far had she walked down the gravel path?

Up ahead, a deer stepped out of the tree line and stared at her. The deer, unconcerned with Jordan's presence, peered over at her with large, dark, blinking eyes. Without warning, it bounded down the path.

The old house shouldn't be much farther ahead. She glimpsed around for the weeping willows Heidi had told her to watch for.

As she rounded a bend in the path, the forest transformed into a vast field. The path widened. Flanking it were rows of tall weeping willow trees. She continued walking in total fascination. The scene reminded her of the grounds of a Southern plantation home. Only this one had been adapted, using trees that would survive the Wisconsin winter.

Up ahead, she saw the outline of a building through the trees. Her feet continued to move forward though her vision remained transfixed on the building before her.

The house was something out of *Gone with the Wind.* A three-story-tall portico was supported by a row of columns that ran the entire length of the front of the house. The second-story windows were doorways, which exited onto the wraparound porch.

Heidi was right. This place was a replica of the Greek revival plantation homes she'd seen down South. All the landscaping was untended and overgrown. Several windows were broken—the bottom edges of the draperies pulled out and blew in the breeze.

The house totally enthralled her. It filled her with longing. A feeling she hadn't experienced since she was a young girl. Jordan remembered sitting in the back of her parents' truck and staring out the window at all the big, beautiful houses passing by. Deep in her heart, she'd craved a solid structure, filled with love, to call home.

Since she enjoyed studying historical architecture, she could almost imagine what the house had looked like in its original glory. Shining bright white and majestic, surrounded by trees and colorful flowers.

Jordan wanted to learn more about its history. Thinking of Eli, she remembered his invitation. *Come at six o'clock.*

She checked the time. Where had the afternoon gone? If she was going to get changed before heading over to the farmhouse, she needed to hurry back.

***

Eli brushed his hair one more time, cursing that he should have gotten a haircut like Heidi had suggested last week. He looked as shaggy as an Irish wolfhound.

Telling himself over and over that tonight was only a simple dinner with Ann did nothing to calm his nerves. Quite the opposite. His pulse quickened every time he thought of her.

Keep it cool, man. You don't want to turn into a blubbering idiot in front of your children.

A knock sounded from downstairs. She was here. After one last look in the mirror, he descended the stairs, ready to welcome the gorgeous and fascinating Ann Dufour into his house.

When he opened the door, his heart stopped at the sight of her. He couldn't breathe.

"Hi. I found a basket in Heidi's closet and packed all the food inside." She raised the wicker picnic basket. Waiting for him to reply, her smile fell. "If you want, I can just leave it here for you and the kids."

"No, no," he said quickly, finally finding his tongue. "Elliot and Lita are excited for you to join us. Come on in." Eli reached for the basket to take it out of her hands. His fingers brushed against the soft skin of her arm. Sparks shot through him.

She quickly released her hold on the basket. "All the smoke has cleared from the house. You'll be happy to know that I won't be baking again." Her laughter echoed through the otherwise quiet kitchen.

What was it about her that had him all twisted up, including his brain?

She'd changed into khaki shorts and a pink button-up top. Sparkly sandals adorned her feet. He noticed her toenails were painted to match her shirt. If she was wearing makeup, he couldn't tell. Not that she needed any. Why mask perfection?

"Lita made a cake this afternoon." He set down the basket by the chocolate frosted two-layer cake on the counter. Suddenly, he felt very self-conscious about the interior of his house. Every room was still decorated in the same dated style as when his parents had lived here.

Ann came over to look at Lita's cake. "Now I feel really incompetent. How old is Lita, anyway?"

"She's only ten, but acts like she runs this place. And sometimes she does."

Ann tucked a piece of her short hair behind her ear. "Lita's a great girl. And Elliot's a wonderful boy. You're a lucky father."

Her words impacted his heart. He *was* lucky to have Lita and Elliot. When his marriage had dissolved, Nikki could have sued for custody. He hated the fact that she'd left them without a fight, but he was grateful they were his to nurture and raise. They were his to protect. "So, what do you have hidden in this basket?"

She came over to join him by the counter. "I brought brats because that's what the meat counter guy recommended. There's a container of potato salad. Don't worry, I didn't make it." Ann lifted the plastic container out of the basket and set it on the counter.

"And what do you plan on doing with these?" He took out a honeydew melon and a cantaloupe.

Smiling, she grabbed them out of his hands. "I'm going to make fruit salad. That doesn't involve heat."

"Can I trust you with a knife?"

"Oh, ye of little faith." Her brows arched over her gray eyes. "How about you just worry about the grilling. I'll call Lita if I need help in here."

He laughed at the look of faux offense on her face. While her lips twitched with good humor, her jaw remained set in stubborn pride.

Eli went out to start the grill. Elliot ran over to join him out on the back deck.

"Hey, Dad, Henrietta hasn't had her calf yet. Do you think something's wrong?"

Elliot had taken on the job of naming every cow, heifer, and calf on their farm. Sometimes, the names he came up with were very fitting. Other times, they were downright hilarious. "Henrietta is fine. I checked on her this morning. Let's give her a little more time."

"Okay," he said with a sigh. "Do I need to shower before dinner?"

Eli sniffed his son. "You bet. We have company tonight."

Elliot's face perked up. "I thought we were supposed to leave Ann alone. Why don't you have to leave her alone?"

"It was her idea. Well... she wanted to make dinner for us, so I invited her to join us. I was just being nice."

He didn't miss the flash of doubt in Elliot's eyes before the kid ran inside the house to shower.

Eli followed him in to check the progress in the kitchen. Ann was alone, which meant Lita must be still hiding in her room.

Instead of calling to her, he went upstairs and knocked on her door. "Lita, Ann's here. She'd like your help with the fruit salad."

No answer. He tried again.

Knock, knock, knock. "Come out of your room. We have a guest."

After a brief pause, Lita cracked opened the door. "I'm not feeling good." She went to close the door.

Eli stuck his foot in the opening. "You were fine earlier when you made the cake. I expect you to come downstairs and join us for dinner."

"Why?" Her angel face scowled up at him. "You don't care about me. All you care about is wanting Ann to think we're the perfect family."

"I'm pretty sure Ann knows our family is far from perfect. What's really going on?" He pushed the door open to see a bedroom in chaos. Clothes were scattered on the floor. Her dolls were off the shelf and tossed in a pile in the corner of the room.

"I called Mom." Lita sniffled and sat on her disheveled bed. "I asked her if she'd take me with her."

"What did she say?" Eli already knew, and seeing his daughter heartbroken left him angrier than ever.

Wiping a tear from her cheek, Lita looked up at him with clear eyes. "Mom said that I need to stay home with you. Being on the road with the band is no place for a kid."

"I'm sorry." What else could he say? *I told you so?* He kept a firm rein on his temper while mentally yelling curses of frustration. How could Nikki not know how much pain she inflicted?

"If it's no place for kids, then why is she there? Why doesn't she love me?" As she began sobbing, her small shoulders shook.

"Mom does love you and Elliot. It's hard to understand sometimes why people do the things they do."

No one ever told him how hard parenting would be. Lita was right. Nikki put herself first. She'd run off to pursue her own dreams, even at the cost of her children.

But Eli couldn't deny his responsibility in the whole mess. He'd been the one who'd insisted on moving back to Wisconsin. He'd refused to sell the farm, knowing that Nikki was miserable living there.

When she'd told him she was leaving, he hadn't taken her seriously. By the time he realized their marriage was really over, it was too late. Nikki had emotionally removed herself from the family long before she'd physically left.

"Remember that I love you, more than anything else on this earth. Aunt Heidi loves you. And I'm pretty sure Elliot does, too, even when you two are fighting."

Despite her tears, Lita smiled. "I'm sorry about the mess. I promise I'll clean it up after dinner."

Eli stood. "Don't worry. How about we go make sure Ann hasn't burned the kitchen down? Okay?"

A giggle escaped. "I like her."

"She's pretty cool… for a girl."

Lita hopped off the bed. "Pretty cool or just pretty?"

What a little tease. "Don't start, young lady. Or no Bay Beach for you tomorrow."

They went downstairs to find Ann had cut all the melons into small chunks, thankfully without bloodshed.

He must have looked surprised.

"I'm not totally useless in the kitchen." She set the knife on the counter, and then popped a piece of melon in her mouth. "*Mmmmm,* yummy," she sighed. A drop of juice hung from her bottom lip until she licked it away.

Eli's eyes almost exploded from their sockets. That mouth. Those lips. He had to fight to maintain control.

"Dad," Elliot ran into the kitchen through the back door. "The grill's smoking."

Shoot. He'd forgotten to put the brats on. Now the grill was smoking hot. Just like the woman lighting up his shabby kitchen.

"See, you're not the only one who makes smoke when they cook," he said to Ann. "Though no brats were harmed. Not yet, anyway."

Thirty minutes later, the four of them were seated around the scuffed-up kitchen table. Lita sat on one side of Ann, Elliot on the other. Ann seemed to enjoy their company. She even laughed at the kids' corny jokes.

"These are so good." Ann reached for another brat.

"Where are you putting all that food?" Eli was astonished at the amount she'd eaten. By the looks of her, Ann had the diet of a field mouse. "You have a hollow leg to fill up?"

Blushing, she shrugged her shoulders. "I guess I'm not used to being able to eat whatever I want."

Lita gave him a funny look then turned to Ann. "How come you don't know how to cook?"

"Lita." Eli nudged his daughter with his elbow.

"Oh, that's okay." Ann set down her fork. "I don't have to. I have people who plan my diet and cook my food." Her happy features dulled. She set her lips in a tight line.

Controlling how much food she ate and wasn't allowed to cook her own meals. Add the fact that she was trying to hide from someone, and Ann fit the classic profile of a battered woman.

"Are you rich?" Elliot mumbled while wiping his mouth with his arm.

Her gaze dropped to her plate. "Depends on what you mean by rich. If you mean that I have a lot of money, then yes. But there are other ways a person can be rich. Love and family make you rich. Having a place to call home makes someone rich. Even simply being happy with what life has handed you makes you rich."

"You're absolutely right." Eli felt a strong urge to protect her from whoever had hurt her. "Love and family are more valuable than gold."

Ann stayed quiet through the rest of their meal. She listened to Lita's chatter and Elliot's stories, but most of her good humor had vanished.

Once they'd cleaned up the dishes, she went to leave. "Thanks for the great dinner. I haven't eaten that well in a really long time."

"But you can't leave," Lita said. "We haven't had dessert, yet."

"Can you save me a piece? I should get going."

"But why? If you leave, Dad's going to go sit in his chair and fall asleep. And all Elliot wants to do is play with his dumb toy tractors. It's so boring here." Lita pleaded her case well, using her words in combination with some award-winning dramatic acting. Her head tipped back and she let out a long sigh. "Save me."

"I'm sorry, honey, but I'm really tired. I'll see you tomorrow, okay? Maybe we can do our nails or something."

"Dad's taking us to Bay Beach tomorrow. I'll let you know when we get back."

"Sounds like a plan." Ann opened the screen door. "Thanks for inviting me to join you. Have a good night."

The screen door banged closed behind her. With both kids watching Eli like a hawk, he couldn't escort her back like he wanted to.

After spending time with Ann, his nightly routine of dozing off in his chair, and then heading up to his empty bed felt painfully lonely.

Chapter Seven

When the ringing from Jordan's cell jolted her out of a good sleep, she blindly slapped her hand on the dresser until she made contact. She didn't open her eyes to check the caller ID before she answered.

"Hello," she mumbled.

"Jordan? What's wrong?" Phil's concerned voice sounded through the phone.

"*Hmmm.* Nothing." She propped herself up on her elbow. "You woke me up."

"It's ten o'clock. You must be enjoying your vacation."

"I was having the best dream. I was just a normal girl, living in a normal world."

Phil laughed. "Sweetheart, you'll never be normal."

"Funny." She huffed and rubbed her eyes. Very slowly, she opened her lids to see, yes, the time was really ten a.m. "What do you need?"

"I'm just checking in. Making sure you're all right. Lacy told me your trip hasn't gone exactly as planned."

"Yeah, the storm really screwed things up, but you know what? I'm learning to roll with the punches."

"I take it you haven't been recognized yet?" Phil asked before another voice sounded in the background. "Doreen says hi and to enjoy your break. You deserve it, kid. Just don't make it too long."

If Phil was the closest thing Jordan had to a father, his wife, Doreen, was like her mom. She'd moved into their home as a teenager and become part of their family. "Tell Doreen I'm staying at a dairy farm in Wisconsin. I even helped feed the calves the other day. And no one recognizes me here. Must be my stellar disguise."

"You're a natural beauty, Jordan, and I'm glad you're able to see yourself like I do—the little brunette girl who cast a spell over me, a hardened music manager, with nothing but her angel voice."

Jordan rolled out of bed. Her feet shuffled across the carpet, stopping in front of the full-length mirror attached to the back of the door. "You're the one who hired that team of hairstylists and makeup artists to begin with. Add a personal trainer, dietitian, and publicist, and I can't even go to the bathroom without someone giving their opinion."

"I know. Back then, we were trying to build your career. Now, you're a big enough star you can tell them all to take a flying leap, if that's what you want." Phil's laughter came through loud and clear. So did the sound of Doreen yelling out her agreement.

"Isn't that what I'm doing?"

"Right now, you're hiding."

She fluffed out her short hair with her fingers. *Maybe I'll keep my hair like this. A new look for a new Jordan Ann Spencer.*

Phil cleared his throat. "We're worried you're getting burned out. Your breakup with Henry is all over the news. Don't worry, though. Your publicist team is working overtime to discredit the lies that spoiled brat is telling."

"What's he saying?" Of course, Henry would talk to the media. Another failed relationship for Jordan, the emotionally unsteady country star.

"It's all utter nonsense. We have it under control. You relax. That's an order."

"I've been writing a lot. Have a couple new songs in the works." Sitting back on the bed, she curled her feet under her. "I want my next album to get back to the basics. You know, like more acoustic instrumentals. Get rid of that pop, techno-sound the producers keep pushing."

They talked for a little while longer, and then Jordan ended the call with a promise to keep working on her new album. She planned on walking over to the old, abandoned mansion later, wanting another chance to study the architecture.

She would not allow herself to worry about what the media was saying about her today, knowing they'd report a different rumor tomorrow. In truth, she'd finally found a small slice of happiness on a farm in Wisconsin. And she had the hots for a man who worked with his hands, not a rich, pampered pretty boy.

Go ahead and print that, stupid tabloids. No one would ever believe you.

***

Eli was up before dawn in order to get all his chores finished so he could take Lita and Elliot to Bay Beach. Even the kids were awake before their alarms. They headed out to the barn without even a peep of protest.

He couldn't remember the last time he'd taken them somewhere for a fun day. That was usually Heidi's gig. He'd always stayed behind because there was so much to do at home.

Well, he made a promise, and barring the heifers escaping again, he wasn't going to break it.

After a quick shower, he dressed, and then rummaged around for a ball cap that was somewhat clean.

"Hey, Dad." Elliot came walking into his bedroom, holding something behind his back. "What's Ann doing?"

On a shelf at the back of the closet, he found a new Milwaukee Brewers hat. He folded the lid a few times to loosen it up. "I don't know. She didn't say last night."

Elliot wiped his nose with his arm. "Can I ask if she wants to come with us?"

"Use a tissue," Eli scolded. He noticed something clutched in Elliot's hands—a bouquet of flowers. "Did you pick those?"

"Uh-huh." Elliot nodded his head. "In the field behind the barn. They're for Ann."

Eli noted the tinge of pink on his son's cheeks. *Does my nine-year-old, the boy who still thinks girls have cooties, have a crush on Ann?*

Like father, like son. An overwhelming love filled his chest. Elliot possessed a sweet, caring nature. Something Eli strived to emulate, though often fell short.

"Why do you have flowers for Ann?" he asked, even though he already knew. Looked like the kid was one step ahead of his old man.

"Because she's nice. Can she come with us? Please?" Elliot shook the flowers in an attempt to resuscitate his bouquet. A few orange petals fell to the carpet.

This little trip was supposed to be family time. Only the three of them. But he had to admit, the idea had merit. While the kids were running around from ride to ride, he'd have someone to hang out with. A pretty someone.

"How about we walk over to Aunt Heidi's house and see if Ann's outside. If she is, then we can ask her. She might not want to be bothered, though. Don't be disappointed if she says no."

"Ann's said she'd never been to Bay Beach before. I'm sure she'll want to go."

When they got downstairs, Eli didn't find Lita in the kitchen, or in the family room. He hadn't seen her since she'd gone off to do her chores.

"Do you know where Lita is?" He hoped she wasn't pouting in her room. It seemed these days any little thing set her off. As hard as he tried, he didn't understand her mood swings.

"She's outside, waiting to leave. She said she was going over to say hi to Ann."

Hadn't he instructed both of them to leave Ann alone? She was looking for privacy, and that seemed to be the one thing lacking from her stay here. He wouldn't blame her if she found somewhere else to hide away.

He went outside with Elliot at his heels. The sound of singing stopped him in his tracks—Lita's voice. He'd know that sweet sound anywhere.

Ann must be accompanying her with the guitar. For a minute, he stood still and listened. Lita had great pitch, and her voice rang clear. She was singing a song he'd never heard before, which could be anything recorded in the last ten years. Since moving back to the farm, he'd been completely out of the music scene. The only station he listened to played classic rock.

He waited until the song ended to approach the house. Lita looked at him from the porch swing with a huge smile on her face.

"You sounded wonderful." He clapped for both of them.

Lita stood from the swing she'd been sharing with Ann. "Ann's really good at the guitar. Almost as good as you, Dad."

Ann smirked. When she looked up at him, her eyes sparkled. "Then I think your dad should play something, because I don't believe anyone plays better than me."

A challenge. One he couldn't ignore. He did still have his pride.

She handed her guitar over to him, and his rusty fingers strummed the strings. Eli hadn't played in years. He kept too busy to indulge in hobbies.

"What song?" Lita asked. She held an imaginary microphone up to her mouth.

The image of her mother, standing on stage and holding a real microphone, made Eli's stomach clench. Lita was so much like Nikki. He couldn't deny it—as much as he may like to.

Elliot got seated next to Ann and handed her the flowers.

"Thank you so much." She gingerly took them out of Elliot's hand. "They're beautiful. I'll put them in a vase with water once I go inside." Ann leaned over and gave him a peck on the cheek.

The boy's already flushed cheeks turned bright red. He glanced over at Eli with a huge smile on his face.

Smooth moves, kid.

Laughing, Eli strummed a G-chord. "How about 'Gimme Shelter,' by the Stones? You remember the lyrics, Lita?"

She shook her head. "I know the first verse and the chorus."

Ann relaxed back and set her elbow on the armrest. She looked so incredible he almost started playing a love song. He had to stop that kind of thinking. Nothing good would come of it. Ann would be gone soon. She'd probably leave tomorrow, which would be for the best—for all of them.

Eli started playing the opening chords to a Clapton classic. His confidence rose with Ann's smile. The guitar felt like a natural part of his body. The melody flowed through him, and Lita began to sing. She hit all the notes with spunk.

Eli strained to hear Ann quietly humming in the background. From what he could tell, she had a nice voice, even if it was restrained. When he got to the guitar solo part of the song, he didn't hold back. Elliot, Lita, and Ann clapped with encouragement. By the time the song was done, he'd broken out into a sweat.

"Impressive." Ann reached to take back her guitar. "So, who played better?" she asked Lita and Elliot, who'd both taken seats on the floor of the porch.

"Dad." Elliot cried out, with a smile for Ann. "But you played well, too."

She ruffled his shaggy head of hair. "Your dad still has some rock-n-roll flowing through his veins. Eli, I bet you could get gigs at the local bars."

"Those days are over." Eli missed them, though. And playing brought back the rush. He could almost hear the crowd cheering. Looking at Lita and Elliot, he knew they were the only ones he cared about pleasing. They were more important than a stadium filled with thousands of fans.

Ann picked up a notebook she'd earlier placed on the floor. She closed it, but not before Eli caught what looked like handwritten poetry. Or song lyrics?

"I'm sorry we interrupted you," Eli said to Ann while ushering his daughter down the stairs.

"It's no bother. Actually, I was the one that called Lita over. I wanted her opinion on something."

Lita squirmed out of his grasp and started back up the stairs. "I liked the second one. It seems happier."

"Thanks." Ann smiled. "You guys have fun at Bay Beach."

Elliot jumped up from the ground to the edge of the porch, and then grasped onto the porch rail so he wouldn't fall back. "You want to come with us?" He peered at Ann from over the rail. "Dad said it was okay. They have tons of rides at Bay Beach. Last time, when we went with Aunt Heidi, I went on the Scrambler ten times in a row. Then I threw up all over Aunt Heidi's new shoes."

"Well… that does sound like fun," Ann said. "But I don't want to intrude on your family day."

Eli really wanted her to come along. Maybe simply for some adult company in the sea of wild children. "You wouldn't be intruding. But I understand if you have something else you'd rather be doing."

"It's not that." Ann sighed.

Was she afraid of being out in public? "You could borrow one of my hats." He handed her his Brewers hat.

She seemed to hesitate before reaching out to accept his offering. A true smile brightened her entire face. "Okay. I'll come along, but no Scrambler for me. Let me grab my sunglasses." Ann opened the front door before looking back over her shoulder at Elliot. "And no throwing up on my new shoes."

***

Jordan was in love with Eli's talent. She'd hire him to be in her band in a heartbeat. That was, if he wasn't a single-father dairy farmer from Wisconsin. She believed him when he'd told her his musician days were over.

Sitting next to him in the front seat of his truck, Jordan tried hard to keep her vision straight ahead. But with Lita and Elliot talking loudly in the backseat, she found herself turning around to engage in conversation with them. Then her gaze would linger on Eli—his yellow T-shirt stretched taut over his chest and shoulders. *Wow.* He looked good enough to be the hero in one of her music videos.

She could picture the opening scene. Jordan would be a damsel in distress, dressed in a regency ball gown, engaged to an evil man she didn't love. And while her song played in the background of a masquerade ball, she'd see Eli for the first time. Their gaze would lock across the room. He'd ask her to dance. As they ran off together into the night, the end would fade to black.

Giggling at her silly mind and rather terrible directing skills, she focused her attention on the road ahead.

The trip to Green Bay lasted about forty-five minutes, just long enough for Jordan to be grateful she didn't have to listen to Lita and Elliot fight about who was touching whom for another minute.

After they parked, Eli guided them to the ticket counter. "The rides here are cheap, so the kids will keep busy." He paid for a huge stretch of tickets, and then divided them between Lita and Elliot.

"So where are we going first?" Jordan asked.

There were kids everywhere, and shouts of fun and laughter filled the air. She was glad she'd agreed to come instead of staying behind to explore the abandoned mansion.

"Ferris wheel." Lita pointed over to the lighted circle, spinning at a moderate pace. "Then can we get lunch, because I'm starving."

Jordan was hungry, too, but she hadn't wanted to say anything. On this trip, she was their guest. Simply going along for the ride, so to speak.

"Sounds like a plan." Eli walked beside Jordan. "You want to ride, too?"

"No, thanks. I got my fill of carnival rides growing up."

His brows arched. "Did your parents take you to places like this a lot?"

She approached the metal fence that surrounded the Ferris wheel and tipped her head to see the very top. "Something like that. They worked for a carnival company. We traveled around, mostly in the South. I grew up with one of these in my proverbial backyard."

Lita and Elliot ran ahead to get in line, arguing about who got to be first.

"That must have been cool." Eli rested his forearms on the top of the fence.

"Not really." She shrugged. "I didn't have a real home. Not a traditional one that stayed in one place. A traveling carnival is not the best place to raise kids. Some of the people my parents worked with were very nice. Others, not so much."

Why was she telling him all this? Eli probably thought she was a freak.

"You turned out all right." When he smiled at her, small lines crinkled around his eyes. "Who taught you how to play guitar? You were jammin' with Lita back home."

Home. His home. Not hers. She needed to remind herself of that fact. Eli was a fantasy. Not a man who could fit into her real life.

But right now, she wanted to forget logic and pretend she was part of his family. Lita and Elliot were her kids. Eli, her husband.

She shook those thoughts out of her head. "I found a guitar someone had abandoned in a pile of junk. The guy who ran the ring toss game showed me the basic chords. I figured out the rest myself."

Up above them, Lita poked her head over the Ferris wheel carriage. "Hello." She waved vigorously down at them.

Then Elliot's face appeared. "I can see for miles up here."

The wheel started to spin again, and the kids disappeared out of sight.

Jordan adjusted her sunglasses. So far, no one had looked twice at her. Granted, they'd only been here for a few minutes, but there was so much activity around them, she wasn't worried.

Parents were too busy chasing their children around the park to realize there was a country music superstar in their midst.

"I got my guitar as a gift for my tenth birthday," Eli said. "If my dad would have known I'd take off for LA to pursue music when I got older, he probably would have never bought it for me. Dad wanted me to be a farmer, like him. I don't think he ever forgave me for leaving."

She touched his arm in an attempt to comfort, and her fingertips tingled against his skin. "Heidi told me about the accident. I'm sorry you lost both of them so suddenly."

"We never got a chance to make things right before he passed." He looked away. "I had to come back home because I couldn't let the farm be sold off."

Jordan wanted to say something to sooth his guilty conscience. He was a good man who worked hard to do the right thing. Did he realize how rare those traits were in a person?

Lita and Elliot finished their ride and came running toward them.

"Let's get something to eat." Eli replaced his frown with a warm smile. "And then maybe I can convince Ann to go down the giant slide with me." He winked at her.

With an offer that enticing, how could she say no?

Chapter Eight

Eli watched in awe as Ann finished off the last fluffy, pink piece of cotton candy. The girl could eat. Nothing wrong with that. He wondered how she stayed so skinny, though. Good genetics?

"Time's up. The giant slide awaits." He took the plastic bag out of Ann's hands and tossed it into a trash barrel.

"Fine. But if I get sick on the way down, I'm blaming you." Her grin emphasized the cute cleft in her chin.

They walked side by side over to the entrance to the slide. He handed the attendant enough tickets for the four of them.

"You need a sack." Elliot grabbed one for himself before darting up the stairs.

A wave of people came sliding down, crying out with laughter. Each one wore a smile on their face.

"Have you ever been on a slide this tall?" Eli followed behind Ann. They climbed and climbed up the staircase.

"Nope. The carnival company my parents worked for didn't have a giant slide." She glanced at him over her shoulder and shot him a breathtaking smile. "You are about to witness my inaugural ride."

Eli caught his foot on the last step and stumbled. Luckily, Ann had turned to check out the view from the top and hadn't witnessed his humiliation. What was it about her that made him act like a teenaged, love-struck fool?

Once the attendant had given them the go-ahead, they walked over and got seated. Eli took the spot next to Ann, with Lita and Elliot bracketing them.

"One, two, three, go." Lita and Elliot shouted in unison.

Ann clutched her sack and pushed off. She screamed the entire five-second trip down.

When Eli reached the bottom, he glanced over to make sure she was all right.

She stood up on shaky legs. Her laughter burst out, punctuated by throaty wheezing.

Which started Elliot and Lita laughing along with her. Their mood was contagious, and Eli joined in.

"You laugh funny," Elliot said to Ann, once he stopped laughing.

"I know. My sister, Lacy, says I sound like a wild pack of hyenas." She held out her potato sack. "Can we go down again?"

Several hours later, the kids went to stand in line for the wooden roller coaster, while Eli found a shady spot to sit with Ann.

"You having fun?" he asked. Eli was having a blast. How long had it been since he'd felt this happy and content? He hadn't thought about the farm once since arriving at Bay Beach.

They'd gone on almost every ride at least once, with the exception of the little kid ones. Ann had been a good sport, sitting next to Lita on the Tilt-A-Whirl, and sharing a train car with Elliot. The longer they were here, the more relaxed she appeared.

"I am having fun. Thanks for asking me along." She took a sip of soda. Her full lips pursed around the striped straw. "The weather today is perfect."

Eli tipped his head up to the sky. Above them, through the layer of branches and leaves, the sun shone without a cloud to block its glory. He would have been okay with cooler temps, but at least they weren't getting rain.

"I'll start cutting the hay tomorrow, which will take most of my time for the next couple days. I wanted to do something special today with the kids. Normally, Heidi gets all the fun stuff."

"She'll be back tonight, right?" She took off her sunglasses and cleaned them with her T-shirt.

All of a sudden, nerves buzzed in his gut. He felt like a boy on his first date. With each breath, he struggled to expand his tight chest. And when his gaze met hers, he wanted to get lost. He could stare at her all day.

Every time he looked at her, he noticed something else uniquely Ann. She was still such a mystery, and that enticed him.

"Heidi should be home later today," he said. "But don't feel like you have to hurry up and find somewhere else to stay. That is... if you don't want to. Heidi made it very clear that you're welcome to stay with her as long as you'd like."

"If she doesn't mind, I'd like to hang around for a little while longer." She stretched her long legs in front of her, causing her cut-off shorts to ride up a little higher.

Eli fought to control the desire that built inside him. He hadn't been interested in a woman since Nikki, until now. For five years, he'd been happy as a single guy, focused on being a good father and working the family farm. Love, or lack of it, didn't take up much of his mind. Unless he was trying to avoid being set up by Heidi. She must have gone through every single woman in the area in her attempt to find him an acceptable date.

But all it had taken was a few escaped heifers and a bad thunderstorm to bring Ann Dufour to his front door.

Eli decided to go out on a limb and ask the question that had been weighing on him, even if the answer was something he didn't want to hear. He glanced at her empty ring finger. "Are you married?"

Ann's eyes widened and her brows lifted. "No." Her answer was followed by a single chuckle. "Why do you ask?"

He shrugged his shoulders, feeling stupid. *Do I tell the truth? That I want to kiss you, right here, right now?* "Can't a guy just be curious?" The attraction surging through his body jolted him with so much energy, he felt like he'd been roused from a long, deep sleep.

Ann shifted in her seat so she faced him. "Are you still in love with your ex-wife?"

Shaking his head, he folded his hands on his lap. "No. She's remarried, and I'm only interested in what she does for the kids' sake." He raised his head to see her smiling at him. "Are you seeing anyone? I mean—" he stammered. His blood pulsed quick and hot through his veins.

"Like a boyfriend?" Ann broke eye contact, turning her gaze toward something in the distance. "I'm getting over a bad breakup." She stopped talking and quickly slid her sunglasses back on.

"Eli," a woman said, approaching them at a rapid pace. "Hailey thought she saw Lita here. I'm surprised you came with them today. You're always so busy."

Layla Ryan was the mother of Lita's best friend, Hailey. She also was the reason his younger brother, Sam, avoided coming home.

"Hi, Layla," Eli said. "I'm sure the girls will find each other."

Ann scooted away from him, leaving a foot of distance between them. "I'm going to use the ladies' room." She stood and hustled away, with her head bent down.

"Who was that?" Layla pointed in the direction Eli was looking. "Does she have kids in the school?"

He shook his head. "Ann's a guest of Heidi's. I invited her to come along with us."

"I know I've seen her before. What's her name?"

"Ann Dufour. She's not from the area." Eli noticed the dark bags under Layla's normally bright eyes. As a single parent himself, he could relate to playing the role of both mother and father. No one but Layla knew who her daughter's biological father was. She'd never told Sam. And as far as Eli knew, Hailey didn't know his name either. "I heard you'll be graduating college soon."

"One more semester to go. I hope it was worth it."

Eli sometimes wished he was attracted to Layla. She was very pretty and a great mother, but his brother had never gotten over her, and vice versa. Whenever Sam and Layla were together, which wasn't very often, there was no mistaking the sizzle of attraction, along with plenty of anger and mistrust.

"Do you have any job leads?"

Layla's smile brightened her face. "I have an interview next week. There's a new golf course that's looking to hire an assistant manager to help run the clubhouse."

"Good luck, even though I'm sure you won't need it."

"Thanks." She glanced over at a little boy, crying in his father's arms. "Have you heard from Sam lately?"

The boy had stopped crying and now held a mound of cotton candy in his chubby hands.

"He called Heidi to make plans for when she was in Milwaukee. I talked to him for a few minutes. He's busy, as usual. Doing security jobs on nights he's not at the fire station."

He tried to read Layla's face, but she held onto an expression of polite curiosity.

"He always liked keeping busy," Layla said. "Never wanted to sit still, even to watch a movie."

"Why don't you call him?" Eli ventured to guess that idea would be brushed aside, but he threw it out there anyway.

She shook her head. "I'm the last person Sam wants to hear from."

A bird hopped on the ground in front of them, eyeing several pieces of popcorn on the bench. Eli brushed the popcorn onto the pavement, causing the bird to surge forward to claim its prize. "I doubt that. It's been a long time."

"Your brother is as stubborn as you, Eli." She laughed. "And he knows where to find me."

Eli nodded his head. Yes, both he and Sam had inherited a fierce stubborn streak from their father. A stubborn clash of wills had set Eli off on his adventure to LA. It had also brought him back home and was the reason he'd held firm against Nikki's desire to leave.

Lita and Elliot came running out of the exit for the rollercoaster. They were both talking in unison, so fast he couldn't understand either of them.

Eli stood and put an arm around each child's shoulder. "Ann went to use the bathroom. How about we go wait for her? Then, we can see if she wants to ride the swings one last time before we have to leave."

"Hi, kiddos," Layla said. "I guess I should go find Hailey. She talked my parents into going on the bumper cars."

"Tell Hailey I'll call her tonight." Lita climbed onto the bench behind Eli, and then jumped on his back. She wrapped her arms around his shoulders. "Giddy-up, Dad."

Good thing his little monkey was still light. He put a hand under her to hold her up. "Enjoy the rest of your day," he said to Layla. Then he turned to find Ann, the woman who had reignited his belief in second chances.

***

Jordan couldn't stop smiling. After washing her hands in the bathroom, she grabbed a paper towel and dried her hands very slowly.

She caught her reflection in the mirror and watched her smile grow. *Stop that right now.*

What she felt right now for Eli was dishonest. She'd be a horrible person if she let him believe there was a chance of anything romantic happening between them. He didn't even know her real name for crying out loud.

Jordan must make it clear that she wasn't interested. But that was the catch. She *was* interested. *Well, too bad. You made a promise to take a break from men. And falling for a man like Eli would end in disaster.*

But for the first time, Jordan had a man show interest in her as a person. Not the famous singer who had loads of money in her bank account. Or the person who could help him land a record deal. Or the woman who'd make for good press while they were dating, as well as after they broke up.

Deep down burned the simple desire for someone to fall in love with her, without the mirage of fame. And a mirage it was. The Jordan Spencer people read about in news was a caricature.

Her team had built her into a larger-than-life superstar who dated movie stars, other singers, and even a crown prince. Every relationship was made public. Photographed to no end. Speculated about: *Is it real love this time?*

She didn't date guys to get publicity, but there was no doubt her career benefited from the media attention. And so had theirs.

That's exactly why she needed this break. To get away from the circus and rediscover who she was and what she wanted out of the rest of her life. Not get wrapped up with another guy.

She liked Eli, but there was no possibility of a relationship between them. It would never work. Surely he'd want nothing to do with another singer, whose tour schedule kept her on the road for more than half the year.

Tossing the ball of used paper towel in the trash, she sighed. She'd have to go back out there and make it clear to Eli she was only interested in him as a friend.

Jordan walked back outside, imagining the feel of Eli's kiss. Would he taste earthy or sweet? She licked her lips, wishing Eli's mouth was pressed down on hers.

"Ann." Lita's voice jarred her out of her dream world. "Over here." She was propped up on her dad's back. While waving her arm, she bopped him on the head.

He unceremoniously set her down and rubbed the back of his head. "You have the boniest little elbows."

Unfazed, Lita ran over to meet her. "Dad has eight tickets left. Do you want to go on the spinning swings or the Ferris wheel?"

Honestly, she didn't know if she could handle another ride. But the eager look on both Lita and Elliot's faces, along with the cute smile their father wore, convinced her to take one for the team.

"How about the Ferris wheel?" The words had barely left her lips before Elliot and Lita started toward it.

"You don't have to go if you don't want." Eli walked at her side. His long strides kept pace with her. "I can tell we've worn you out."

"You haven't worn me out." Her gaze flickered over him, enjoying the way his body moved with each step. "It's just the last time I was on a Ferris wheel... well, let's say it's not a good memory."

They stopped at the end of the line. Red, blue, and yellow lights flashed above her. She remembered the feeling of her first kiss and the nausea that followed.

"I was thirteen." She decided the story was more funny than embarrassing. "I met a boy, Garrett, at one of the fairs my parents were working. He asked me to take a ride with him on the Ferris wheel." She took a breath. "I went with him, even though I didn't feel right about it. Well, Garrett was a perfect gentleman, but he did give me a quick kiss on the lips when we got to the top. Then I realized why I'd been so apprehensive and I threw up on his lap."

Laughing, Eli waved her ahead into the queue for the ride where Lita and Elliot waited. "That's a very romantic story."

"It was awful. I hope I'm not going for a repeat."

"Then you should ride with me. I have a strong stomach."

After a short wait, Jordan climbed into the carriage, followed by Eli. As he lowered the bar, his thigh brushed against hers. Behind them, Elliot hooted, while Lita gave them a wave.

Jordan waved back, thinking she'd be safer stuffed between the two kids than belted next to Eli. He was a nice man, who deserved a nice woman. One who would be happy living with him on the farm.

The wheel started to spin, a nice slow speed that lulled her into relaxation. Eli slid his arm around her shoulders, with a smoothness she'd only seen in movies.

Her breath halted, and her body flushed with heat.

The guy had moves. She needed to remember Eli Hintz wasn't simply a wide-eyed farm boy from Wisconsin. He'd been part of the music scene in LA. Surely he picked up a few things during his years out there.

Eli stared straight ahead, a crooked smile on his face. He was playing it cool, and she was anything but.

Jordan flitted a glance over at him before turning to look out over the bay. There were numerous sailboats dotting the water's smooth surface. Below them, kids and parents moved back and forth, like a swarm of busy ants.

His fingers rested lightly on her bare shoulder, and the contact energized each nerve on her skin.

Eli glanced at her out of the corner of his eyes. "You doing okay?"

Not if he continued to look at her like that. "Nothing to worry about." She noticed her hands were shaking, so she clenched them together and rested them on her lap. The urge to run her hands across his broad chest became overwhelming. She felt lightheaded and dizzy—reactions that had nothing to do with the ride.

"You said earlier that you'd recently got out of a bad relationship." Eli lost his smile. The muscles in his jaw tightened. "I promise that as long as you stay with us, nobody will hurt you."

How could she reply to those heroic words without flat-out lying, but still maintain her cover? "Don't worry about my ex. He has no idea where I am. I need the time away to figure out what I want. Who I want to be."

"And what do you want?" He leaned in.

The scent of his spicy cologne filled her nostrils. *I want you.*

This was not reality. Right now, she was in the middle of a wonderful dream. She could let herself pretend she was Ann Dufour, a woman falling for a handsome farmer. And when Eli found out the truth about who she really was, everything would crumble.

She inhaled deeply, trying to steady her nerves. His nearness made it hard for her to think straight. Jordan's body had heated to the point she was afraid she'd burst into flames.

"I want to be truly happy," Jordan whispered.

The Ferris wheel stopped, with their carriage swaying at the top. In the one below, Lita and Elliot rocked back and forth, laughing loudly.

Eli unhooked his arm around Ann and brushed his fingers under her chin. Then he took off her sunglasses—her shield. "Tell me what makes you happy."

For a second, she thought he would try to kiss her. She wanted him to kiss her, despite her head's insistence that kissing Eli was a very bad idea. Instead of leaning in, he continued to look at her with eyes that resembled molten gold.

"The same thing as most, I guess." As the wheel started to spin again, Jordan startled and grabbed onto Eli's arm. *Do not touch.* She obeyed her brain's command and dropped her hand.

The curve of his lips tested her self-control.

"Happiness for me is making a living doing something I love while staying true to myself," she said. "Not getting caught up in all the drama that's always thrown my way."

"I think happiness is a choice. Over the past few years, I've tried hard not to get dragged down by all the crap in my life. And I mean that in a very literal sense." He laughed, causing the fine lines around his eyes to deepen. "If it wasn't for my kids, I don't know how I would have survived."

"You're a great father."

"Some days I'm not so sure. The farm keeps me so busy, and I feel like I'm letting them down."

Taking a chance, she rested her hand on his. "They love you. Isn't that the ultimate joy? To have someone to love, and someone that truly loves you in return, without conditions."

"What about you? Do you have love in your life?"

Jordan had her sister, and Phil and Doreen. But she'd never known a man's total, unselfish love. And she probably never would.

Their carriage stopped at the bottom, and the ride operator came running over to lift the bar. A wave of disappointment washed over her.

After she climbed out of the Ferris wheel carriage, she waited for him to do the same. Before they approached the gate, she decided to answer his last question. "I haven't found anyone I can fully trust with my heart yet. I've learned the hard way that true love may not be meant for me."

***

Eli closed the door to Elliot's room. His boy had zonked out the second his head had hit the pillow. After a day spent outside, running from one ride to another, Eli felt he'd do the same once he climbed into bed.

He knocked on the door to Lita's room. She was old enough that he didn't dare enter her room unannounced.

"Come in," she answered.

Opening the door, he saw Lita sitting in bed and writing in her journal. He was often tempted to read what she wrote, but Heidi had warned him that if she caught him, the breach of trust would damage their relationship. But he still wanted a glimpse inside her head. How deep were the wounds caused by her mom's abandonment? Did she dream about running far away from this farm, like he'd done so long ago?

"Night, peanut. I hope you had fun today." He came to sit next to her on the bed.

She closed her diary and leaned over to set it on the nightstand. "Yeah, thanks for taking us." Her eyes still sparkled, despite the busy day they'd had. "Dad, why is Ann staying here?"

"Her vacation rental was damaged by the storm, and her car's still in the shop. Aunt Heidi was nice enough to let her stay at her house. I guess Ann's okay with that."

Lita sat with her legs tucked underneath her body. "I mean, who wants to vacation on a dairy farm?"

He laughed. "True. But I think Ann's looking for privacy. A place to get away. And our farm is definitely out in the middle of nowhere."

"I guess." She tilted her head to look up at him. "Did you kiss her on the Ferris wheel?"

Heat rose to his face. *Where had that question come from?* "No. I don't normally go around kissing girls on Ferris wheels."

"Maybe you should start," she said with a giggle.

He began to tickle her bony ribs. "The only girl who's getting a kiss from me is you." Eli kissed the top of her head.

Wrapping her arms around him, Lita squeezed. "Do you think Mom would be jealous if you got a girlfriend?"

After giving that question some thought, he answered, "I don't think so. Mom married another man."

Lita rested her head against his chest. "I wouldn't be jealous," she whispered.

His heart constricted with love. How had he been so blessed? Despite the pain of divorce, he wouldn't change marrying Nikki. His children were worth it.

"Well, don't worry too much about it." Eli didn't see his status changing anytime soon.

He would have kissed Ann on the Ferris wheel if he'd gotten a clear green light. But he'd noticed her signs of nervousness—from her narrowed pupils to the tight muscles in her face. Once he saw her body language, he knew she wouldn't welcome his advances.

There had been many times today that he'd wanted to push all doubts aside and open his heart. He'd assumed he wouldn't find love again for many years. But the feelings Ann stirred up in him had hit hard and fast, taking him totally off guard. Was it wrong for him to want someone special to share his life with? Could Ann be that woman?

Ann was a fleeting desire. When she left, his fantasies would end. He needed to keep both feet grounded in real life—his kids, his farm, and his already battered heart.

He tucked Lita under a pink sheet, kissed her one more time, and turned off the light. "Good night, princess."

"Night, Dad."

When he closed the door, he heard his cell phone ring from his room down the hall.

He hustled in order to answer the call before it got kicked over to voicemail. Picking the cell up, he saw Heidi's name on the caller ID.

"Hey, you home yet?"

"No, that's why I'm calling. I'm staying in Milwaukee for a few more days."

Alarms sounded in his head. Starting at sunrise tomorrow morning, he'd be out in the fields cutting hay. The job would take at least two days, maybe three. What would he do with Lita and Elliot? They were old enough to stay home alone during the day for a short while when Heidi went to work, but cutting hay meant he'd be gone from sun-up until past sunset.

"I'm starting the hay tomorrow."

"I know. I'm sorry, Eli, but my friend is going through a tough breakup. She asked me to stay. I already called work, and they said I could take the next two days off." She paused. "How about Nikki's parents? They could take the kids until I get back."

The kids' grandparents on their mother's side still lived in the area. He had a decent relationship with them, despite Nikki's abandonment. "I suppose I could ask."

"Or you could ask Ann if you're really in a pinch."

Eli sat on the edge of his bed. Out his bedroom window, he saw Heidi's house. One light was still on. He wondered what Ann was doing.

Eli would much rather spend another day with her than sit alone on a tractor. The job would be more pleasant with Ann sitting beside him, her body pressed against him.

Not a chance. Ann was not looking to settle down on a farm with a single dad. And he needed to protect both his children, but especially Lita, from becoming too attached to a woman who would leave soon.

He cleared his throat. "Ann is staying here for peace and quiet. I'm not asking her to keep an eye on my children, who are anything but peaceful and quiet."

"Lita called and told me Ann went to Bay Beach with you today," she said, true to form. Heidi was never happy unless she was sticking her nose in Eli's business. "Did it ever cross your mind that she might like spending time with your family?"

"Spending the day with the family is one thing. Babysitting is another."

"So you're saying she prefers your company." Heidi laughed. "Good job, Eli. That didn't take long."

"What are you talking about?" His temper rose to match her humor.

"Seducing our guest."

"I'm not seducing her." Running his hand through his hair, he worked to keep his temper from sounding in his voice. He stood and closed the blinds, blocking the view of the house Ann was currently inside. "I'm going to bed. Some of us have an early morning tomorrow. I'll call Marge and see if she's willing to take the kids for a few days. You have fun consoling your heartbroken friend."

"See ya later."

Eli ended the call and found Marge's number in his contacts. Hopefully, she wouldn't mind the last-minute plea for help.

He had a lot of work to do tomorrow and he didn't want to ask Ann to watch the kids. He couldn't allow himself to be distracted by a cute cleft chin and a pair of pretty gray eyes.

Chapter Nine

After the fifth email from her publicist in less than five minutes, Jordan swore under her breath. They were acting like Henry's lies to the press were equal to a nuclear bomb blast. She personally didn't care what he said about her or their former relationship. And he could take the diamond necklace he bought her only a few weeks ago and shove it.

But the interview with a man who had allegedly sold her cocaine was more disturbing. She'd never done illegal drugs, or even had the smallest desire to do so. The media didn't care about the truth. They wanted to believe her strange behavior was something nefarious and not a result of the anxiety brought on by their constant barrage into her personal life.

As another e-mail alert flashed across the screen, she made the decision to delete her e-mail account from her phone. The only people she would respond to were Lacy and Phil. No music producers or record label execs or publicists or stylists. Everyone riding the Jordan Spencer express would simply have to wait until she was good and ready to rejoin civilization.

Today, she planned on going over to get another look at the old mansion. Last night, Heidi had called to tell her she'd be staying in Milwaukee a few more days. She'd also said Eli had asked his ex-wife's parents to take the kids so he could go work the fields.

Jordan had been strangely disappointed that he hadn't gone to her for help. Could be he didn't want to bother her... though, he must know how much she already adored Lita and Elliot.

Oh well, she had plenty to keep her busy. After exploring, she planned on fine-tuning the song she'd started. The lyrics were about a girl falling for a guy who she knew could never be hers. *Hmmmm, wonder where I got that idea from?*

Walking down the driveway toward the road, she saw a tractor in the distance. Must be Eli. A cloud of dust billowed in the air above where he mowed. Should she go over and say hello? Likely, he wouldn't appreciate the interruption.

White, billowy clouds floated in a cerulean blue sky. Every so often, a cloud would shade her from the bright, summer sun. The weather was beautiful. Perfect, actually. A steady breeze carried with it the smells of farm life—ones she was slowly getting used to.

Up ahead, she saw the path that led through the trees. When she stepped underneath the shade of tall oak and maple trees, the air temperature dropped. She picked up her pace to warm herself. The sound of her feet crunching on the previous autumn's leaves was strangely comforting. She was reminded of all the long walks she'd taken around her own property.

Her house outside Nashville sat on fifty acres, most of it wooded. When she'd first bought the property, she'd had hiking trails cleared. When she walked outdoors, surrounded by the beauty of nature, Jordan could leave all the craziness behind. Even if only for an hour or so, the break kept her anxiety manageable.

But when she toured, she was trapped between her tour bus and hotels. Long walks alone were impossible. So, the anxiety crept up, wrapping around her tighter and tighter like she was a rabbit in a snare. The more she fought, the stronger the constriction.

Right here, right now, she felt total peace. A balanced calmness filled her body. She could breathe freely, without the heavy weight of responsibility sitting on her chest.

Ahead of her sat the rows of weeping willow trees. The path widened, leading up to the decaying stairs of the mansion.

She stood about twenty feet away from the house and stopped a few minutes to visually take it all in. The structure looked like something found in the Deep South instead of central Wisconsin. The style was distinctly Greek revival—a classic plantation house, like many built in the early 1800s.

Several windows on the first floor were boarded up. Others held broken glass that resembled snarling teeth. From what she could tell, the wooden siding had been painted white. Now, the color was closer to a dingy gray. Moss grew freely in the cracks and crevices of the boards. A few small trees had taken root in the ground underneath the front porch, reaching up through rotted-out boards.

The urge to go inside strengthened the longer she studied the exterior. But sneaking into an abandoned building would be wrong, right? Then again, who would she be hurting? Except possibly herself.

If she really was going to go inside, she'd have to be careful. One wrong step and she could easily twist an ankle or break a leg, or worse. She took a tentative first step up the marble stairs, then another, climbing the five stairs while holding on to the rickety iron rail.

Once her feet hit the porch, she gingerly made her way around several openings in the flooring until she arrived at the front door. The impressive entry veranda stretched the length of the house. Up above her, dappled sunlight beamed through decay holes in the second-story balcony.

Not surprisingly, the front door was locked. Jordan wiggled the handle a few more times, just in case it decided to change its mind. The door stayed shut, proving to her imaginative mind that the house couldn't be haunted. Didn't the front door automatically swing open in haunted houses? She rolled her eyes at the absurdity of her thoughts and set off to find another way in.

One of the tall windows to the right of the door was intact and slightly raised. She went over and tried to lift the sash. The window creaked in protest, but it finally relented and started sliding upward. When Jordan got a clear three feet of opening, she bent over and swung one leg inside, and then the other.

She now stood in some sort of formal living room, and was surprised to see the interior in decent shape. Even after decades of abandonment, the furniture, though old and worn, looked ready to receive company. A dusty tea set, painted with delicate pink roses, sat on a serving cart in the center of the room. The wallpaper was in fairly good condition, just worn and faded with the passing of time.

She stepped farther into the room, stopping at a built-in bookshelf. Rows of leather-bound books lined the shelves. There was a stack of newspapers piled at the end. She picked up the top one and read the date. December 31, 1950.

Thumbing through the pile of newspapers, she noticed the dates ranged from 1948 through 1951. Most were Manitowoc papers. A few were written in German.

Now even more intrigued, Jordan continued walking around the room, taking it all in. On the arm of a sofa lay a handkerchief, embroidered with the initials ABT.

This room must have served as the formal parlor. She could almost imagine the lady of the house entering through the double doors to entertain her guests. Despite the dust and cobwebs, everything looked set for company.

Jordan walked through a large doorway and into the front hall. At one end was the foyer, while the other led to the back of the house. There was another room directly across from the parlor, so she decided to explore that next.

This room was derelict and sad. With most of the windows either broken or open, the elements had had their way. The carpet squished underneath her feet. Small plants grew on the floor and walls.

The sound of rustling from the heap of dried leaves in the corner made her heart jump. Out of the pile jumped a squirrel. The animal studied her for several seconds, then it climbed up the wall and out the window, obviously unconcerned by a human presence.

Maybe because the house was regularly visited by the spirits of the people who used to live here. She shivered at the thought. *Don't be silly. There's no such thing as ghosts.*

That thought was punctuated by a slamming door. Jordan's stomach leapt into her throat. The bang came from upstairs. She'd wait and explore that level next time. Something up there did not want to be disturbed.

The room she stood in appeared to be a study or office. A few chairs sat at strange angles by the windows, their wooden legs broken. The fabric covering the seats might have been a tapestry of some sort, its design lost among numerous holes.

A massive desk took up the other side of the room. She went over to look at the photographs sitting on the shelves. They were either black and white or sepia toned. Many were of a little girl, maybe around five or six. She was a pretty child, with curly hair and wide eyes. Her smile shone through the old photograph and the passing of time. Other photographs showed an adolescent girl, starting to show a hint of womanhood.

Picking up a yellowed sheet of paper, Jordan turned it over. Printed on the brittle paper was the headline MISSING CHILD, ROSEMARY TURNER, LAST SEEN AT SILVER LAKE SCHOOL. Underneath the text was the picture of the missing girl— the same girl whose photographs lined the bookcase.

She wondered if the girl had ever been found. Hopefully, young Rosemary made it home safe and sound.

She spent some more time moving from room to room, skipping the stairs to the basement and the second level. The kitchen, set in the back of the house, was as ravaged as the rest of the building. A large, brick hearth dominated one wall. The small room attached to the kitchen must have been the pantry. Jars of green beans and tomatoes still lined the shelves.

She wondered what could have happened. The house seemed to have been abandoned in a hurry. A family home one day, a residence for ghosts the next.

Her stomach let out a low growl. How long had she been here? She took out her phone to check the time and discovered it was well past noon.

Jordan carefully crawled out the same window she came in, conscious of the multitude of spiderwebs crisscrossing above her. She didn't have a problem with spiders, or insects, in general. As long as they left her alone, she'd do the same. But the thought of a spider getting a free ride in her hair gave her goose bumps.

Maybe she could ask Eli if he knew the history behind the abandoned plantation house. She wouldn't be surprised if there was an urban legend attached to it. The place was so sadly neglected, she almost hated to leave.

"I'll be back," she whispered to the house. *Wonder if anyone ever thought of buying it and fixing it up?* A historical Antebellum plantation would make a beautiful bed and breakfast. Or even an event center. Jordan pictured a happy couple being married on the front lawn, surrounded by family and friends, the shining white house serving as backdrop. She sighed. How utterly romantic.

On the hike back, she passed Eli in the field. He was outside the tractor, bent over the mower deck. Did he enjoy farming? Or did he do it simply out of obligation? His dream had been to be a professional musician. And from what she heard yesterday, he was good enough to do just that. But he'd never gotten to see that dream fulfilled. He'd moved away from his band and LA to come home after his parents died. Then, he'd lost his wife, who hadn't felt overly attached to either the farm or her family.

Had all the sacrifices been worth the rewards? Jordan couldn't answer that. She'd never had a deep connection to a plot of land and a family's legacy. Her home outside of Nashville was nice, but if she were to sell it and move, she wouldn't lose any sleep.

A voice inside her head nudged to take a chance and walk over to Eli. Might be he'd find her a welcome interruption.

She wasn't one to shy away from taking a chance. If he seemed cranky, she'd just turn around and leave. Simple as that.

But her feelings for Eli were anything but simple. He did things to her insides. Good things. Confusing things.

What would it feel like to fall in love so deeply, there was never any doubt you'd spend the rest of your life together?

Jordan took a deep breath and veered off the road, stepping onto the field and straight toward the man she wished held the answer.

Chapter Ten

Eli kicked the mower one last time, hoping his anger would be enough to dislodge whatever was stuck in the blades.

Stupid piece of crap. The worst part was he was stuck with the thing for the foreseeable future. He had years left on his settlement with Nikki. Since they'd been married when he inherited the farm, she was entitled to half of his share in the divorce. He didn't have the cash to pay her outright, so he was stuck making quarterly payments. The result—new equipment was not in his future.

Many nights, he went to bed asking himself if keeping the farm was worth it. All the early mornings. Every long, hard day. By night, he was so exhausted, he could hardly walk up the stairs… and he still struggled to pay the bills.

The settlement with Nikki was ridiculous. That fact that he had to buy her out of half of his inheritance left him fuming. *She'd* been the one to walk away from *him*. But he was grateful that she hadn't sued for custody of Lita and Elliot. The money he could live without. He wouldn't last a day without his kids.

Eli swore when he heard the crunch of approaching footsteps. Probably Fred Schmidt, the farmer whose land butted up against his. Fred liked to check up on Eli. Some days, Eli appreciated his concern. Others, the unsolicited advice got under his skin.

And today, when his temper was ready to boil over, he did not want to listen to Fred's lecture on the proper care of farm machinery.

"Is it break time?" A feminine voice sounded from behind him.

Relief, along with a feeling less pure, flooded his body. Eli turned to face her. Ann was a most welcome sight. His lips curved in a smile.

"No breaks anytime soon," he said. "The mower's stuck—again."

"Is there anything I can do to help?"

"No. Unless you have a magic wand to summon up a new mower." He guided her over to a sliver of shade on the other side of the tractor. The July sun sizzled the air around them.

She leaned against the tall tractor tire, which came up to the top of her head. "Sorry, my magic wand has been acting up. If I ask for a new mower, chances are you'll get a donkey instead."

He laughed, something he found himself doing a lot when he was around her. Ann had a sense of humor and wasn't afraid to tease him.

"Best we not take the chance. I don't need another mouth to feed." Eli took off his cap and used it to fan his face. "Why are you out here?"

"I took a walk to go see the old mansion hidden in the woods. Heidi told me about it. I can't believe someone built that beautiful house and then just abandoned it."

"The old Turner place?" He knew the stories about that house. How it was haunted by the ghost of the little girl who'd gone missing all those years ago. They'd never found her, and her parents had moved away, leaving the huge place to sit empty.

"I actually snuck in through an open window. Have you ever gone inside?" Her eyes glistened.

He could sense her excitement. "In high school, we used to go over there and hang out. A group of us stayed overnight on a dare." Eli and his friends had made it through the night, but just barely. At night, the house was even creepier than during the day, and that was saying a lot. There'd been plenty of strange noises echoing through the dark. Although, most had come from his friends' snoring.

"I stayed on the ground floor because I couldn't get up the nerve to go upstairs," Ann said. "Not after I heard a door slam shut." She shivered. "Do you know about the missing girl, Rosemary?"

Despite the heat, his chill returned. "How did you hear about her?"

"I found a poster they made."

"There are all sorts of stories about what happened to her," he said. "Some say she was murdered. Others blame her parents. Then, there are stories that she was kidnapped by her mother's kin, and they took her back to live in Georgia."

"So, what actually happened?"

He shrugged. "No one knows. I think the case is still unsolved."

"That's so sad. And that majestic home has been left to rot away." She glanced over her shoulder in the direction of the mansion, which was hidden from view by the dense woods.

"Every once in a while, someone inquires about buying the property, but nothing ever happens. I guess no one cares enough or wants to invest that much money into a crumbled-down house."

"Someone should care." Ann turned back to face him and smiled. "Have you had lunch?" she asked. "I was going back to make myself something to eat. I could bring some out for you."

"I packed a cooler to take on the tractor. But thanks, anyway."

"Then what are you doing for dinner?" Little beads of sweat formed on the skin above her upper lip. She wiped them away with the short sleeve of her shirt.

Looking over his shoulder, he gave his mower the evil eye. Knowing how finicky it could be, he'd be working in the fields well past dark. "I'll eat when I stop for the day or skip dinner if it gets too late."

Ann shook her head, causing her hair to float around her face. "I'll bring you something to eat. I'm not going to let you starve. Where will you be around six?"

"Hopefully not still here."

She pulled out her cell phone. "Give me your number. I'll call you when I have the food ready?"

Common sense told him that he should decline her offer. Nothing good would come from spending more time with her. But he enjoyed her company too much to put up a fight. Plus, she was offering to feed him.

After she entered his number under her contacts, she wished him luck, and then waved goodbye. He was left to count down the minutes until he saw her again.

***

Jordan answered the call on the first ring. "Hey, sis. How's Deutschland?"

"German," Lacy answered. "It's *wunderbar*."

She put down her pen and notebook. "Make sure you go to the Hofbräuhaus beer garden in Munich."

"We'll be in Munich tomorrow. My travel buddies will always stop for a beer." Lacy paused. "Um… Bob called me yesterday, and I was debating whether to tell you. I hate to bother you with this—"

Jordan's stomach sickened at the mention of their dad. "Whatever the problem, we share it together, just like always."

Their system for handling their parents was simple. Lacy played defense, handling calls from them and keeping them away from Jordan. She, on the other hand, used her money and influence to stop them from threatening either Lacy or her.

Bob and Jane only bothered her when they were in desperate straits, which was hard to imagine since she'd given them a lot of money several years ago, with their signed promise never to demand another penny.

Lacy sighed deeply. "Bob wanted both of us to know that the media is contacting him, asking about your past history with drugs. Between Henry's allegations of drug use and the false reports you've checked into rehab, the story's spinning out of control."

"Ugh," Jordan groaned. "Why do people always want to believe the worst? You know I've never used coke or heroin, right?"

"How dare you even ask me that? You're as likely to do drugs as I am. Growing up, we saw firsthand how evil drug addiction is."

"I talked to Phil yesterday. He said there's some drug dealer claiming I'm a frequent customer. Phil didn't say anything about reports of me checking into rehab." Jordan sat on the sofa and rubbed her temples with her forefingers. Reporters were probably making inquiries at every drug and alcohol rehab center in the country. Didn't they have real stories to chase? Stories that shed light on real-world problems. But gossip about Jordan's life earned website clicks, and that's what made them money.

"People have noticed you've gone off the grid," Lacy said. "No one has seen you since the concert in Milwaukee. Combine that with the drug story Henry's telling, and they're speculating. Let them. You don't owe them anything. Enjoy your time alone. You deserve it."

"You deserve a nice vacation, too. I'm sorry you have to deal with this mess."

"No worries. After the call from Bob today, I turned my phone off. When I powered it back up to call you, I did not look at my texts, voicemails, or e-mails."

"Did Bob ask for more money?" Jordan asked.

There was silence on the line.

"Lacy?"

"No, he didn't mention money. He told me about the reporters bothering him, and then he said Mom's cancer has spread. I guess it's pretty bad. The doctors gave her only a few months to live."

Jordan felt no reaction. Most people would have a rush of emotions when they found out a parent was dying—sorrow, anger, depression. But Jane was practically a stranger to her. The last time she had seen her mother was seven years ago, and that was a brief, insignificant exchange.

"Bob wanted us to know," Lacy said. "So we could make peace with her before she's gone."

Peace. What would either Bob or Jane know about peace? She could still feel the sting of Bob's belt on her back and the burn of her tears as she begged him to stop.

"Her cancer doesn't change anything." Jordan stood and went over to the window. She allowed the warm breeze to flow over her face. Outside, she saw the small form of Eli's tractor moving in the distance. He must have fixed his mower.

"Focus on healing yourself," Lacy said. "I'm going to get ready for bed. It's getting late here."

"Sleep tight. Love you, Fart-Face."

The sound of Lacy's laughter filled Jordan's ear, soothing her anxiety.

"Love you, too, Butt-Breath."

Jordan ended the call and noticed the time. She'd promised Eli dinner and had no clue what she'd make. Though, cooking was probably not a good idea. She did *not* want another kitchen fire. She could drive to the little grocery store in Sterling and check out their deli. Maybe grab a bottle of wine.

A nice picnic dinner sounded like a good plan.

An hour later, she stood in front of the deli counter, scratching her head. There were so many choices. At home, her dietician and cook handled her meals, and when she traveled, Lacy made sure the venues and hotels had the proper food and beverages. Every calorie was counted, along with nutritional value. She'd become obsessed with staying slim.

That's why these last few days felt so incredibly freeing. She'd eaten brats, hamburgers, French fries, cotton candy, ice cream, eggs, and bacon. And it all tasted *so good*. For once, she stopped stressing over her figure and enjoyed life.

"What can I get you, sweetie?" the lady behind the deli counter asked with a friendly smile. Her gray hair was pulled back into a tight bun. A white paper hat topped her head.

"I'm not sure. I'm planning a picnic. What would you recommend?" Didn't hurt to ask.

The woman pointed to the warming bin at the end of the counter. "Broasted chicken is a favorite. Easy to transport and not too messy to eat. Get some pasta salad and coleslaw for the sides and you'll be good to go." She glanced back at Jordan. "How are things over at the Hintz farm?"

How in the world did the deli lady know where she was staying?

Jordan's heart rate increased. She struggled to breathe. If she was discovered, her nice, quiet retreat would come to a screeching end. The media would flock to this small town and camp on the street in front of Eli's farm. He'd know she had lied to him about her name. About her entire identity.

Betty—as her name tag read—smiled. "That's rural life. Everybody knows everything about one another. Fred—he owns the farm next door to Eli's—came in here yesterday saying Eli and Heidi had a cute little lady staying at Heidi's place. And since you're new around here, and definitely a cute little lady, I figured it was you. When the most exciting thing around here is the annual Firemen's Picnic, it doesn't take much to get our lips wagging." She grabbed a bucket and went over to the chicken. "How many you feedin', sweetie?"

"Umm." She suddenly felt very self-conscious. If she said two, Betty would think she was planning a picnic with Eli. Even if that was exactly what she was doing, she still didn't want their business spread across the local grapevine. "How about you give me enough to feed five?" Jordan could leave the leftovers in Eli's fridge.

Betty gave her a half smile. "You sure, sweetie? Aren't Lita and Elliot gone to their grandparents?"

Jordan's face heated with embarrassment. She shouldn't care about the assumptions of a stranger. It's not like she was planning on putting the moves on Eli. She was only feeding a busy farmer. Nothing wrong with being a nice person.

"Five it is." Betty put a lid on the bucket of chicken, and then filled a large container of pasta salad and another of coleslaw, all without waiting for an answer.

She hoped Eli was hungry.

Betty slid the items across the stainless-steel countertop. "Anything else I can get for you?"

"No, thank you." Jordan set the food in her shopping cart. "Have a nice day."

"You, too, sweetie."

"Oh. I do have another question for you," Jordan said, turning back. "Do you know the story behind the old Turner mansion?"

The woman's brown eyes brightened. "Everyone around here knows about the Turner place. Some say it's haunted. But I don't believe that hogwash."

"The style of the house seems out of place for this area."

"William Turner built that house for his wife, who he met down in Georgia. Annabelle was her name, and William built their home as a replica of the one she'd grown up in."

"That's so romantic. And it explains the Greek revival style."

Betty nodded. "Their daughter's disappearance made all the papers. Even the ones in Milwaukee. Everyone had their own opinion about what happened. That house is a magnet for speculation." She pulled out a dish towel and started cleaning off the counter.

"Did they have any suspects?" Jordan couldn't contain her curiosity. During her last concert tour, she'd gotten addicted to watching true crime shows.

"Nope, not that I heard. William and Annabelle moved away with their other child, a son. They left all their belongings behind. I remember people saying that nobody knew where they'd gone. They just vanished."

Jordan didn't remember seeing any pictures of a boy in the study, only the ones of Rosemary. Very interesting. "Thanks for the info."

"Anytime, sweetie. And you say hi to Eli for me. I hope you two have a nice picnic." Betty winked before adjusting her paper hat and walking away.

As she made her way to the wine aisle, she imagined the gossip that would start if she bought a bottle to go with the chicken. Single dad Eli, being romanced by the woman who crashed in his front yard. She could almost see the story in the Sterling newspaper. At least it would be an improvement from the current headlines about her.

Deciding to throw caution to the wind, she grabbed a nice bottle of white wine.

After checking out, Jordan loaded up her haul and headed back to the farm. Inside the safety of the car, she began to sing what she'd been working on earlier that day.

> *"From the moment I met you, I knew you'd break my heart*
> *Your gold eyes melted my defenses right from the start*
> *I have no choice but to follow this through*
> *Nothing's sweeter than kissing you."*

Chapter Eleven

Ann's text came at six on the dot, saying she was on her way with dinner.

Eli could finally put his cell away. He'd been checking his phone obsessively all afternoon.

Even with the earlier issues with the mower, he'd made good progress. Tomorrow would be another full day. By day three, he should finish before dinner time. That was, if his equipment didn't break down again.

Last he'd heard, Lita and Elliot were having fun at their grandparents' house. He'd asked one of his hired hands to take over the kids' chores. Eli hoped they were enjoying the rare opportunity to sleep in.

Ten minutes later, Ann drove up in the ATV. She looked so cute, bouncing up and down in the seat as she navigated across the field. After parking next to the tractor, she climbed off and went around to the back.

He joined her and caught a whiff of his favorite food, broasted chicken. Picking up the picnic basket, Eli's stomach growled. "You're my hero."

"If I'd known you were starving to death out here, I would have come sooner." Ann took the blanket and a pink bag. "Where's a good place to set up?"

He led her over to a grassy area adjacent to the field. The ash trees that grew there would provide some shade from the late afternoon sun. Eli peeked inside the bucket of chicken and inhaled the delicious aroma.

For the next hour, he wanted to eat, relax, and enjoy Ann's company. How had he gotten so lucky? His dinner companion was not only drop-dead gorgeous, but also possessed a kind heart. Kind enough to have brought him enough broasted chicken to feed his entire extended family.

After a few flaps of the blanket into the air, Ann let it glide down to the earth. He set the picnic basket in the center.

Along with the chicken, she brought a large deli container of coleslaw, a bag of chips, pickles, a store-bought cake, plates, forks, and napkins. Last, she retrieved antibacterial wipes.

Eli watched her set up their little picnic. She was so earnest in her preparation that he couldn't help but feel a deep sense of endearment. What kind of man would hurt her? He knew he'd risk his own safety to protect her.

"Help yourself." Ann spread out her hands and sat back on her heels.

"Will you hand me the bottle of wine?"

Her cheeks flushed as she passed him the bottle. "I didn't know what to bring to drink. I figured wine would be the easiest." Ann's gaze flickered over to him. "Although, don't drink too much. I'd hate to see you get a ticket for a DTD."

"What's a DTD?" Eli popped open the wine.

"Drunk Tractor Driving." Laughing, she held out two cups for him to fill. Ann smirked and raised her eyebrows. "Do you think that's a real thing?"

"No, I've never heard of a DTD." He laughed. "Don't worry about me getting behind the wheel of my tractor drunk. I'm way too obsessed with making straight lines when I mow."

Ann's smile shot like lightning straight to his heart. One look from her left Eli weak with desire.

He wanted to hold her close, so she'd feel safe in the protection of his arms. Maybe then, she'd share her story.

The buzz of cicadas provided background music. Every so often, the wind gusted from across the field, blowing Ann's brown hair.

She had pretty hair, cut to fall right at her jawline. The style framed her face and gave her an innocent, almost girlish look.

"Heidi said you have a brother, Sam." Ann scooped coleslaw onto her fork. "Does he live around here?"

He finished chewing the chicken in his mouth before answering. "Sam lives in Milwaukee. He's a firefighter for the city."

"Is he the youngest?"

"He's the typical baby of the family. Sam is five years younger than me and one year younger than Heidi. Growing up, Sam could set the barn on fire and I'd get the punishment. He was in the car when our parents died. I struggled to get him to finish high school, afterward."

"I imagine that was a tough decision for you to move back home. You took on a lot of responsibility. There was the farm and your own family. But also caring for your teenage brother and sister." She twirled her wine glass in her hand while shifting closer to him. "I hope you gave yourself time to grieve."

His heart squeezed with sorrow at everything he'd lost when that car ran the stop sign and plowed into his parents' car. Fate had a cruel sense of humor. Before Heidi's panicked call, he'd thought he'd had it all—a beautiful wife, a child on the way, an up and coming music career. Their band had just picked up their first major gig. They'd been on the verge of being noticed.

And he'd walked away from it all, dragging Nikki with him.

Eli let out a long breath. "I didn't have time to grieve. There was too much to do. Still is."

Leaning forward, she set her hand to rest on his. "Do you miss music?"

His gaze dropped to the red plaid blanket and their connected hands. He swallowed hard. "I do," he admitted. "I loved playing the guitar. In high school, that's all I wanted to do. Nikki and I formed a band after we started dating. She loved the spotlight. I was happy to stand in the background and sing backup. We left for LA shortly after high school graduation, against both our parents' wishes. We thought we'd be the next big thing."

She didn't laugh, like he expected. Instead, she tipped her head so her flinty eyes were locked onto his. "I think you had a lot of courage to follow your dreams. And you also had both courage and wisdom to come back home when your family needed you. You should make time for music, though. Lita's a good singer, and with the proper training, she could really be something."

"That's what worries me. She's too much like I was at that age. Always searching for a way off the boring farm. I want her to do something she loves, but not because she wants her mom's attention."

Why was he sharing parts of himself that were so deeply personal? He never talked about his fears and shortcomings, even with his own family. Ann was practically a stranger... but that might be why he felt so comfortable sharing with her.

Ann's hand remained resting on his. The skin of her palm was so smooth compared to his calloused hand. Heat from her touch pulsed through his body. The urge to kiss her was a strong drug.

"I am not a parent," she said. "So, take what I say with a grain of salt, but don't project your own fears onto Lita or Elliot. Your kids are smart and good. I'm certain that when the time's right, they'll choose the path that's right for them."

He smiled. "I'm so thankful they're growing up here and not in LA. I don't know what I would have done if Nikki fought for custody."

At the sound of his ex-wife's name, Ann withdrew her hand and set it on the blanket. "How could she have walked away?"

"From the start I knew Nikki didn't want to move back to Wisconsin. When she finally relented, she was miserable. *I* chose this life for us. She filed for divorce because I wouldn't compromise. Lita blames me for her mother leaving, and she's right."

Her lips pulled down in a frown. "No, you're not to blame. Lita will understand that someday."

Several seagulls flew overhead. Their cries pierced the air, giving voice to his own heartache.

"Nikki would have never been happy here." Eli noticed the sun had begun its descent. He should get back to work, but this time spent with Ann seemed more important.

"You were here. Her children, too." She moved her body to within inches of his own.

Eli reached up and ran a strand of her silky hair between his fingers. "We weren't enough."

Ann's lips were so close. All he had to do was lean slightly forward and he'd taste the sweetest dessert. The honking of a horn sounded behind him, startling them both. Eli turned his gaze toward the road to see the beat-up truck of Fred Schmidt.

Fred kept on driving, but the moment had passed. Clenching his hands, Eli moved his body so he was at safer distance from Ann. Giving in to temptation would be wrong. He needed to know more about her before he got too involved.

"That's enough talk about me," Eli said. "I know you live down South. There's no mistaking that accent. But you never said where."

She started putting away the leftover food back in the basket. "A little town in Tennessee. You've probably never heard of it."

"What do you do for a living?"

Her head lowered, and she appeared to hesitate. "I'm not working right now. Kind of in between jobs, so to speak."

Why was she so evasive about answering his questions? "Do you have any other siblings, besides Lacy?"

"It was just the two of us growing up. We had to look out for each other. No one else would." She lowered the lid of the basket and stood. "That's enough depressing information about me. I'm ready to accept payment for this meal."

"Payment?" All sorts of provocative forms of payment flashed in Eli's mind. His face heated with Ann's mischievous smile.

"A song." She laughed. "I want you to sing me a song."

Eli rested his forearm on his knee. "That's a steep price for one meal."

"But it was a good meal, right?" She raised her face up to the sun. Its rays washed over her skin, giving her a golden glow. "My guitar's in the ATV. Be right back." And with that, she bounded away.

The ringing of a phone sounded from the corner of the blanket. He looked over to see Ann's cell light up with a call. A picture of a man filled the screen. The guy's neck was as big as Elliot's waist. He looked like a member of a motorcycle gang. The name under the picture read *Cole Dufour.*

Was this the man Ann was running from? They shared a last name. Ann had said she wasn't married and that she'd just gone through a bad breakup. Was Cole her ex-husband?

Eli's blood boiled at the thought of Cole laying a hand on Ann. This guy might be built as solidly as a '64 Mustang, but Eli would not stand by and let her be hurt.

Moments later, Ann came back holding her guitar, and then handed it to him. "Your choice of song."

He watched her sit cross-legged on the blanket, looking as innocent as a child, and instantly calmed.

"I'm warning you… I'm very out of practice."

"Then let's get you back in practice." The cleft in her chin deepened with her smile. "One song at a time. Starting now."

"Fair enough." Eli strummed a B major chord and began the intro to "Bed of Roses." Nothing worked better on the girls than Bon Jovi.

He sang, trying not to overdo it, which was proving difficult. Not only because he felt truly alive when he played, but Ann gave the lyrics new meaning. He'd give anything to be lying on a bed of roses with her instead of the middle of a farm field.

***

If Jordan hadn't been sitting down, she certainly would have swooned. *Holy cow.* Elijah Hintz had a voice that melted her insides into a puddle of mush.

She'd heard this song a million times, performed in corner bars and even by Jon Bon Jovi himself—but she'd never heard it like this. Eli's voice was deep, with a hint of hoarseness, like gravel wrapped in a silk scarf. Every word rolled off his tongue with such feeling. Jordan became totally lost in the song.

If they would record a duet, she knew it would do insanely well. He had the whole package—good looks, charisma, and talent. Jordan clasped her lips shut so she wouldn't sing along.

The final cord echoed around them, and he watched her. Was he looking for her reaction?

Wouldn't he be shocked to know her first instinct was to jump over and tackle him to the ground, and then kiss him until they both forgot their own names? Instead, she simply clapped her hands and smiled.

Eli didn't know her real name. Truth felt like a glass of cold water dumped over her head. She gulped down the rest of the wine in her glass. Little chance alcohol would take the edge off the ache in her heart.

His place was here, on the farm. Hers was in Nashville and touring all over the world. He had made a commitment to give his kids a sense of hard work, safety, and home. Jordan's life was a rollercoaster, full of paparazzi and the occasional stalker. Together, she and Eli didn't mix. He'd turned his back on her lifestyle. If he'd held firm when his wife wanted to leave, surely he wouldn't change his mind because of an attraction to her.

From the short time she'd known him, she could tell he was a man of his word. When he made a decision, he stuck to it, and Eli felt obligated to his parents to keep the farm in the family.

"Your turn." Eli handed her the guitar.

When he came close, she inhaled deeply. He smelled like grass and dirt. Before today, she would have recoiled at those scents. Now… she wanted to bathe in the smell. She'd pay good money for someone to make an Eli-scented essential oil.

Jordan accepted the guitar with trepidation. Playing wasn't a problem, but if she sang and he recognized her voice, she'd blow her cover.

"I can't follow your performance." Jordan strummed the guitar, not paying attention to the chords. "You were amazing." She'd love to have him on stage with her. They'd make a great team.

"Lita told me you were working on lyrics. How about you sing me that song?"

No way. Those lyrics were about him. They were the beginning of a song she now thought of as "Eli's Song." "It's stuff I've been writing to fill the time. It's really no good."

Eli moved to sit behind her. Reaching around her body, he covered her hand with his and moved them over the strings of the guitar. "Come on." He nudged her with his knee. "Play me anything then."

His body was too close to think straight. She couldn't even remember how to play the guitar. Jordan took several deep breaths. The melody for a classic Simon and Garfunkel song floated into her head. She knew then what to play.

"April come she will,
When streams are ripe and swelled with rain…
July, she will fly,
A love once new has now grown old."

Jordan held back on her vocals and even sang out of tune.

"Beautiful," Eli whispered in her ear. "I love Simon and Garfunkel. There's a distinct quality about your voice, and I think with some training, you'd be amazing."

"Thanks." Jordan set down the guitar, hiding a smile. She used every ounce of willpower not to turn in his arms and press her lips against his. She cleared her throat. "I should really let you get back to work."

He rose to stand before her. "You're probably right. The hay's not going to cut itself." Eli took off his baseball cap and ran his fingers through his hair. "Thanks for dinner. I appreciated the break... and the company."

After they loaded the items in the back of the ATV, Jordan hopped in the driver's seat. "Let me know if I can help out with the morning chores, since the kids are gone."

He scratched at the scruff covering his chin. "Heidi called earlier. She's coming home tomorrow. I guess her friend got back together with her boyfriend. Crisis averted. For now."

"That's good." She nodded and turned the key in the ignition. "Catch you later, Eli."

Before she could make her getaway, he brushed his lips across her cheek.

As he walked away, back to his tractor, she noticed a bit of swagger in his step.

Cocky man. Who did he think he was—Brad Pitt? Jordan had met Brad, and she had to admit that Eli was better looking. And from the looks of the smirk on Eli's face as he climbed into the seat of the tractor, he knew it, too.

***

The sliver of a crescent moon hung high in the sky—a martyr to the shadows of the night. Jordan sat outside, enjoying the darkness. In the distance, the hum of a tractor traveled through the air. Must be Eli, still working, well past sundown.

Crickets chirped in a constant buzz, reminding her of the sound created by an excited concert crowd.

The warm summer wind also carried the now familiar scents of the farm. Scents that she had found disagreeable when she'd first arrived were now strangely comforting. They were smells of life, and home, and a family legacy.

Earlier, she'd noticed a missed call from Cole. She pressed his contact button, causing his picture to pop up on her screen. His scowl highlighted the scar running down the right side of his face. Every time she asked him how he'd gotten it, he always had a different story. She figured the real story was too hard to tell, even for a tough guy.

Her bodyguard did his best to look mean and intimidating. That was part of his job, after all. But Jordan knew the big teddy bear he hid inside. Cole had put himself between her and crazed fans too many times to count and he always had a hug for her after every show.

"Hey, sweetcakes," Cole answered. "You finally get a free minute to call me back?"

"I was enjoying a picnic supper when you called."

His baritone laughter traveled through the phone's speaker. "Who's the guy? Do I need to come rough him up? Don't end up with another loser. The kind you attract like a bullet to the head."

"You're not coming and roughing up anybody. I had an innocent picnic with a friend." Although, her fantasies about Eli were not exactly innocent.

"Tell the guy sharing your blanket that I will break him if he breaks your heart."

Jordan sighed. "I appreciate the offer, but I'm fine. So… why did you call?" She put emphasis on the word "you." "Not to check-up on my nonexistent love life, I hope."

There was a rustling in the background, along with distinctly feminine laughter.

"Cole, am I interrupting something?"

Cole Dufour was to women what Michael Jordan was to basketball. And he loved them right back. Jordan often wondered why Cole, a former Marine Raider, would want a job as a bodyguard to a starlet. But he was devoted to her. And because of Jordan's devotion to him, he lived a very full and interesting life.

As Jordan's personal bodyguard, Cole made a healthy amount of money, got to travel the world (no war zones included), and had plenty of time off to pursue other activities. From what Jordan could tell, many of those activities involved beautiful women.

"No. A few buddies came over to watch the baseball game. One of them brought his girlfriend." He paused. "I just wanted to check up on you. I heard you never made it to Door County. You really stuck on a dairy farm?"

"I'm not stuck. It's actually been relaxing here."

He laughed. "I'd pay money to see you, Jordan Spencer, milk a cow."

"I'm not working on the dairy farm, you goofball. And they have machines to do the milking, by the way. But I did bottle feed a calf. They are so cute. What if I build a little barn by my house and got some calves, and maybe a chicken or two? I could have my own little farm."

"And what about when you travel? You're gone for six to eight months out of the year."

"Don't burst my happy bubble." She stuck out her bottom lip, even though Cole couldn't see her. "I want a farm."

"Whatever you want, princess. Excuse me for being the voice of reason."

"And I love you for it." Jordan inhaled a deep breath of fresh air. Her lungs filled, along with her heart. In the short time here, she'd become very attached. Leaving was going to hurt.

"Hey. You worked intelligence in the Marines, right?"

"Why? You want me to dig up some dirt on Henry?"

"Henry doesn't matter. Can you look into a girl named Rosemary Turner and see if you can find out some information about her family? Her parents, William and Annabelle, would have lived in a town called Sterling, Wisconsin. Rosemary disappeared in 1951. They never found her. The family moved about six months after her disappearance, leaving all their possessions behind."

"You don't think we're going to solve a seventy-year-old missing persons case, do you?"

"Of course not. I love a mystery, and I've been exploring their abandoned house. I'd like to find out who owns it now. If you find anything, let me know."

"Sure thing, Sherlock Holmes." Cole muttered something under his breath. "Sorry. The Cubs' best hitter just struck out. So, are you really doing okay?"

"I'm in a good place. Not one anxiety attack since I got here. I'm happy."

"Good." A bang sounded in the background. "I got to go, sweetcakes. Keep it up. I'll talk to you again soon." He hesitated, and then said, "And let me know if you need me. I can be there in a few hours. Okay?"

"Okay. Thanks, Cole." She ended the call and looked back up at the moon. It held steady in the sky as it rotated in sync with Earth.

Kind of like Cole.

And then there was Eli.

A man who stayed fixed in place like the stars, while her world continued to spin.

Chapter Twelve

Since Heidi wouldn't be home until later in the day and Eli was busy in the fields, Jordan made a return trip to the Turner mansion. Today, she'd made a promise to herself that she would conquer the second floor. From the outside, there looked to be a third floor, too. Jordan wasn't crazy enough to go all the way up there. At least not today. One story at a time. And if she saw anything paranormal, she'd run straight out the front door.

She climbed through the same raised window as before. The drawing room still looked worn and dirty—but what did she expect? A ghost hosting a tea party?

Making her way into the foyer, she gazed at the wide staircase. At one time, it must have been grand. Now, the carpet runner was a faded red and covered with dirt and leaves. Dust coated the sweeping mahogany banister rail. Above her hung a crystal chandelier, still clinging onto some of its glory. A beam of light streamed in from one of the high windows and struck the crystals, throwing a rainbow of prisms on the walls. They made a trail for her to follow up the stairs.

How could she not follow a trail of rainbows? Jordan took one step at a time, proceeding with caution. The boards under her feet creaked and groaned but remained intact.

The hallway extended off both sides of the staircase. She decided to go left. The hall was gloomy and covered in shadows. Some sunlight found its way through the open doors, along with a lone window at the end of the hallway. At one of the open doorways, she peeked inside the room. With trash and brush scattered on the floor, it appeared to be a home to wildlife. Jordan heard scratching coming from under the bed and she promptly closed the door.

In the third room she entered, Jordon found a perfectly preserved bedroom. The stillness of it all made her skin crawl.

A row of dolls sat on an upper shelf, staring back at her with unblinking glass eyes, making the whole scene seem even more disturbing. Hung above a canopy bed were block letters that spelled out ROSEMARY. Beautiful floral wallpaper lined the walls. Everything about the room was in pristine condition—especially when comparing it to the rest of the house. Each of the five large windows was still intact. Even the color of the wallpaper seemed vibrant.

Rosemary's bed was made, with a faded white coverlet pulled up to the pillow shams. A teddy bear rested against the wooden headboard. Jordan left the room, closing the door behind her. A wave of sadness washed over her and a few salty tears ran down her cheeks to land on her lips.

This grand house, which once held so much love and life, was now haunted by sorrow. A missing girl. Her parents and brother leaving behind almost all their possessions. *Why?* Hopefully Cole would find some information about the Turner family.

She spent a few more minutes investigating the rest of the rooms on the second floor.

At the end of the hallway, she discovered the master bedroom. Most of the windows in the master suite of rooms were broken. The air inside smelled of mildew and rot.

She sneezed three times and stepped back into the hall. A board underneath her foot snapped, making her jump. Jordan needed to remember to be careful. This was an old, rotting house. She'd gotten so lost in exploring that she'd forgotten about safety.

After descending the stairs, she went back into the kitchen. In the corner of the room sat the door to the basement. No way would she'd go down there all by herself. Maybe she could convince Eli or Heidi to come with her.

She wasn't a chicken, just practical. Who knew what dangers lay hidden in an old basement?

Walking back to the front of the house, she imagined what this house would look like fully restored. With so many rooms, it would make a fabulous bed and breakfast. She'd seen plenty of homes like this in the South turned into tourist destinations and event centers. Would the same concept work up here?

What if *she* were the one who brought this house back to life and gave it a new purpose? The idea had merit. With all her other responsibilities, she just didn't know if she could devote herself to such a big and important project.

But wasn't the point of her time away to take a deep look at her life and reprioritize, if necessary? Maybe a project totally separate from her music career was exactly what her heart needed.

Checking the time, she decided to head back to the farm.

As she walked down the long driveway, she wondered what Eli was doing. Last night, she'd dreamed about him. They'd been a family, with one of their own on the way. Only a fantasy. A false hope conjured up by her romantic mind.

Eli was too good of a man to get dragged into her life. The one waiting for her back in Nashville. Her real life.

***

"So, what did I miss?" Heidi asked while accepting a glass of wine.

Jordan picked up her own glass and took a sip. "A fun day at Bay Beach. Other than that, Eli's been busy with the hay cutting. And with Lita and Elliot away, I've been kinda bored."

Heidi laughed. "But I thought you were looking for a quiet getaway. Wasn't that why you were heading to Door County?"

"Your family has a way of worming themselves into your heart." The statement was true, and she'd miss the Hintz family when she left. "How was Milwaukee?"

"Summerfest was fun, though dealing with the crowds is a struggle. I was unsure about going, but my friend convinced me to try. She promised we'd leave if I began feeling panicky."

"I don't like crowds, either." Jordan followed Heidi out the back door. She sat on one of the chairs on the porch. Being famous meant she couldn't go anywhere without being approached by fans. One or two she handled fine. But when groups surged around her, pure panic followed. In those moments, all she wanted to do was fall to the ground and disappear. There'd been times in those situations that she hadn't handled herself well. Another negative headline for troubled star Jordan Spencer.

"There are a lot of things that trigger anxiety for me." Heidi set her glass on the wrought iron coffee table. She turned her gaze toward something in the distance.

The farmhouse, which stood like a dark centennial across the backyard, was blanketed in the growing twilight. The hum of Eli's tractor still reverberated through the air. The kids would come home tomorrow from their grandparents'.

"I try to avoid most social situations," Heidi said. "Eli tells me I just need to get out more. He doesn't understand what constant anxiety physically does to my body."

Jordan did. "I was diagnosed with an anxiety disorder five years ago, but I had issues for years before that. I thought it was just a part of normal life. Something I had to deal with."

"I know." Heidi turned her head to face Jordan. "Except for work, I spend most of my time at home. This is the only place I can fully relax and be comfortable. Eli worries that he's holding me back from living some exciting life. He doesn't understand that even if he didn't need my help with the kids and the farm, I still wouldn't want to move away. I like my life here. I'm happy."

Jordan itched her nose, which had begun to tickle. Not being able to hold back any longer, she let loose a trifecta of sneezes.

"Do you have allergies?" Heidi asked.

"Not normally. Must be whatever Eli's stirring up." She hoped she wasn't getting sick. Jordan pulled out a tissue from the pocket of her shorts and blew her nose in the hopes of dislodging the offending pollen. "If you're happy with your life, that's great. Don't feel pressured to be someone you're not. Happiness is a valuable commodity. Something money can't buy." Her money had provided her comfort, not happiness. That, she knew, needed to come from the inside.

"I'm glad you're here." Heidi's smile deepened her dimples. "You're welcome to stay for as long as you can put up with my crazy family."

"Your family is great. And I'd really like to stay for a little while longer, as long as it's okay with you and Eli."

"I have a confession." Heidi's smile faded, replaced by a worried frown. "And I hope after I tell you, you won't leave."

Jordan's body tensed from years of defensive instinct. "Why?"

"Because... I know who you are." Heidi took a deep breath. "The first morning, when we were having breakfast, I thought you looked familiar. It wasn't until I saw a promo poster for your concert at Summerfest that I put it together. You're obviously looking for some anonymity, and I promise I won't tell anyone that Jordan Spencer is staying at our farm. That is, if you still want to stay."

Her heart sank. "I suppose you've heard the allegations of my drug use and erratic behavior." If so, would Heidi want a troubled country star around her family? And what about Eli?

"I'd be lying if I said I hadn't, but I don't believe everything I read. When I was at Summerfest, I talked with some people who'd been at your concert. They said you sounded amazing. I wish I'd been there to hear you sing."

From the time she'd spent with Heidi, Jordan had judged her as a woman with a discerning head and caring heart. Exactly the type of friend she needed as desire grew to unburden her soul. "That night was the final concert in a tour that lasted four months. I was tired, stressed out, my ex-boyfriend threatened to call me out as a crazy woman, and my anxiety was so high, I wanted to rip off my own skin." Since then, thankfully, she'd found peace. Her body and mind were in the process of healing. "My sister convinced me to hide away for a while and decompress. So, after the show, I cut and dyed my hair, and she rented a car for me so I wouldn't be followed. I guess you know the rest of the story."

"The Jordan Spencer I've gotten to know is kind and genuine. I wouldn't ask you to stay if I didn't believe that."

"Will you tell your brother?" Jordan couldn't ask her to lie to Eli. But the thought of losing his friendship left her wanting to cry. Deep down, she knew he'd find out eventually, but she didn't want her fantasy world crashing down so soon.

Heidi's brows rose in reaction to the question. "I don't see a reason why Eli needs to know. Though, I don't think it would matter to him if you're Ann Dufour or Jordan Spencer. He'd like you the same." She winked at her across the darkening porch.

"There's nothing going on between Eli and me."

"Why not? I haven't seen him this interested in a woman in a long time."

"That interest will disappear the second he finds out who I am." The truth burned her lips. "Ann isn't real, and Jordan comes with a boatload of problems. First, my career is the same as his ex-wife's. Her desire to be a touring singer is the reason she left her family."

"When my therapist talked to me about opening myself up to dating, she said that nobody is perfect, but love purifies. If a relationship is meant to be, the two people find a way to make it work."

"I don't think my being a famous country music singer is something Eli will overlook." Jordan shifted in her seat. Her secret was out. Could she trust Heidi to keep it?

Although Jordan hadn't known Heidi for long, she reminded her of Lacy. She was pretty sure those two would get along well.

She reached over to shake Heidi's hand. "Let's start over. I'm Jordan Spencer. I live outside of Nashville, and I'm a country singer."

Heidi accepted the gesture. "Hi, Jordan. It's nice to meet you. I'm Heidi. I hope you're enjoying your vacation here at the Hintz Dairy Farm. I know the accommodations aren't what you're used to—"

"Stop." Jordan smiled. "The accommodations are perfect. Thanks for not letting this change things. Well, I'm sure they will, a little. But despite the fame, I'm really a normal girl, struggling to get through this thing called life."

"Then come on, normal girl." Heidi stood. "Let's do a normal girl thing and refill these empty wine glasses. How does reality TV and chocolate ice cream sound?"

"Sounds like a fun, normal evening."

***

Eli finished cutting the hay by noon on the third day. Once all the equipment was cleaned and put back in the shed, he settled himself at the kitchen table to start another unpleasant task—paying bills. He was reading over his health insurance statement when Elliot and Lita burst through the back door.

"We're home," Lita shouted the obvious.

"Why didn't Grandma and Grandpa come in?" Over the years, Eli had developed a good relationship with Nikki's parents. He even included them in holiday celebrations and birthdays. So, it surprised him that they left without touching base.

"Grandma needed to get to her hair appointment." Lita took a cup out of the cabinet and went to fill it up with filtered water from the refrigerator.

Elliot dumped his duffle bag on the floor and ran upstairs.

"Hey, dude, come back here and pick up your stuff," Eli hollered after him.

A door slammed in reply.

"What's wrong with Elliot?" he asked Lita. Disrespectful behavior was not typical of Elliot, who was usually happy and even keeled.

Lita peered at him from over the rim of her glass. She finished taking a drink, and then came over to sit by Eli. "Mom called while we were at Grandma's. When it was Elliot's turn to talk to her, he started crying. I think he's embarrassed."

"Elliot looked upset, not embarrassed." What had Nikki said to their son?

"He's just being a big baby." Lita's smile contrasted with Elliot's foul mood. "Mom feels really bad about not coming to see us this summer so she asked Grandma and Grandpa for some money so she can fly home. Isn't that great?"

He felt the familiar punch of dread in his gut. Why did Nikki do this? She'd get their children's hopes up with promises, only to disappoint them. How many more times would he have to dry their tears? He knew how to mend cuts and scrapes, but how did he help heal broken hearts?

"What did Grandma and Grandpa say?"

"They didn't say for sure, but they want Mom to come home. Maybe if she sees how grown-up Elliot and I are, she'll want us to visit her in LA or go along to some of her concerts."

"Lita." He was unsure how to proceed. Being the bad guy wasn't new to Eli, but he still hated it. "Don't get too excited. Your mom doesn't always follow through with everything she says."

"You sound like Elliot. He called Mom a liar." Lita picked at the hot pink polish on her fingernails. Tiny flakes fell onto the table. "He told her that he wished she wasn't our mom and he didn't care about seeing her. Then he said he hated Rick and their band."

Eli wasn't a fan of Nikki's new husband, but he never shared his feelings with his kids. "I'll go talk to Elliot." He pushed back the chair to stand, and then went upstairs. Stopping in front of the door to his son's room, he hesitated. In some ways, Elliot's pain was harder to care for.

With Lita, all her feelings were verbalized and straightforward. If she was mad, he knew why. When she was hurt by something Nikki had done, she would tell him, even if that meant screaming out all her pain back at his face. At least he knew what he was dealing with.

Elliot was so much like Eli's dad—quiet and steady. He could always count on Elliot to do his chores without complaining. And when he was done, he'd stay in the barn and continue to watch over the animals.

Even as a nine-year-old boy, Elliot was sensitive and nurturing. If Elliot had acted out, he must be hurting—a lot.

Eli knocked, and after not receiving an answer, he opened the door and stepped inside.

Lying on his twin bed, Elliot's body was still.

"Hey, buddy." Eli sat next to his son's prone form. "Lita told me about your conversation with Mom. I'd like to hear from you what happened."

First, he sniffled. Then, Elliot rolled onto his side. Tears welled in his eyes. "I don't care about Mom and I don't want to talk about her."

Eli ruffled the boy's curly mop of hair. "I see you're upset. Whatever you're feeling, you can tell me."

"Mom acts so nice on the phone. She tells me she misses me and can't wait to see me. All she does is lie. I don't want her to come here. She left all of us and she can stay gone forever."

His son's words stung Eli's heart. Elliot had lost all faith in his mother. He'd given up hope she'd ever love him the way he deserved.

Eli wrapped Elliot in his arms. "When Mom left, we all had to be brave. I'm doing the best I can as your parent. You and Lita have been disappointed too many times, and I don't blame you for being mad. I believe one day, Mom will look back and regret missing out on such a wonderful boy."

Elliot sniffled. "I told her you had a girlfriend and were in love. Mom got mad."

Great. He could only imagine the conversation he'd be having with Nikki later. He'd have to explain that Elliot was mistaken. Ann was not his girlfriend

He liked Ann, a lot, and so did the kids. But his feelings wouldn't develop past the puppy love stage. Ann was too much of a mystery.

Eli kissed the top of his son's head. "It's okay to feel upset, but remember how much I love you."

Elliot buried his face into Eli's chest. Deep sobs racked his small body. Wrapping his arm around him, Eli pulled Elliot close.

"I want to believe Mom when she says she's coming to see us, but what if she doesn't?"

"Let's take one day at a time, okay, buddy? She misses you and Lita, and maybe things will work out this time. If they don't, we'll deal with it together, as a family."

The two were quiet for a few minutes until Elliot managed to calm himself. He sat up and wiped his eyes with the sleeve of his shirt. "Did Henrietta have her baby, yet?"

Laughing, Eli stood. "Why don't you go out to the barn and find out for yourself. Just be back in the house by six for dinner."

Elliot raced out of his room. Seeing his animals would brighten his mood.

Eli stood in the doorway and took several deep breaths. He needed to get his emotions back under control before he went downstairs to Lita. An unexpected rage filled his veins. His entire body grew tense, like a rattlesnake ready to strike.

Going into his bedroom, he softly closed the door with strained control. He opened the closet door and looked at the top shelf. Carefully, he slid off a photo—a photo of Nikki and him on their wedding day. He barely recognized the boy standing in front of the altar in a Las Vegas chapel. Eli finally turned his gaze to Nikki. His fist clenched in response.

"How could you do this to them?" he asked her image, his voice tearing from his throat in a horse whisper. "You told me you loved me... that you loved our children... and now I would give anything to erase you from their lives."

Nikki's face, frozen with a happy smile, stared back at him.

He tore the photo from top to bottom, and then again across each half. Taking each quarter, he shredded it. Eli dropped a handful of the colorful confetti in the trash can.

He needed to go outside and clear his head. A long walk would work out some of the negative energy that burned inside him.

Movement outside his window caught his attention. Heidi and Ann were walking up to the front of the house.

Seeing Ann instantly dampened his temper. Elliot had told Nikki that Ann was his girlfriend, but how could a young boy understand the intricacies of falling in love? Eli didn't even understand his own heart.

Yes, Ann was a beautiful and nice woman. But Eli had learned the hard way that trust needed to be earned. And if he were to fall in love again, it would only be after he was confident of her faithfulness and commitment to not only himself but more importantly, to his children.

Eli needed to keep guard over his heart until he understood Ann better. Who was she running from? And did she feel the strong connection between them? He'd have to take a risk in order to find out.

If she broke his heart, he'd survive. But he wouldn't stand by and watch his kids become attached to Ann, only for her to leave them with more empty promises.

Chapter Thirteen

When Jordan saw Eli descend the stairs, her heart sank in reaction to the frown on his face. His shoulders were hunched like they supported the weight of the world. The moment his gaze connected with hers, his lips twitched with a smile.

The usual pulse of attraction hit her chest, along with a new feeling—complete relaxation and comfort. Being with Eli was like coming home after a long day at the recording studio, changing into pajamas, and crawling into bed. His presence was a safe place for her. And in her world, those people were few and far between.

He came to stand by her side. "We have an hour before supper. You fancy taking a walk with me?"

"But, Dad, Ann was just going to do my hair." Lita followed her statement with a long sigh.

"I promise to do it after we eat, okay? Your hair isn't going anywhere." Jordan gently tugged a handful of Lita's blonde locks.

"Fine. Will you do my makeup, too?"

"Lita," Eli's deep voice warned. "Don't push it."

She rolled her eyes at her dad, and then smiled sweetly at Jordan. "Enjoy your walk."

Eli held the door open, and Ann walked outside. He quickly met her at the base of the porch stairs and took her hand "Let's go this way."

Walking side by side over a rolling hill, she enjoyed the feeling of his rough hand encasing her own. They continued in silence down a long stretch of grass that cut between two fields. On one side grew corn. The other, soybeans.

When they reached a narrow passage through the corn field, Eli guided her to turn left. Jordan strolled next to him, their bodies separated by a row of thigh-high corn plants. Every so often, he'd swing their connected hands over a tall, leafy stalk.

The buzzing of insects and the crunch of their shoes on the dirt were the only sounds carried in the air. For Jordan, this place was heaven on earth.

He stopped and turned to face her. They were standing in the middle of the corn field, like the only two people in the world.

Eli placed one large hand on either side of her hips and pulled her toward him. Being the gentleman that he was, he gave her several seconds to back away. The heat of his golden eyes melted her body until she was unable to move. His gaze shifted to her lips before his mouth descended on her.

Time stopped. Every sense in her body—smell, sight, taste, touch, and sound—were all focused entirely on Eli.

He engulfed her. Took her in and made her whole. His kiss was gentle yet demanding. Innocent as a teenager's, yet as passionate as reunited lovers. Their kiss was the very essence of music.

Eli filled her heart.

His mouth continued to move over hers and he wrapped his arms around her waist, pulling her closer.

Jordan's body molded against him. She lifted her arms so her hands rested on his broad shoulders. Then she raked her fingers through his wavy hair, loving its silky texture. Her lips traveled across his jawline before nipping at his earlobe.

Inhaling sharply, he grabbed a fistful of her shirt. He growled and angled his head to reclaim her lips.

When their kiss ended, he kept his gaze focused on her. "Did you feel that?"

"*Mhm.*" Full words escaped her. That kiss—she'd never felt anything that intense before.

"You drive me crazy."

"Ditto." She brushed the side of his face with the palm of her hand. After kissing Eli, how would she ever give him up?

"What's going on between us?" His mouth curved into a slight smile.

"I don't know," she whispered.

Eli placed a finger under her chin. "I can't deny that I'm incredibly attracted to you, but I have unanswered questions. Will you let me in?"

His words shot like a bullet and shattered her heart, sending pain radiating through the rest of her body. How could she continue to deceive him? But how could she explain the truth? Panic gripped her at the thought of seeing the passion is Eli's eyes dim.

For the first time in a very long time, she enjoyed being treated like a regular person, and she did not want that to change. Not here. Not in the one place she'd found a sense of peace.

She cleared her throat. "I'm leaving in a week, so I think it would be a mistake to let things go further between us. I like you... but my job keeps me very busy."

"Too busy for me." A statement, not a question. His sexy lips pressed together in a straight line. Thin furrows bracketed either side of his mouth. "Are you still involved with your ex?"

"No. I want nothing to do with him. Ever." She inhaled deeply, trying to calm her nerves. "But I have obligations back home that need attention. I don't want to lead you on, Eli."

"Thanks for being honest with me. I guess this is the part where you say we can still be friends." He stuffed his hands into the front pockets of his shorts.

Lifting her hand, she touched his arm. "I want you, more than I should admit. But your life is here." She swept her arm over corn plants. "With Lita and Elliot. My life won't fit into that."

His gaze drifted over the field, toward the distant horizon.

"Eli," she said in a soft voice. "I wish things were different." She wished that more than words could ever express.

Turning to face her, one corner of his mouth lifted with a smile. "I can't blame you. Farm life is tough. A lot of women run the other way. Nikki's a prime example."

"Nikki's a fool." Jordan took hold of his hand and entwined her fingers through his. "Honestly, I think farm life is very attractive. I've been more relaxed and happy here than I've been in a long time."

"Elliot thinks we're in love. Or at least that's what he told his mom." Eli kicked a clod of dirt with the toe of his boot.

"Oh, no. I hope that didn't cause problems with Nikki."

"No more than usual." He brushed back a few windblown pieces of her hair off her cheek. He took a deep breath and closed his eyes for a beat, and she knew she'd hate the words he was planning to say next. "Kids have a way of seeing things us jaded adults are blind to. That's why I think you should find another place to stay for the rest of your vacation. After everything Lita and Elliot have been through with their mom, I don't want them believing you'll remain a part of our lives."

Nausea rolled in her stomach. Eli feared she'd hurt Lita and Elliot. Of course, she'd never do that on purpose, but hadn't she just told him she'd be too busy to keep in regular contact? "You want me out of your life?"

"No, I don't. But you will leave, either now or a week from now. It would be easier if we didn't get any more attached to you than we already are."

"Oh," she whispered. What had she expected? She and Eli would have a harmless fling, and then wave goodbye? Eli was a father of two very perceptive children. He was only protecting them from false expectations.

Jordan took several steps away from Eli. She needed to put some distance between them before she dissolved into a puddle of goo. "My car's fixed and will be delivered tomorrow morning. Is it okay with you if I stay until then? Or I'll ask Heidi to give me a ride into town tonight. I'm sure I can get a hotel room until I find a rental house—"

"Of course you can stay until tomorrow morning." He raked his fingers roughly through his hair. "You must think I'm a jerk."

"I understand. Your kids are lucky to have you." She forced a smile. What she would give for a father who had loved her the way Eli loved his children. "I'll come up with an excuse for Lita and Elliot."

"Ann." His voice sounded strained. "I'm sorry."

Eli reached for her, but she stepped farther back. She wrapped her arms around her body—an ineffective armor against heartache.

"Would you mind giving me some time alone?" she asked. "I promised Lita I'd style her hair. Would it be all right if she came over to Heidi's after dinner? It won't take long."

He closed his eyes and nodded his head. After taking a deep breath, he turned and walked away.

Once he'd disappeared over the hill, Jordan's eyes filled with tears. Fear had stilled her tongue from telling the truth. Yes, she was a coward. She couldn't bear Eli turning on her the way Henry had done only weeks earlier.

At least with her lie still intact, they could part as friends. She did the right thing to let him go.

She had no other choice.

**

"You did what?" Heidi's voice was low and even, which filled Eli with more dread than if she would have shouted the question.

He'd seen that feral look in her eyes twenty years ago, right before Heidi had stabbed him with a pitchfork for dragging her dolls through the field behind the tractor.

He stood before his sister outside the livestock barn. Evening had quickly fallen, and he'd sent the kids inside to wash up for bed. "I thought it would be best." Reliving that kiss with Ann was not something he wanted to do, but his body would not let him forget. His heart pumped fire instead of blood at the memory of her delicious mouth and body.

"Best for whom?" Tipping her head, she glared at him.

"Lita and Elliot. Do you understand how hard it is to deal with their emotional roller coaster every time Nikki pops into their life? I can't handle them being disappointed by someone else."

"So, you plan on locking them up? Never let them form an attachment with anyone because, heaven forbid, they might be hurt in the process?" She paced back and forth. "How about you tell me the truth? *You're* the one afraid of getting hurt. You're falling for Ann, and it's got you running scared."

He clenched his hands at his sides. "This isn't about me. Don't you dare tell me what's best for my children."

"And don't you dare tell me who can stay at my house." She raised her small fists, looking like she was ready to do some damage. "Ann wounded your male pride. Get over it."

"My male pride has nothing to do with it." After his heartbreak over Ann's rejection, he did not want to fight with Heidi. Apparently, though, he had no choice but defend his decision.

"Lita and Elliot like Ann, but she's not their mother. Don't punish Ann for Nikki's actions."

"Elliot seems to think I'm in love with Ann. And I wouldn't be surprised if Lita's planning our wedding."

Heidi slapped her hand on her forehead. "Oh, no. They want to see their dad happy and in love. How terrible."

"Your sarcasm is not helping." Eli's frown, along with his foul mood, deepened. "What am I supposed to do when Ann continues to evade my efforts to get to know her better? Oh, except for the one thing she's made crystal clear... she wants nothing to do with us after she leaves."

"She never said that." Heidi's hard expression dared him to challenge her. "Have you ever considered that Ann's scared to open up to you? And if she did, that you wouldn't accept the real her?"

"That's ridiculous."

She reached over to lay her hand on his arm. "I trust that after some time to think things over, you'll make the right choice." After kissing his cheek, she ruffled his hair and walked away.

Later that night, Eli got a call from Nikki, just as expected. Because they were in different time zones and sleep schedules, he'd been deep asleep when his cell rang.

"Hello." Eli tried to wake up his brain. He'd been having a good dream about Ann. She was now just a dream, and he clung to memories of time with her like a drowning man would a life vest.

"Did I wake you up?" Nikki didn't sound very concerned.

"What do you want?" *Let's skip the false pleasantries and get to why you really called.*

"I heard you're getting married. Isn't that kinda quick, Eli? You've known her for what, a week?"

He rubbed his hand over his face. "Elliot told you some things that aren't true. I'm not getting married. I'm not even dating."

"Why would he lie to me?" She huffed. "How dare you bring a strange woman into their lives without discussing it with me?"

You're a good one to talk. Nikki had gotten married without discussing it with Eli. She hadn't even bothered to inform the kids until months later. But then again, her husband rarely saw Lita and Elliot. "I'm not dating Ann, and we're not getting married. She's actually leaving tomorrow." Saying those words physically pained him. His chest ached with regret. Why had he been such an idiot and asked her to leave? Was Heidi right? Had he reacted to his hurt pride?

"Then why would Elliot tell me you two are in love?"

Being awoken to Nikki's inquisitions gave him a splitting headache. "Elliot was upset."

"I told him I want to come home and see him. I would have thought he'd be happy about that."

The deep voice of her husband sounded in the background, and Nikki replied something Eli couldn't make out.

Eli decided enough was enough. He wanted to go back to sleep. His five-a.m. alarm would not stall because he'd been up half the night on a phone call. "Are you really coming, or just telling them that to be their hero for a few days? Just remember that I have to pick up the pieces when you break your promises."

"For your information, I bought my plane tickets. Rick's coming, too. My mom's treat. Isn't that great?"

Not really. "I swear, Nikki. If you back out again, I'm going to find you and make sure you really understand the damage you're doing."

Her laughter sounded like the grinding of gears. "I sure hope you're not threatening me, Eli. I'll be there in five days, so you better learn your manners. By the way, do you think Rick and I can stay at your house?"

"No," he said with finality. "I'm going back to bed."

"Good night." Nikki made a kissy sound before ending the call.

How had he ever been in love with her? Sure, she was pretty, and he'd been a horny teenage boy who hadn't seen past a beautiful face and hot body. The first few years of their marriage had been great, living the rock-star life in LA. They'd been happy. Or as much as he knew of happiness.

His parents' death had changed everything. But if he were honest with himself, things would have changed regardless. Nikki had been pregnant, and Eli remembered trying to convince her that he needed to quit the band and get a real job. She'd fought him, saying that once the band would get noticed, they'd have all the money they'd need to raise a family.

Their marriage had deteriorated from there. They were both stubborn. Neither one of them wanted to give.

So, when Nikki told him she was leaving, he hadn't been surprised. What had shocked him was the fact she had abandoned their children. Even at the lowest point in their relationship, he never would have thought she'd be capable of walking away from them.

Enough obsessing about the past. Eli rolled over in bed and closed his eyes.

Back to that dream about Ann.
Now, where was I?

Chapter Fourteen

"I'm sorry if we've bugged you, but please don't leave." Lita stood before Jordan's car with the palm of her little hand resting on the hood.

"You have not been a bother. I've really enjoyed getting to know both you and Elliot." Jordan slid her guitar case in the backseat. Earlier that morning, the repair shop had driven her car over to the farm. Now, parked next to Heidi's house, the rental looked as good as new, which it should for the large total of the repair bill. She'd paid cash, brushing off Heidi's insistence that Jordan should put in a claim with their insurance to cover the damage. "I found a nice rental right on Lake Michigan. There, I'll be out of everyone's way."

"You promised to stay here for two weeks—and it's only been one. Why did you change your mind?" She narrowed her eyes at Jordan. "It was Dad, wasn't it? He said something to you last night. That's why you missed dinner, and you were so quiet when you did my hair."

Jordan did not want to cause any more strife for Eli. Although, he did kind of deserve it. "Don't blame your dad. This is my decision." She came over to put an arm around Lita's shoulders. "You have my cell number and my e-mail address. I promise to keep in touch."

"I know all about adult promises."

"You can always count on mine." Jordan would make certain to protect the girl's tender heart. And that's why she was leaving. Someday, she'd come back for a visit not as Ann Dufour, but as Jordan Spencer. She'd love to be able to fully explore Lita's voice. Arrangements could be made for her vocal coach to come along and give both Lita and Elliot lessons. "I mean it, honey. Don't assume my leaving early has anything to do with me not caring about you."

"Yeah, it has to do with Dad."

Jordan decided she best bypass talk of Eli altogether. She wrapped the girl in a snug embrace. "I will miss you. Keep working hard and good things will come your way."

Tears filled Lita's eyes. "Bye, Ann. Don't forget about us." She spun around and ran across the yard to the farmhouse.

Jordan sighed deeply. Nothing about this morning was going well. Elliot and Lita were upset. Heidi refused to speak to her brother. Eli had gone off to the milking house, probably to avoid having to say goodbye. She hated to admit it, but her leaving now was best for family harmony. Once she was gone, their lives would calm down.

Going back inside, Jordan found Heidi sitting at the kitchen table.

She twirled a coffee mug in between her palms. "You all packed?"

"I think so. Let me know if you find anything I've left behind. Or just keep it." Jordan sat across the table from her. "I hope to come back someday for a visit. That is, if it's okay with Eli."

"Eli isn't king around here. I purchased this house from him with my own money, which means he has no right to ask you to leave. You are my guest."

"I respect his feelings." Jordan's were a jumbled mess. The familiar fingers of panic crawled over her skin. "You've been a good friend, even after you found out who I really am. I appreciate that more than you'll ever know."

Heidi stood and wrapped Jordan in a strong hug. Tears flooded her blue eyes. "I'm going to miss you. Lita and Elliot will miss you, too. But it will be the worst for my blockhead of a brother. He'll have the hardest time dealing with your absence. I can only hope that someday you two will get another chance."

"Maybe." Probably not, but Jordan would never forget Eli.

After saying goodbye to Heidi, Jordan left to go find Elliot. She didn't want to leave without giving him one last hug.

***

Eli might be stubborn, but he wasn't stupid, and asking Ann to leave was up there on the top ten list of the stupidest things he'd ever done. Right underneath his failed attempt at riding the

Frederickson's bull when he was sixteen. For that adventure, he'd earned a broken arm and bruised pride. If he let Ann go today, he would not only hurt his family, but he'd have to live with the guilt of knowing he'd acted like an entitled jerk.

Now, he hoped Ann would listen to his apology, instead of slamming the car door in his face, like he deserved. Even if that meant groveling at her feet.

As he walked out the front door of his house, he saw Ann's car still parked by Heidi's place. Good. She hadn't left yet. He still had a chance to put things right.

Last night, Heidi had called the motivation for his actions correctly. When he'd kissed Ann, he'd felt the earth tilt under his feet. The spark they'd made had been amazingly hot. He'd never craved a woman as much as he had Ann. But then, she'd been honest with him, practically raising a giant red stop sign.

And his reaction—hurt and anger over her rejection. When he'd stopped sulking long enough to really think about it, he was grateful for her candidness. He had to admit that telling him those things had probably been as hard for her to say as it was for him to hear.

He'd just stepped onto the porch when he halted at the sound of Ann's voice. Not wanting to disturb her, he waited until she was finished. He peeked through the window to see her pacing around the family room, holding her cell to her ear.

"Everything's fine, Cole." Her voice drifted through the window screen. "The place I'll be staying at is out of the way, not even you will be able to find it."

His blood boiled with the mention of Cole—Ann's ex. Sounded like he was still trying to locate her. He watched Ann frown as she listened to the caller.

"Don't you dare come." She waved her hand in the air. "No, I mean it. And you're not going to beat anyone up."

If that man laid a hand on her, Eli wouldn't hesitate to rush to her defense. He took a step and the floorboard creaked under his foot.

Ann glanced through the window at him and her scowl deepened. "I need to go. Bye." She ended the call and marched to the door. Once she stepped outside, she gazed stoically at him. "I'm leaving now if that's what you came over to check on."

"No." He stuffed his hands into the pockets of his jeans. How had he made such a mess of things? Oh wait, he knew. He'd been too focused on his own feelings. Eli had been sure she'd fallen for him as hard as he'd fallen for her. He'd been wrong. Time to man up. "That's not why I'm here. Not to make sure you're gone." His gaze dropped to his scuffed work boots. "I want to let you know you can stay."

When he raised his head, he saw her staring wide-eyed at him.

She raised her delicate, cleft chin, even as it trembled slightly. "Wait... what?'

Beg, man, if you have to. "Yesterday, when I asked you to leave..." He sighed. "I wasn't thinking clearly. That kiss... it rattled my brain." *Along with other things.* "It was a jerk move on my part. I want you to stay on for the rest of your vacation."

"While I appreciate the offer, I've already made other arrangements. I'm not staying somewhere I'm not wanted."

"But you are wanted." *More than I'll ever admit.* "Heidi, Lita, and Elliot have enjoyed having you here. And you're Heidi's guest, so technically I had no right to ask you to leave."

She brushed past him and descended the stairs. "How magnanimous of you."

Eli hustled to follow her as she made her way to her car. When she swung the door open, he moved to put his body between it and Ann. "Stop and hear me out."

"Why?" The depths of her granite-colored eyes sparked with cold fire. "You have no right to command me to do anything. I'm not one of your children or a worker on your farm."

This was not going the way he'd planned. How had he so grossly underestimated the feisty spirit hiding underneath her sweet smile? "I'm not commanding."

"Oh, yes, you are. That's what you do, Eli. You're the master of the universe." She raised her eyebrows in a challenge. "And I don't take orders from anyone, so move out of my way."

What could he say next that wouldn't stoke her temper any further? "Please." The word stuck in his throat. Was she right in her accusations? Sure, he barked out orders because he had a lot to do and didn't have time for debate. He needed people to follow his commands quickly. That's how the farm, and his family, stayed afloat.

"Please, what?" She crossed her arms over her chest. Her foot tapped on the gravel driveway.

He inhaled deeply. "Please stay."

"Why are you here? You must have a million other things to do."

"Nothing that can't wait." That wasn't true. He did have a million things that needed his attention. But nothing as important as making things right with Ann.

She tried to shove her way past him, with no effect. "I've already said goodbye to everyone. Just let me go."

"You didn't say goodbye to me." His mouth turned down in a pout.

"That's because we said our goodbyes yesterday." She pushed his arm, but it stayed firmly in place.

"What do I have to do to convince you?" Eli considered the possibilities. Kissing her again was right at the top of his list. Why was he a glutton for more punishment? "You were honest with me yesterday. And after I'd just dealt with more Nikki drama, I overreacted. I want to protect my kids from more hurt, but I understand that this time, I was the one who hurt them. They like you, and you've been kind to them. I trust that you wouldn't do anything to cause them more pain."

"But I will, Eli. You were right. I'll leave, either today or in a week." She turned her head to gaze across the yard to the old farmhouse. Her body sagged, seeming to have lost all its fight. "I haven't been completely honest with you about who I am. So, I do agree that it's best I leave now, before things get more complicated."

"What are you running from?" He rested his large hand on her narrow shoulder. "Maybe I can help."

Her lips gave a slight smile. "I'm not running from, so much as traveling to a destination. I just don't know where the journey will take me. My life has morphed into a monster that I can no longer control. I took this break in order to find myself and figure out what I want my life to look like. The only thing I know for certain is I don't want the monster, not anymore."

"I'm sorry." He stepped away from her car, knowing that he couldn't hold onto her if she wanted to fly. "You deserve to be happy, and I thought you were happy here. If you want to leave, I won't stand in your way." Leaning over, he kissed her soft cheek.

As he turned to walk away, Ann put a hand on his bicep. "Are you really okay with me staying on? You're not just saying these things because your family is angry with you?"

He grunted with laughter. "I'm used to being the target of the tribe's unrest. Trust me, I'm too stubborn to be bullied into doing something I don't feel is right. Even by my own family. If you want to stay, you have my blessing. The only thing I ask is that we both make it clear to Lita and Elliot that there is no romantic relationship between us."

"Thank you," she said softly. "For your trust. All of you have come to mean a lot to me. Can you give me a few minutes to think things over?"

Eli wished more than anything that he meant something more than a friend to her. But if friendship was all she was offering, then he'd be a fool not to accept. "I'll be over in the red barn. Come get me if you'd like help carrying your stuff back into Heidi's."

He left her then, hoping that wasn't the last time he'd see the lovely Ann Dufour.

Chapter Fifteen

Jordan marched back and forth in front of her car. She couldn't make herself get inside and drive away. Yet, she hadn't come to the conclusion that staying was the smart choice.

Why did Eli have to be such a frustrating, overbearing, but overall wonderful man? *Ugh.*

After minutes of indecision, she finally decided to use her phone-a-friend and ask for help.

Cole picked up after the first ring. "Well, that was fast. Can't get enough of me?"

"Guess what just happened." Jordan didn't wait for his reply. "Eli came over to tell me that he changed his mind. I'm allowed to stay now."

He chuckled. "Of course, he did. Eli's a man."

"What's that supposed to mean?" By this point, Jordan was sick of dealing with *all* men. She should have tried to get a hold of Lacy.

"It means that you're a beautiful, sexy woman, and that can make a man do some strange things. And then you kissed the poor sucker and broke his heart. Jordan, give the guy a break."

"He kissed me, and I didn't break his heart." But she should have given more thought to his feelings about their situation, instead of just her own.

"Yes, you did," Cole said. "Regardless, the offer still stands. I'll come beat him up for you. No one upsets my Jordan and gets away with it."

"Cole." Her anger then turned to laughter. He had a way of doing that—reducing her boiling rage to a simmer then to lukewarm anger, and then finally, she was cool and relaxed, laughing at his silliness. "What should I do?"

"That's not my call. You need to figure this out on your own. What does your heart tell you?"

She stopped pacing and listened to the voice inside her. The one she'd started to pay attention to again. "That I should stay."

"Then there you go," Cole said. "Unpack your bags."

"But how do I keep from falling in love with Eli? Every time I'm around him, my brain shuts down. I can't start another doomed relationship. Not with him."

"Not every relationship is doomed."

Jordan sighed. "No, just mine."

"Sweetcakes, you just haven't found the right match for your special heart."

His words brought tears to her eyes. "I love you, Cole."

There was a brief pause. "Love you, too, Jordan. Call me if you need me."

After she ended the call, Jordan felt a lightness lift her body. She'd stay for one more week. Her focus—shining happiness into her life, and the lives of those around her.

She strolled to the barn and went inside, searching for Eli. After a brief hunt, she found him in the pen of a calf, bent over in examination.

He lifted his gaze at the sound of her footsteps on the cement aisle. "Hey. This little lady isn't feeling well." Rubbing his hand across the calf's head, he exhaled. "She's running a temperature and doesn't want to stand."

"Poor thing." The calf gazed up at her with huge, brown eyes. "What will you do for her?"

"I'll call the vet and have him take a look. Don't worry. We'll have her feeling better soon." Eli stood and exited the pen. "Have you come to a verdict?"

She clasped her hands behind her back, mostly to stop the impulse to reach out and touch him. "After much deliberation, I have come to the conclusion that if you're fine with me hanging around, then I will cancel my other reservation. I'd like to stay. We're both mature adults. Well, at least one of us is."

Eli laughed. "I won't ask which one of us, but I can probably guess." Pulling his ballcap out of the back pocket of his jeans, he shook it out and put it on his head. "I'm glad."

"So, we're good?" No use wishing for what her heart craved. She'd have to be content with his friendship. Although, when he looked so ruggedly sexy, in dusty blue jeans and a too-tight T-shirt, he was a hard man to resist.

"Yeah, we're good." He tipped his head toward the open barn door. "I'm heading over to the milking parlor. You want to join me?"

"You bet." She'd never seen a modern milking parlor before. And an added bonus, she'd get to spend some time with Eli.

She followed him outside and climbed into the passenger seat of the ATV. After a short ride, they arrived at a large, metal building.

"My dad built this facility about twenty-five years ago in order to increase his herd size." He pulled on a door on the side of the building and held it open for her to enter. "Over the past few years, I've bought all new milking equipment. Most of the process is automated. I also expanded the pasture to give the cows plenty of time outdoors."

Jordan stepped inside and was amazed at the large, open space filled with cows lazily munching on their feed. "Wow. This is huge."

His face beamed with pride. "Farming is a very complicated business these days. It takes a lot of work to keep this whole operation running."

Eli guided her down one of the long aisles and introduced her to three of his farm helpers. Running a farm was a twenty-four-hour, seven-day-a-week job, and she gained a new respect for Eli's work ethic.

After her tour, Eli drove her back to Heidi's. With a wink and a grin, he left her to head back to work.

What a shameless tease.

And just like that, one more defensive wall around her heart came crumbling down.

***

Two days later, she got it in her head to try cooking again. She wanted to prove to herself she could pull it off, *without* setting the kitchen on fire. Spaghetti shouldn't be too hard. Plus, Heidi had all the ingredients already in the pantry. *Just don't burn the water and you'll be fine.*

As she browned the beef to add to the sauce, her mind drifted to Eli. Since the day she'd almost left, he'd maintained a friendly manner toward her, but gone were the long looks and flirty smiles. He was a man of his word. Such a rare thing in her world.

Not that she still didn't have the burning desire to curl up in his arms and bury her head against his chest.

When Heidi came home from work, she was tasked with the job of rounding everyone up for dinner. She came back a short while later with Lita and Elliot in tow.

"Eli wanted to shower and change his clothes before coming over." Heidi pulled out a stack of plates from the cabinet and began setting the table. "He should be here soon."

Jordan's stomach fluttered at the thought of sitting down to dinner with him, all freshly washed and smelling like spicy soap. Her heart jumped when he came walking through the back door, his curly hair still damp.

"Something smells good in here." He smiled at Jordan.

Lita went over to guide him to a seat at the table. "How did you get here so fast? Did you even use soap or just stand under the water for a few seconds?"

Eli laughed. "Hey, that's my line."

"I'm glad you hurried because I'm starving." Heidi poured two glasses of wine, one for herself and the other for Jordan.

Thankful, Jordan accepted the glass and took a sip. The pressure of cooking this simple spaghetti dinner had frazzled her poor nerves.

Once everyone else was seated, Jordan proudly brought a bubbling pot of sauce to the table.

"Did you turn off the stove?" Eli asked with a grin.

Setting the pot down on a macramé trivet, Jordan smiled down at the man who still didn't trust her in the kitchen. Well, none of them did, but that was beside the point. "I'm not sure. Why don't you go check? Then you can bring the garlic bread back with you."

He stood and gave her a slight bow. "As you wish."

"We should watch *The Princess Bride* tonight." Lita scooped spaghetti noodles onto her plate. "I love it when Wesley says that to Princess Buttercup."

"That movie has too much kissing." Elliot scrunched up his nose. "Dad promised I could play my drum set."

Eli set the garlic bread on the table. "Only if that's okay with Aunt Heidi and Ann. They'll have to listen to you play, too, since your drums are in Heidi's basement."

Heidi shrugged and sprinkled parmesan cheese on top of her spaghetti. "It doesn't bother me."

Elliot turned his attention to Jordan. "I keep my drum set over here because Aunt Heidi has a nice basement. Dad's got his electric guitar down there, too."

"I'd like to hear both of you play." Jordan twirled noodles onto her fork. Taking a deep breath for courage, she tasted her creation. Not bad. Even better than her personal chef's spaghetti. Although he didn't use meat in the sauce, and the noodles were some sort of vegetable protein concoction. So maybe the bar wasn't *too* high.

"Yeah, Eli," Heidi said with a wink directed at Jordan. "We could have a concert. Elliot on drums, you on electric guitar, and Lita can sing."

Lita wiped her face off with a napkin. "What about Ann? She sings really good. I've heard her."

"Let Ann enjoy the show." Heidi held up a forkful of spaghetti and smiled. "Good job on dinner, by the way. I think you've got potential."

Jordan laughed. "Thanks. I might try my hand in my own kitchen when I get back home." She hadn't stepped on the scale, but she was pretty sure she'd put on at least ten pounds in the last week and a half. Not that she cared. She liked the feeling of a full stomach.

Eli's face clouded over, and he dropped his gaze down to his plate.

She wondered if he thought about their kiss as much as she still did. *No use going there.* Those thoughts would only lead to heartache, and she'd had enough of that in her love life.

"Maybe we should watch *The Sound of Music* later. Y'all are a very Von Trapp family." Jordan tried to coax a smile out of Eli. "You'd make a wonderful Captain."

"Not likely." A corner of his mouth twitched. "Christopher Plummer was in a league all his own. I'd never be able to come close."

"I could be Liesl. *I am sixteen going on seventeen,*" Lita sang.

"Oh no, you're not." Eli's scowl started a chain reaction of giggles, and soon laughter filled the kitchen.

After they'd eaten and cleaned up the kitchen, Jordan followed the crowd down to the basement for the next act. The big rock-n-roll show.

Heidi's basement was designed to be a party space. A large bar with six stools took up part of one side. Fixed on the wall was a large TV, along with various sports memorabilia. Elliot's drum set was placed in the far corner.

As he pulled out the five-piece set, Elliot hummed with excitement. Eli went into another room before coming out with a shiny, black electric guitar. He set it down and went back to get the amp.

Jordan got seated on the leather sofa facing their makeshift stage. *This was going to be good.*

***

Eli hadn't played his electric guitar for a very long time, but the weight of it felt good in his hands. He remembered playing sets with Nikki, who stood at the front of the stage. She was always the star of the show. And he'd had no problems with that arrangement. Being famous had been her dream. She'd been the one who'd insisted they move out to LA. Not that he'd put up much of a fight. Eli had been eager to put miles between him and the family farm.

Now, his fingers strummed over the strings once again. The sound of the chords reverberated out of the amp. He could feel the vibration in his chest. A sensation that pulled him back in time.

Eli missed this part of him—the part that loved making music. It didn't matter what kind, although he still hated country western. The act of blending notes together to produce melody was as close to magic as he'd ever get.

Following Elliot's rhythm of the drums, Eli played. He didn't think about the chords or the sound; he let his fingers have free rein.

The two of them together sounded great. He glanced up and made eye contact with Ann. Inside his chest, his heart beat as strongly as the bass drum behind him.

How had he let himself fall in love with her? Even after Ann had told him that her life had no room for him, he couldn't stop his growing feelings. The seed had been planted in the part of his heart that craved someone to share his life with. Roots had already taken firm hold.

There were so many things about Ann that were still such a secret. But when she smiled at him, like she was doing now, he felt like he'd known her all his life.

Eli stepped aside to give Elliot the spotlight. Elliot's thin arms whipped around like they were made of noodles, banging and clashing until Eli thought he'd go deaf.

Once finished, Elliot came around the drum set and took a bow next to his dad. Ann, Heidi, and Lita gave them a standing ovation.

"That was wonderful," Ann said, coming up to Elliot. "You're a natural on the drums. Have you had lessons?"

Elliot shook his sweaty head. "No. But I want to soon. Dad says I have to get my grades up next year then he'll let me take lessons."

"Study hard. You have a natural talent for rhythm. My drummer would be very impressed." Ann bit down on her lip.

"What do you mean... my drummer?" Eli asked while powering off his amp.

"Oh... I mean my friend is a drummer. He plays in a small band back home. Nothing you would have heard of." She rocked back and forth on the balls of her feet. "Do we get another song?"

Eli noticed the pout growing on Ann's face and second guessed unplugging his guitar. "Maybe we can do an encore performance another night. Elliot and Lita still have a few things to do yet tonight. We take their animals to the fair tomorrow."

"We're in 4H." Lita rolled her eyes. "Dad promised I don't have to do it next year. I'm showing three Holland Lop rabbits at the fair. Elliot has a Guernsey heifer and Holstein cow."

"We have to take them for judging," Elliot said. "Ginger's going to win a blue ribbon."

"I start baling hay in the morning." Internally, Eli groaned at the thought of his alarm going off at four a.m. "Then we'll load up the livestock to take over to the county fairgrounds. You're welcome to come along, Ann."

"I'd only get in the way." Ann started for the stairs.

Heidi followed her up. The two women whispered back and forth.

When they got upstairs, the kids said good night to Heidi and Ann, and took off running toward the barn.

"I promised Lita I'd help her brush her rabbits." Heidi slipped on her tennis shoes. "You two take a break and relax."

Before Eli could say a word, Heidi was out the door and skipping across the lawn.

"I know what she's doing, and I'm sorry." Eli couldn't stop his smile. As much as he wanted to be mad at Matchmaker Heidi, there was a secret part of him that was grateful. Time alone with Ann was hard to come by.

"What do you mean?" Ann fidgeted with the few dishes left on the counter.

"Never mind. How about we go outside? It's finally cooling off out there, and I could use some fresh air."

"Aren't you afraid one day you're going to OD on fresh air?"

"Nah." He held the door open for her and enjoyed the view as she walked past. "I love the outdoors. Even in winter, except for during blizzards. I draw the line at wind chills below zero."

"How is it possible to get that cold? As a Southern girl, I'm allergic to the cold."

He laughed and almost reached over to take her hand. Pushing back the impulse, he crossed his arms.

"Which way?"

"If you don't mind, I'd just like to sit on the porch. I'm kinda exhausted from making dinner." She pointed toward the sun, still a fiery ball of orange in the sky. "I hate to see another day come to an end."

So do I.

They sat on two of the rocking chairs on the front porch. Ann crossed one long, tan leg over the other.

Eli forgot how to breathe. After several seconds, his brain started working enough to form words. "Nikki's coming to visit the kids. I wasn't sure if they'd said anything to you, yet."

"Lita mentioned it. She's afraid her mom will cancel."

"Neither kid has much faith in Nikki's word. But I think this time she's really coming. She should be here in three days."

Nikki hadn't been here in over a year. When she'd told him yesterday that she was still planning on coming, he couldn't believe his ears. From the questions she'd asked over the phone, he had a suspicion her motive for coming home wasn't only to see Lita and Elliot. Nikki seemed overly interested in Ann. He'd repeated over and over again that he was not dating Ann, but Nikki wouldn't listen.

If he would have known all it took to get Nikki to visit her kids was Eli dating another woman, he would have played that card long ago. Not that he would have really dated, just like he was not really dating now. Although, the stunning woman sitting next to him made him want to change his status.

"That's good that Lita and Elliot will spend time with their mom." Ann glanced over at him. "I'll try to keep out of sight. I don't want my presence to cause any problems."

"Don't worry about it. Nikki will pick up Lita and Elliot, and then she'll be gone." He hoped, anyway. Nikki hated the farm and everything it stood for. He couldn't imagine she'd want to spend any more time here than she'd have to.

"You and Elliot were really good down there." A smile once again lit up her face.

He was thankful for the change in subject. The last thing he wanted to think about now was his ex-wife. "Thanks. Elliot took to the drums like a seed to good soil."

"Both your children are musically gifted. And their father sure knows how to rock out on a guitar. Man… you're lucky there were other people around because otherwise I would have tossed a pair of panties on stage." Her laughter echoed through the still air.

Eli felt a flush of heat move through his body. "Oh, I've had my fair share launched at me. The red, lacy ones are always my favorite." He winked over at her. Two could play at this game.

A pink blush tinted her cheeks. "Sorry, all I have are big, white cotton."

He highly doubted that.

Bird songs drifted across the breeze. A blue jay flew across the front lawn and came to rest on a branch in the large oak tree. The sun was hovering just above the horizon line. Soon, the stars would begin appearing in the variegated deep blue sky.

"Tell me one thing about yourself, besides the fact you wear granny panties," Eli said with a grin.

"Funny." She shifted in her chair. "I'm really not that interesting."

"Indulge me."

Appearing to think it over, Ann rocked in the chair.

She wore a pink top and black and white polka dot shorts. Since the air had cooled off, she'd put on a white sweater before coming outside. Eli wasn't an expert on clothing, but her simple outfit seemed to be well made. Even her sandals, he could tell, were made of high-quality leather. Her being wealthy would explain her noble bearing. Sometimes he could almost see a tiara on her head.

"Well, you already know that my parents worked for a carnival company," she said. "I use the term 'company' very loosely. My sister and I traveled around with them. But I guess you could say our home base was a little town in Mississippi. That's where we'd go when my folks had a break from gigs."

"You have a great Southern drawl." Eli loved listening to her talk.

"I've worked hard to temper it. Not get rid of my accent completely, but I've learned to turn it on or off, depending on the situation. And when I'm comfortable, like I am now, I don't think about it, so my drawl is more pronounced."

"You didn't have a good childhood?"

"My sister Lacy was the one bright spot in my life. Along with singing. I loved putting smiles on the faces of the people who'd stop and listen." She pressed her lips together and stopped talking.

Which made him wonder what she wasn't saying. Why did she still hold back parts of herself?

But Eli had no right to her secrets. They belonged to her.

He wasn't usually the type to glower over things he couldn't have. With Ann, though, he found himself becoming more and more dejected. Eli wanted her. And the fact that she only wanted him as a friend left him feeling like a boy who discovered there was no Santa. Nothing in his life seemed as fascinating anymore. His work days seemed to drag. Getting out of bed in the morning was a struggle. All the work around the farm felt like a smothering blanket.

"Music is a gift," Ann said. "The melody, the lyrics… they connect people. They can make people happy, or sad, or motivate them to interact. Music can make people jump up and down or put tears in their eyes. Being able to do that is like holding a magic wand. It's as close to true magic as I think is humanly possible."

"That's exactly how I feel when I perform. I haven't found anything like the rush I got when I stood on stage. The music from my guitar was part of a larger creation. Nikki needed the acknowledgment of the crowd. I only wanted their energy."

Ann nodded her head. "Someday, you'll watch your children on stage. You're so lucky to get to share your love of music with them."

A fleeting image of his dad's broad, weathered face came to his mind. As much as they had fought, Eli sure missed his father. He'd been gone for so long, Eli had a hard time remembering the sound of his laughter or the way he grunted when he was mad. "My dad never heard me play, I mean really play. He'd been too busy to come to any of my school band concerts, and when I got older and started the band, he disapproved. His passion was the farm, something I grew to resent. Now, it's too late."

"You can't change the past with your own father, but you are affecting the future with your children. They both know you will love and support them, no matter what." Ann rested her hand on his shoulder.

"I wish my dad knew I came home. I'd want him to be proud of what I do every day to keep this place running." Eli swallowed hard, trying to push down his emotions. "The last time we talked, he told me this farm was my family legacy. I owed it to the family to stop goofing off out west and come home. And you know what I said in reply? That I didn't want anything to do with a family legacy that was more important to him than his own children. That was the last thing I said to him."

"You didn't know." Ann's fingers kneaded his tense shoulder muscles.

"It shouldn't have mattered. He was my father, and I should have shown him more respect." Eli would give anything to have one more talk with his dad. To tell him everything that had happened over the past ten years. About Lita's beautiful singing voice, and Elliot's love of the farm and his animals. He'd tell his dad that he now understood why he'd spent so many hours working, from before sun-up to past sundown.

He understood the challenges of balancing the roles of farmer and father.

And some days he felt as if he were failing at both.

***

Jordan rose and went to stand behind Eli. She set a hand down on each of his strong shoulders, ones that seemed to carry the weight of the world, and she began working out the knots in his muscles.

He groaned as she pushed deeply into his unyielding flesh. "Don't stop," he muttered.

She laughed and kept massaging. "You're as tightly wound as a guitar string around a tuning peg."

"You'd be too if you hauled seventy-pound bags of feed all day."

"I know your father would be proud of the man you've become," Ann said. "Don't let guilt and regret become more important than gratitude. You've got a lot of things going for you, Elijah Hintz."

He laughed, and then groaned again as she dug her knuckles into a particularly resistant knot of muscles. Eli's head tipped back and he closed his eyes.

As she worked, she took the time to appreciate how well built he was. His broad back and shoulders stretched the white T-shirt he was wearing. Each arm rounded with a mound of bicep muscle, which had been built the honest way—by hard, manual labor. Even his forearms were muscular and covered with a dusting of sun-bleached hair.

He also had a great neck. One she could imagine kissing, up and down the curve of his spine. And his legs were the best pair she'd ever seen on a man. His whole body was sculpted like a statue of a Greek god.

Looking down, she saw his brown hair curled at the nape of his neck. He could use a haircut. Her fingers itched to run through his locks.

Eli was almost perfect. Well-built and good looking. A kind man and a loving father. He worked hard but knew how to have fun.

He was everything she ever wanted in a man. Yet, he was nothing she could ever have.

His first obligation was to his family and farm.

Jordan Spencer traveled most of the year. Between touring, promotional stuff, and flying to work with other producers, she was rarely home for more than a week at a time. She wouldn't be able to give the kind of commitment Eli needed in a partner.

Then there was her track record with men. She'd never had a romantic relationship with a man that had worked well. And most had ended badly, with leaked photos and stories to the media, public fights, and emotional breakdowns. Although Eli didn't seem like the kind of guy who would try to make a buck off of her, Jordan had learned a long time ago that people's sense of right and wrong shifted with enough money and media attention.

Yes, she was high maintenance. She had anxiety issues. She expected a lot out of the few people she let into her life. People accused her of being aloof and snobbish. Other country musicians called her a sellout when her music sounded too mainstream.

Did that mean she'd never find love? She wondered if she was destined to live her life alone.

Jordan gave Eli's shoulders one last squeeze before lifting her hands and cracking her knuckles. "Feel any better?"

He stood, and then turned to face her. "Better than I've felt in a long time. Thanks, for everything. Dinner, sitting through our little performance in the basement, and the shoulder massage."

She didn't remember moving, but she found herself wrapped in Eli's strong arms. Settling her head onto his chest, Jordan absorbed the beat of his heart. Soon, her own heart synced to his rhythm. His solid body was warm, almost hot, and she melted against him.

His lips brushed the top of her head. "I should go check on the kids. They need to get to bed soon."

"Always the one keeping everything running. When do you take a break and relax?" She breathed in his earthy scent. *I want to stay in your arms forever. Don't let me go.*

"I don't." Eli let his arms fall to his side, and Jordan suddenly felt chilled. "Maybe someday, when I'm old and gray. But for now, if I stop, the whole operation crumbles apart."

"I can appreciate the pressure." She was the center of the Jordan Spencer enterprise, and she feared losing everything she'd worked so hard to achieve. Her absence, even for two weeks, was having an impact on the people who worked hard to keep her business running. But if she hadn't taken the drastic step of taking a break, her mental health would have made it impossible for her to continue.

"I hope you can come to the fair with us." Eli descended the porch stairs. "I'm sure Lita and Elliot would love it."

"We'll see." Above them, a few stars twinkled in the inky sky. How long had they been out here talking?

"Good night, Ann."

"Night, Eli."

Jordan stood at the corner of the porch, watching Eli stride across the lawn. "My real name is Jordan Spencer," she whispered into the twilight. "I'm a country singer from Nashville." She paused to clear her throat. "And I think I've fallen in love with you."

Chapter Sixteen

The next afternoon, Jordan helped Lita put her rabbits into their respective carriers. Elliot and Eli loaded the bovines into the stock trailer.

Once all the animals were set, Eli pulled Jordan aside. "You're welcome to come with us. I know it's not the most exciting thing, but seeing all the 4H kids set up for judging is pretty cool."

Eli was such a wonderful dad—he made her ovaries ache.

She'd wanted to say yes, but decided not to risk discovery. Plus, she'd convinced Heidi to come explore the Turner mansion with her.

"Thanks for inviting me. Heidi and I already made plans."

"Okay." He tossed his truck keys into the air, caught them, and then clutched them in his fist. "Catch ya later."

Eli climbed into the driver's seat, looking good enough to eat.

While Jordan fought the urge to run after them, she waved goodbye to Lita and Elliot, who rode in the backseat of Eli's truck. Seconds later, the truck turned onto the road and they were gone.

"My brother's sweet on you." Heidi approached Jordan. "Since Eli's divorce, he's only been on one date, despite a lot of women's efforts to lasso him. He's shown no interest in romance, until now."

"You understand nothing can happen between us, right? He doesn't even know my real name. Once he finds out I've been lying to him the whole time, he'll hate me." Jordan walked toward Heidi's car.

They'd decided to drive to the abandoned mansion in order to save time.

Heidi grunted as she tossed her bulging backpack in the backseat. She'd filled it with a few granola bars, two water bottles, an old film camera, pen and paper, a plastic bag, rope, and binoculars.

"Are you sure we need to bring all that stuff?" Jordan asked.

"You never know what dangers or paranormal activity we'll find." Heidi rubbed her hands together and smiled.

"Whatever you say, Indiana Jones."

Heidi climbed in and turned the ignition key. "Nice distraction, but back to Eli. He'll understand why you kept your real identity a secret." She put the car in reverse and did a quick U-turn before heading down the driveway. "He's happy whenever he's with you, Jordan. For the first time since Nikki left, he's really happy."

Jordan was happy when she was with him, too. That still didn't change the reality of the situation. "The last thing I want to do is mislead anyone. Eli knows I'm leaving, and I have a busy life to get back to. He knows there's no possibility of us seriously dating, so we've left things as friends."

"And I'm sure he'll respect your wishes. It breaks my heart to see both of you act so stubborn."

Sighing, Jordan turned the car's vent to blast the AC directly on her face. "He won't leave the farm. And I'm heading back to Nashville in a few days, and then I'm off to Las Vegas for a country music awards show. My career is important to me. I've stepped away for a break, not forever."

"The only reason Eli keeps this farm going is out of a sense of obligation." Heidi slowed down for a tractor she'd approached from behind. The thing was pushing twenty miles per hour. Instead of passing the tractor, whose driver kept swerving to the right to let them, Heidi putzed along behind it. They were in no hurry.

"He talked to me about his relationship with your dad before he passed. There's a lot of guilt there, but do you really think guilt is the only reason he stays and runs the farm?"

"Eli talked to you about Dad? Wow, he never talks about him, even to me and Sam. He'll reminisce about Mom, but never Dad." Heidi peered over at her. "He does feel guilty for how he acted toward Dad. And he wants to do right by his own children. Then there's me, the one who's the most attached to the farm. I'm sure Eli wants Sam to come back someday." She frowned, and her voice held a touch of sadness. The tractor turned off onto a field, and Heidi accelerated. "If it wasn't for the family, I think he might have sold it a long time ago."

Jordan rested her head on the window. "I wish things could be different. Like I said before... my life isn't normal. Normal people don't have paparazzi stalking them every time they leave their house, or heaven forbid, go on a date."

"So, what's it like to be Jordan Spencer? You're not anything like the news articles."

"Drama sells. Some of the things are true, some are fabricated. Did you see the story several months ago about my meltdown in a grocery store? I'd just spent an hour being harassed by five photographers. I couldn't take it anymore, so I started yelling, and then sobbing. My bodyguard finally had to physically remove them. Of course, two photographers sued me for that."

"That's horrible." Heidi scowled. "I hope they didn't get any money from you."

Jordan laughed. She could laugh about it now. "My attorney settled out of court. Seeing Cole drag two grown men out of the store by their shirt collars was worth a few hundred thousand."

"Oh, my." Heidi took her gaze off the road long enough to gawk at Jordan, open mouthed.

Jordan watched them approach the wooded area, and then she saw the overgrown driveway.

Heidi turned into a tunnel of green. They drove until the path became too narrow then she stopped the car. After Heidi retrieved her backpack, they started walking down the shaded path.

"I never set out to be famous," Jordan said over the screech of a blue jay. "Phil, my manager, discovered me singing at a local fair. He treated me like an adult, not a kid he was trying to pull one over on. I had lots of those types. Some even offered my parents money for me to do things other than sing." A chill crawled over her skin at the memory. "But Phil was different. He really saw me as a person. He appreciated my voice not only for what it was, but what it could be."

"I remember reading somewhere you emancipated from your parents." Heidi moved to the side to avoid a few overgrown branches that blocked her way.

"I emancipated when I was sixteen. At the time, I was living with Phil and his wife, Doreen. I'd released my second album. I was making a lot of money, and of course, that's when my parents suddenly became interested in my well-being. Although, they didn't care about *me,* only my money. I made the decision to sue for emancipation on my own, and Phil and Doreen gave me guidance and support. And when Lacy turned eighteen, she came to live with me. Phil and Doreen treated both of us like their own daughters."

What would her life have been like without Phil? She shivered at the thought. He'd proven to her over and over again that there were still good people in the world. Without him, Jordan would have lost her faith in humanity a long time ago.

"Do you still write a lot of your own music?" Heidi asked.

"I did at the beginning. Then music producers and record labels got involved, and I lost some of that creative control. I've been working on a few songs while I've been here. I think I'm going to insist my next album go back to my roots."

"A lot of people, myself included, will be happy to hear that." Heidi brushed a few curls off her face.

Jordan laughed. "My heart is pure country."

"To be honest, I really didn't like a few of your more recent songs." Heidi's cheeks dimpled with her smile. "But I loved your music when you first started. I still have your first CD. It was called JORDAN, right?"

Jordan nodded. She'd been fourteen when she'd recorded that album. So young. So pure and innocent. She remembered the joy of going into the recording studio to sing. She'd never felt so free.

Heidi's grin widened. "I still know all the words to 'Country Redemption.'" She began to sing.

After the first few notes, Jordan joined in.

Fresh air and farm fields
A boy sitting on a tractor next to me
Hayfields and rows of corn
As far as the eye can see
I was lost but now I'm home
My country redemption is where I want to be
I've been lost in the city
Wandered in far-off lands
But no place is my heart free
Like when I'm in the country.

They finished the final high note with a fit of giggles. Heidi had a good voice, once she got warmed up.

"I remember sitting up all night writing that song," Jordan said. "My producer didn't think it would do well. He said it was too hokey. But Phil backed me up and *Country Redemption* became my first number one hit."

"Stupid record producer… *pfft*. What did he know? My mom loved that song. She'd turn it up on the radio every time it came on. She called it her anthem."

Warmth bloomed in Jordan's chest. When she'd started singing, she'd done it purely to connect with people's emotions. Her music had connected with Heidi's mom. That meant so much to her. "I wish I could have met your mom."

"Mom would have loved to have met you, too."

The path widened ahead of them. Before them lay rows of weeping willow trees.

They were almost there.

"I wish I could go back in time," Jordan said. "To when I first started. The industry was still fresh and new to me. The media treated me with respect. Now, my love life is a running joke. They bet on how long each new love interest will last." Jordan understood human nature. People loved to build others up, just to tear them down. She was America's sweetheart one day, a prima donna heartbreaker the next. On Monday she could do no wrong, and on Tuesday they'd report she was a drug addict. Yes, that did weigh her down. She didn't want to care, but she did.

"You need to make better choices in men," Heidi grunted. "Henry Morrison? Really? I'm sorry, but *what* were you thinking?"

Laughing, Jordan whacked her on the arm. "He has the most amazing blue eyes." And when those eyes had been turned on her, she'd gone weak. "But you are absolutely right. I knew he was an egotistical jerk before I started dating him. To be fair, though, I didn't know he was a liar."

"What you need is a good, honest, regular guy. Someone who will treat you like a queen and who loves you for who you are on the inside."

Jordan knew exactly where Heidi had looped back to, so she decided to start playing a little offense. "And what about you, Miss Heidi? When's the last time you got hot and heavy with a man?"

Blushing, Heidi looked down at the toes of her shoes. "I'm not the dating type."

"What's that supposed to mean?" Jordan stopped walking. "You're not a nun, are you?"

"No. Not officially." She chuckled. "I don't want to be. I just have a hard time around guys, like face to face. I get all awkward and weird. It usually doesn't end well."

"Awkward and weird, huh. Nerves get the best of you?" Jordan smiled understandingly at her new friend. The jitters were a third wheel on all of Jordan's dates.

The plantation mansion appeared like a ghost from behind its veil of weeping willow trees. Today, the sky was full of gray clouds. Without the sunshine, the cool, monotone lighting made the house appear even more forlorn than usual.

"I can't believe I let you talk me into this." Heidi tipped her head to take in all three stories.

Jordan found a porch step that wasn't crumbling and took a seat. "Can I have a water bottle?"

"And you made fun of me for bringing this backpack." Reaching in, she handed one over.

"I simply questioned why we need a Boy Scout survival kit."

Heidi sat next to Jordan and took a drink herself. "A while back, I signed up for an online dating site. I didn't get much notice, but I do chat with a couple of guys regularly."

"Online dating is a great option. As long as you're careful."

"I haven't met anyone face to face. I'm just not ready for that step. Maybe if I find a guy who I really connect with." Heidi took another drink. "The thing is… I don't want to move away from the farm. It's not only that Eli needs my help; I love my life there. It's my home. My safe place. If I ever do get married, it would be to a guy who'd be willing to move in with me."

Jordan studied Heidi's pretty, round face. With her sandy blonde hair and bright blue eyes, Jordan was sure she didn't have trouble attracting men. But Heidi wasn't looking to date for the sake of dating. When she did give her heart away, it would be one and done.

"You signed Eli up for online dating, right? How many requests did he get?" Jordan asked.

"Oh, I don't remember. At least a hundred. He only had it up for a few days."

"A *hundred*?" She shouldn't be surprised.

"Well, I did exaggerate about his qualities in hopes of drawing a bigger crowd. I put down that he loved watching romantic comedies, long walks on the beach, and cuddling with his cat." Heidi giggled. "And the best part—I used a photo of him shirtless for his profile. He almost murdered me when he found out."

"I can understand why." Jordan stood and offered Heidi a hand up. "He thinks you're on a mission to get him married off."

Heidi gave a dimpled smile. "As God said to Adam in the Bible, 'It's not good for man to be alone.' Eli does a good job hiding it, but he does get lonely."

"I understand exactly how he feels."

***

"I have a surprise for you," Eli told Lita and Elliot as he pulled his truck into the county fairgrounds.

"Is Mom here already?" Elliot asked with a hint of caution in his voice.

Eli couldn't blame either kid for doubting whether their mom would really show up this time. They'd both been pretty quiet about Nikki's visit.

"Nope. Try again."

"Did Ann say she's staying longer?" Lita asked.

He wished. Ann had told them she was leaving to go home in three days, and he worried about her. Would she return to a dangerous situation? Before she left, he would sit down and talk to her about his concerns. If there was any doubt, he'd offer to escort her home. In order to keep her safe, of course.

What was he thinking? He couldn't take off now, during the middle of the summer growing season. He'd never taken the kids on a summer vacation. How many times had Lita asked to go to Disney World? Or Elliot begged to go to Great America so he could ride the roller coasters?

The needs of the farm always came first. But for how long? Before he'd knew it, his kids would be grown. They'd be gone, and he'd be left alone in that big, old house.

He shook his head to clear those thoughts from his mind. Lita and Elliot were still here. He needed to remember not to take that for granted.

"Nope," Eli said. "One more guess."

"Just tell us." Lita exhaled a long sigh. She slid her bare feet off the back of the passenger seat and started putting on her socks and shoes.

"Fine. You two are no fun. Uncle Sammy is meeting us here. He's staying for the weekend."

Ear-piercing screams filled the truck cab. Uncle Sammy was near rock-star status in Lita and Elliot's eyes. He was tall, handsome, always funny, and a big-city firefighter. *How do you compete with that?*

"I knew he was coming." Elliot bounced up and down in the backseat. "He always comes to the fair."

Eli pulled the truck up alongside the cattle barn and parked. Before he turned off the engine, both kids jumped out and sprinted toward Sam, who stood in the shaded entrance.

A smile crept on Eli's face. He loved his little brother, even when Sam showed him up. He thought of Ann, and his smile morphed to a frown. Maybe he should have a little chat with Sam and explain that Ann was off limits this weekend. No need for both Hintz boys to get their hearts broken by the pretty girl with large gray eyes.

"How are my favorite flying monkeys?" Sam had both Elliot and Lita crawling up either side of his body. Good thing the guy was six-foot-five.

Eli closed the door of the truck and walked over to join the mayhem.

"Ginger is going to win a blue ribbon," Elliot said while hanging with his arms around Sam's neck.

"So are my rabbits," Lita talked over her brother. "I'm sure Beatrice will win Best in Show. Since I don't have to do 4H next year, I want to go out with a bang."

Sam now had both kids hanging from him like he was a jungle gym. How could he hold both of them like they were still toddlers?

Seeming finally to have had enough, Sam bent down to set each child back on their feet. "How about we get your animals set up? Unless you just want to stay here and climb on me all day?"

Lita rolled her eyes, which made Eli smile. Nice she did that to someone else once in a while. He patted Sam on the back. "Thanks for coming early."

"I had a long weekend. Thought I could use a break."

The bags under Sam's normally bright eyes made him look years older. His smile appeared as shallow as a mask.

"Everything okay?"

"Yeah." Sam nodded. "We had a big fire a few weeks ago. You might have seen it on the news. It was a rough one. A couple kids died."

"I hadn't heard. You talk to someone?" Eli asked, even though he already knew the answer.

Turning away, Sam grunted. "We had someone come sit down with each one of the guys who were at the scene. Nothing she can do. Those kids are still dead."

Luckily, Lita and Elliot were already away by their respective animals. He didn't want them overhearing. Eli took hold of Sam's arm. "Don't try to be a tough guy. After everything you've been through, it's not a sign of weakness to get help."

Sam had been a passenger in the car when their parents had died. He'd held Mom in his arms when she'd taken her last breath. Now, he was fighting to save others. But at what cost?

"How about we save the psychoanalyzing for later." Sam grinned. "Let's get these animals unloaded so we can head home. I'm starving."

They worked for about an hour. Elliot found pens for his cow and heifer, and fussed over them like a mother hen. He made sure they had plenty of fresh straw and a full bucket of feed. Each cow even got a peck on top of their furry heads from Elliot before he left.

Sam helped Lita brush her rabbits, before settling them inside their cages. Then, she walked the aisles, checking out the competition.

"You need help baling?" Sam asked once they were all done in the livestock barns.

"I still have the south field to do yet. They're predicting rain on Sunday, so I need to get that hay bundled up ASAP. Plus, I promised the kids I'd spend a day with them at the fair. So, yeah, I could use some help."

Sam adjusted his baseball cap. "Then good thing I still remember how to drive the John Deere. Don't worry, old man. I got your back."

Must be nice to show up, help around the farm for a few days, and then go back home. Eli wasn't so lucky. But then again, that had been his choice. He could have sold the farm and left for the city, too. He'd stayed for his family. The farm was a part of their blood.

Sam helped Lita climb inside the truck then closed the door behind her.

She rolled down the window. "Are you following us home?"

"Only if your dad doesn't drive like an old lady." Sam tapped her on the nose. "See you there."

Eli started the engine and put the truck in drive. Before he took his foot off the brake, Sam came up and pounded on the driver's-side window.

Sighing, he pushed the button to lower it. "What?"

"Heidi said something about a girl staying with her. Is she still there?"

Eli didn't like the smirk on his brother's face. "Ann's not a girl. She's a woman. But yes, she's still there." He paused. "Why?"

Sam wiggled his eyebrows. "Is she hot?"

Giggling sounded from the backseat.

Amusement turned to annoyance. "Don't even think about it, fire-stud."

"This Ann might be just what I need to help brighten my spirits."

Lita leaned forward between the two front seats. "Dad's got dibs on her already."

"What does dibs mean?" Elliot interjected. He rested his arms on Eli's headrest.

"It means," Sam drawled. "That your dad thinks this lady only has eyes for him. Well, she hasn't met the better looking younger brother yet."

Eli pushed Sam's elbows off the windowsill, causing him to lose his balance.

Sam recovered quickly. "Now you got me curious." He winked at the kids. "I'll make sure to beat you home."

Raising the truck's window, Eli blocked out the nonsense coming from his brother's mouth.

"You two get your seatbelts on."

The truck shook as Lita and Elliot bounced around in the backseat. When they finally got settled and buckled in, he took his foot off the brake.

He needed to beat Sam home. There was no way Sam would be introduced to Ann without him present.

Sam played fast and loose with women, and Eli didn't want to see Ann swept up in Sam's charm. People always like Sam better than Eli, and normally he was all right with that.

But not this time.

Chapter Seventeen

Jordan carefully walked across the rotting floorboards of the covered porch, over to the opened window. She crawled inside, directing Heidi to follow her lead.

Now, both women stood in the drawing room. Heidi spun in a circle, her jaw hung slack. She turned her gaze to Jordan. "This is amazing. I've only seen the house from the outside." Lifting a dirty sheet, she revealed a painted wooden rocking horse. The paint might have been bright and fresh at one point, but over time, it had chipped and faded.

A tickle built inside Jordan's nose. She waved her hand in front of her face, trying to hold back the sneezes that were building. They came anyway.

The loud noise scared some little critter, which rustled through the pile of leaves in the corner of the room.

Heidi continued moving around the room. She picked up a delicate-looking white teacup painted with pink flowers. "I think it's so weird they left all their stuff behind. The Turners must have been the wealthiest family in the area."

"And no one has returned to claim it. I can't believe the house hasn't been totally looted by now." Jordan exited the drawing room and went over to the study, with Heidi close behind.

"It's mostly local kids who sneak in, and they only take a thing or two as a memento. Otherwise, besides the locals, no one else really knows this place is here."

Going over to the bookshelf, Heidi glanced at a row of pictures. "I can almost see them living here. The little girl running into the study to tell her dad something exciting, her mom, coming in behind her with a plate of cookies and tea."

"I know," Jordan said. "Everything is dusty and dirty, but I half expect to hear the family enter. I guess that's what intrigues me about this house. That it's so beautiful, yet so sad and neglected. I feel like it's waiting for someone to come along and care for it again. Turn it back into a home." That was exactly the idea tickling her brain. Not a home for herself, although she'd love to live in a historical home someday, but a place to share with the community. She wanted this house to see joy again.

They continued exploring the house, chatting quietly as they worked their way through the decrepit rooms, though Jordan couldn't help but feel almost as if sound itself could disturb the foundations.

Jordan exited the final room and slowly led their way down to the basement.

"Think we'll find any demons hiding down here?" Jordan sent Heidi a mischievous grin and laughed at the look she got in return. Heidi was obviously more spooked than she had let on. "Come on, aren't you curious? If we're going to find anything—it'll be down here." Jordan took the last step with a flourish and stepped onto the packed dirt floor. Squares of daylight shone in through several high-placed windows. The room was practically empty, besides three shelves that rested against one cinder-block wall. On the shelves were some glass canning jars, filled with what looked like tomatoes.

At the far end were two doors. Jordan walked over to the one on the right.

"Perhaps a little curious," Heidi said as she shone the flashlight right in Jordan's face, only to laugh when she ducked away from the offending beam. "But I'm still not planning on opening either of those doors with you."

Jordan snorted inelegantly and pulled the door open. For all the drama, it was actually not that surprising to find the small room completely empty.

"Nothing here." she called out to Heidi. "Only way too many creepy crawlies," she added under her breath and turned to the other door.

She yanked it hard, though it didn't seem to want to move. She pulled a few more times, opening it little by little. Once she had about a two-foot opening, she slid inside the room. Her flashlight illuminated a room full of stacked boxes, toys, and children's drawings.

"Heidi," she called out. "Come here."

"Why?" Heidi's voice sounded muffled.

"Because I'm being eaten by demons."

"Really?"

Jordan waited to respond until she heard the sound of approaching footfalls. "Please, take your time. The demons are now using my bones for toothpicks."

Heidi's laughter floated through the open door. "And you seem to be taking it all pretty well." She stopped laughing when she caught sight of the interior of the room. "What's all this?"

"I don't know." Jordan went to the wall and studied the drawings. Some were done in colored pencil and very detailed. Others looked like they were created by a young child with crayons. "Do you think the kids came down here to play?"

"I can't imagine why? They had a beautiful house and nice bedrooms upstairs." Heidi picked up a faded rag doll. The smile on the doll's face drooped. Its red yarn hair had been chopped unevenly. The doll, after years of sitting in a dark room, seemed to have lost all hope to be reunited with its little girl.

Jordan opened the lid to one of the boxes. Inside, she found stacks of papers—doctor's reports. They were from various medical professionals—family doctors, surgeons, and psychologists. They were all for Rosemary.

A few doctors had noted Rosemary's psychiatric condition. Jordan read the letter from a psychologist. He'd written about his growing concern over Rosemary's safety, and the safety of others around her.

Another letter requested parental permission for electric shock therapy. The form was unsigned.

"Heidi, you have to see this." Jordan lifted up a stack of papers and set them down on the box. "Did you hear any stories about Rosemary Turner's mental condition?"

Heidi shook her head. "No, I haven't." She ran her finger over one of the medical reports.

"Back when these medical reports were written, they had a limited understanding of psychological disorders." Jordan's gaze skimmed over another set of doctor's notes. "People who suffered from those types of problems were treated very poorly. See here, they wanted to put her in a mental hospital. Rosemary was just a teenage girl."

"Poor thing." Heidi's hands trembled as she set down a folder.

Jordan took another long look around and felt a wave a sadness wash over her. The sting of tears burned behind her eyes. This house, as grand as it still was, held so much sorrow. The feelings were as much a part of the structure as the wallpaper and furniture.

"Maybe Cole managed to find something," Jordan said as they made their way back upstairs.

"Cole? Your bodyguard?"

Jordan nodded and took out her cell phone, then showed Heidi a photo of Cole. They were standing together on the Great Wall of China. "He's a former Marine and looks like a brute. Over the years he's worked for me, we've become very good friends."

A smile crept across Heidi's face. "He's hot. Anything ever happen between the two of you?"

Jordan laughed, glad to finally shed some of the oppressive feelings their excursion had brought up. "When I first met him, the thought did cross my mind, but the more time I spent with him, the more he felt like an overprotective big brother than a potential lover. Plus, he's too good at his job to risk losing him if things didn't work out. But don't worry, Cole doesn't suffer from a lack of female attention. There are a lot of women who go gaga for the dangerous, bad-boy type. And that's Cole—motorcycle, leather, scars, and tattoos."

Heidi sighed. "He's perfect."

Pressing his name in her contacts, she put her cell up to her ear and heard ringing.

Just like she expected, Cole answered right away. "What's wrong now, Jordan?"

"Nice to talk to you, too."

"Sorry, I'm working on my bike." The sound of clanking metal sounded through the phone. "What do you need, sweetcakes?"

She smiled at his term of endearment for her. Sometimes, she wished she had fallen in love with Cole. He was a good man. But he had an absolute avoidance of committed relationships. According to Cole, sliding a ring on his finger was the same as a metal choke collar. Could that be the reason why her sister kept her feelings for Cole unspoken? Lacy wanted a husband and kids someday, not a playboy boyfriend who was allergic to serious relationships.

"Have you found any information about the Turner family?"

"The what family?" His deep, baritone voice held a hint of teasing.

"Don't play games with me, Cole. We're at the house now and we found something in the basement."

"Who's we? Did you drag Eli along for the ride?"

"No. I'm with Heidi. His sister." Jordan walked across the dining room and gazed out the large windows. The backyard stretched over the ground like a blanket of emerald fabric. Tall trees that were likely hundreds of years old held sentry duty over the property. Their branches swayed with the light summer breeze. She pictured a wedding gazebo set in the open field toward the back.

"Give me a second," Cole said. "Let me go wash off my hands and grab my notes."

She heard the sound of running water, and then the rustling of papers.

"I'm getting out of here," Heidi called out. "Being inside this place is giving me the creeps. I'm hearing voices, and they're not coming from you."

"Let's go back outside." Jordan agreed that she'd started to feel weird, too. Her skin was itchy and hot one moment, chilled the next. And she continued to see movement in the shadows of each room, like something was following them.

They both crawled out the drawing room window.

Once outside on the porch, Jordan took in a deep breath, filling her lungs with fresh air.

Cole's voice sounded through Jordan's cell phone. "Okay," he said before clearing his throat. "I pulled together as much info about the Turner family as I could find. William Turner was a native of the Manitowoc area. He made a lot of money in the shipping and lumber industry. He met Annabelle during a purchasing trip to Georgia. The story is she turned down multiple proposals from William because she didn't want to move north. So, William built an Antebellum-style plantation house in Wisconsin in hopes of gaining her hand in marriage."

"She must have said yes." Jordan went to sit next to Heidi on the porch steps. The wind had started to pick up.

"Annabelle married William Turner in 1935. She moved into the house you're currently exploring soon after the wedding. What I gather from old news stories is that she didn't socialize much.

Although, I did read an article about a large party she threw after her daughter's birth. I'll send it to you. It has some nice black and white photos of the exterior and interior of the house. There's a private trust that now owns the house. Not much information on that."

Jordan's excitement started to build. Thank goodness for Cole and his researching skills.

"Did you find anything about the daughter's disappearance?"

"Hold your horses. I was just getting to that." His deep, baritone laughter sounded through the phone. "Rosemary's disappearance was a big news story. Her parents waited to report it to the police until she'd been missing for two days. And then, they weren't very cooperative with the authorities. I did an open records request and got the police reports for the investigation."

"*Ohhhh.*" The anticipation was killing her. "What did they say?"

"The case is still unsolved. Six months after their daughter went missing, William and Annabelle took their son, Willy, and moved away. The police came over to the house one day and everyone was gone. The only living family member left is Willy, William Turner II. He was in a bad auto accident about twenty years ago and is living in an assisted living center in Macon, Georgia."

"I wonder why he just let the house rot." She brushed back strands of hair that had blown on her face.

"Don't know," Cole said. "Could be the house held too many bad memories."

"Thanks for doing this for me." Jordan stretched her legs in front of her. "You are the best."

"I know." He chuckled. "Have you talked to Lacy lately?"

"Not since she got back from Germany. Why?"

"Just making sure she made it home safe." Cole cleared his throat.

"Why don't you call her?" Jordan said. "I'm sure she'd love to tell you all about her vacation." Good thing Cole couldn't see the smile on her face. She knew Lacy had a huge crush on Cole. And she suspected Cole had feelings stronger than friendly concern for her sister. The night of her final concert show, when they'd been all together in Jordan's dressing room, she noticed the way Cole's gaze followed Lacy's every move, like he was memorizing everything about her.

Jordan sighed. *Oh, unrequited love. Why must you torture us so?*

Now, that was a great start to a new song.

"I don't want to bother her," Cole said. "When will you be home?"

"In three days. See you soon." She ended the call and raised her gaze to take in the beauty of her surroundings one more time. The long, low branches of the weeping willow trees swayed in a choreographed dance. "You ready to head back?" Jordan asked Heidi.

"I just got a text from Eli asking where we were. Sam's home," Heidi said with a huge grin. "You get to meet my little brother."

Panic crept inside her chest. What if Sam recognized her then told Eli? "Do you think Sam will know who I really am?"

Heidi's blonde eyebrows shot up. "I'm not sure. He's kind of like Eli, not really into pop culture. But if I get the sense he does, I'll pull him aside and explain. Don't worry." She patted Jordan on the shoulder. "Eli's not going to find out until you're ready to tell him."

"Thanks." Jordan walked alongside Heidi back to the car.

Her thoughts drifted to Rosemary Turner and the mysteries surrounding the abandoned plantation house. Then, inevitably, they focused back on Eli and her heartbreak when the time came to leave his farm. And Cole, Lacy, Phil, and Doreen—the only people in the world she fully trusted. Heidi and Eli were beginning to move into that small circle.

Was it too much to hope for that she and Eli would remain friends?

Who was she kidding? Jordan was in love with the man.

Her head told her to be reasonable. A person didn't fall in love so quickly. She was just experiencing another one of her flights of fancy. Meet a cute guy and get swept away by his charm.

But what she felt for Eli seemed different. He didn't want her for her fame and money. He wanted her for who she was on the inside. That was a special gift.

What was her poor heart going to do?

Chapter Eighteen

Eli and Sam walked down one of the long aisles in the dairy barn. Eli wanted to show his brother the improvements he'd made since the last time Sam had been home, six months ago.

"The new machines were a good investment. More milk with less manpower. How much did all this set you back?" Sam kicked at a few pieces of straw covering the cement floor.

Normally, the aisles were kept pristine. Which meant either Elliot or Lita had passed this way recently. Even Lita loved to pet the dairy cows and sneak a few hugs when she thought no one was looking.

"I took out a loan to buy the equipment. The increased productivity will offset the interest cost. That is, if milk prices don't continue to drop." The fluctuating prices of milk always weighed heavy on Eli's mind. He not only had to make enough money to feed and care for his livestock, he had a family to support, farm hands to pay, and then there were his payments to Nikki. It would take another four years to pay off her portion of the farm she received from the divorce.

"You've done a good job, but is this what you want to do with the rest of your life?" Sam scratched at the dark scruff growing on his face. "Dad would understand if it wasn't."

Eli knew that Dad's opinion didn't matter anymore. He was gone. But that didn't relinquish Eli's feelings of responsibility. If he sold his family's heritage to strangers—most likely a corporate dairy operation—he'd have failed in his duty.

"I'm satisfied with my life. It's good, honest work. And Lita and Elliot are growing up with a strong work ethic." Eli patted the rump of a large, black and white Holstein. The cow craned her neck to look back at him and let out a bellow. "These girls are my family, too. I couldn't sell them off."

"You always were a big softy."

Large fans mounted from the ceiling blew air through the building. The sliding doors on either end were opened, letting in fresh air to keep the herd cool. Eli noted that one of the cows in the central pen walked with a limp. He'd have to come back after dinner and check on her.

His phone buzzed and he pulled it out of his pocket. "Heidi said the pizzas were delivered. We should go home now if we want to eat while they're hot."

"Is the girl staying with Heidi there?" Sam grinned, showing off his perfect teeth.

The look on his brother's face annoyed Eli to no end. He would not allow Sam to flirt with Ann. No way.

"I assume she'll be there." Eli shrugged, trying to show he didn't care either way.

Sam studied him then laughed. "Man, you're a goner. Don't worry, I won't hit on your girl."

"She's not my girl."

"Then why did Lita say you had dibs on her?"

"How am I supposed to know? Lita's ten. I don't understand half the things that come out of her mouth."

"This Ann must be special to have pulled you out of monkhood. I was seriously starting to worry about you."

They stepped outside the barn into the warm, late-afternoon breeze.

Eli grunted. Why did his little brother always have to be such a pain?

"Dude." Sam nudged him with his elbow. "How far did she let you go?"

"Shut up. We're not in high school anymore." Eli punched Sam on the arm, hard. He needed an outlet for his frustration.

Apparently, so did Sam, whose fist flew into Eli's gut.

Eli fought down the urge to heave.

They traded jabs, with Sam landing the final blow on Eli's jaw.

"Okay, you win." Eli rubbed his jaw. "You still play dirty."

Sam laughed and hung his arm around Eli's neck. "And you still fight like an old man."

Lita came running out the barn door. "Boys," she huffed. "Stop acting like children. Take me home before our pizzas turn to ice."

"Has she always been this dramatic?" Sam asked.

"You have no idea what it's like to raise a preteen girl." Eli couldn't stop smiling at Lita's eye roll.

Sam swung Lita onto his back. "You roll your eyes at me, sweetheart, and they'll get stuck that way."

"Oh, please. If that's the case, Dad's face is going to get stuck in that goofy grin he has whenever he's with Ann." Lita kicked Sam lightly on the sides. "Giddy-up."

The two of them took off toward the truck laughing loudly before Eli could reply.

***

Inside the outdated kitchen of the farmhouse, Jordan counted out six dinner plates. The back door suddenly opened, blowing in the unmistakable scent of the farm.

Voices drifted in as well. She recognized Elliot's and Lita's, and the rumble of Eli's deep laugh. But there was a new voice she hadn't heard before.

Must be Sam.

He stepped into the kitchen, and Jordan nearly dropped the stack of plates she held in her hands. The smile he sent her was a million megawatts of pure charm.

Sam Hintz was tall and lean, a stretched-out version of his older brother. Standing side by side, she noticed both men had the same chestnut brown hair. Eli's was longer, with a touch more curl.

As Sam sauntered toward her, Jordan stepped forward.

"Hey, there. You must be the Ann I've been hearing so much about." Sam took the plates out of her hands and set them on the table.

"And you must be the little brother I've been hearing about." Her gaze drifted up and down his tall body. "But you don't seem so little to me." She let out a giggle and mentally kicked herself. This was Eli's brother. Jordan glanced at Eli and saw the scowl on his handsome face. *Jealous?*

Sam headed over to the pizza boxes, flipped up the top on one, and sniffed. "Yum… Hawaiian style. Ann, I hope you've been enjoying your stay here at the farm. Although, I never figured a dairy farm in central Wisconsin as a huge vacation destination. Maybe Eli should start a bed and breakfast."

Eli snorted in response.

"Well, I was heading to Door County when I got lost and crashed into the ditch in front of the farm. Your sister was kind enough to let me hang out until my car was repaired. I liked it so much I decided to just stay for the rest of my getaway." Jordan took a slice of pepperoni then sat between Lita and Heidi.

Eli placed himself directly across the table from Jordan, his plate piled high with pizza. "Those heifers caused a lot of trouble that night." He took a bite of pizza and chewed, the whole time keeping his gaze fixed on Jordan.

The heat of it had her squirming in her seat. Did anyone else notice how he was looking at her? Like pizza wasn't the only thing he was hungry for.

"Ann and I went over to the Turner mansion this afternoon," Heidi said. "She actually talked me into going down to the basement."

"What's the Turner mansion?" Lita asked.

"No place you need to go." Eli leveled a fatherly look at her. "Aunt Heidi and Ann shouldn't be going there either."

Heidi nodded her head. "That's right. You listen to your father and stay away from the spooky, old, abandoned house. There's nothing there but rotten floor boards and ghosts."

"Ghosts?" Elliot's eyes widened like golden disks. "I've always wanted to see a real ghost."

"There's no such thing as ghosts, kid," Sam said. "Except for the ghost of the little girl who lived in that house and went missing. She didn't eat all her dinner and a monster came and snatched her up in the middle of the night. Now, she guards the house and haunts anyone who dares enter."

Both Lita and Elliot stared at Sam, wide eyed and slack jawed.

"Don't listen to your uncle's nonsense," Eli said. "There's no such thing as ghosts."

"Well..." Heidi grinned. "We did hear someone crying in the basement."

"Stop, you two," Eli snarled. "Or I'll be waking you up tonight when my kids have nightmares."

"Can the ghosts travel from that house to ours?" Elliot asked with a slight shake in his voice.

Jordan patted his hand. "I promise there were no ghosts." Picking off the last pepperoni on her pizza, she set it down on the plate, next to the others. She only ate cheese pizza. A quirk she carried from childhood. Not that she'd eaten much pizza growing up. Sometimes, though, vendors would give her food for singing by their stand. There had been days when those gifts were the only food either she or Lacy got to eat. "I have a friend who's doing some research on the Turner house. It's owned by a trust. The son, Willy, is the only surviving family member. He became handicapped after a bad car accident a while back."

"They should bulldoze it down," Eli said. "That place is a hazard. I'd hate to think of Lita or Elliot sneaking in there like we used to do."

"Or we are now." Heidi sent him a sweet-as-sugar smile. "It's really not so bad, Eli. A few rotted-out steps, but it's mostly home to critters. I'd hate to see that beautiful house razed because no one cared enough to fix it up."

"I might buy it. I bet they'd sell it for the right price." Jordan's mental health might benefit from a project that didn't involve the music industry. Plus, she'd have the perfect excuse to come back and see Eli, Heidi, and the kids.

Eli arched his brows. "Restoring that big of a house would take more money than it's worth."

"But imagine how wonderful it would look all fixed up. I could restore the mansion to look like it did when it was first built." Jordan set down her pizza. "I could turn it into a bed and breakfast combined with a wedding venue. Or sell it to someone who wants to live in a Southern plantation home."

"Why would anyone want to live in a plantation home in Wisconsin?" Sam asked. "No offense, Ann." His smile included an amazing set of dimples.

Jordan felt herself blush. If only Eli was so unabashedly flirtatious. Then again, if he was, she'd be in even more trouble. "We'll have to find out who holds the title for the house, first. I just hate the thought of that beautiful house falling apart."

"Can we go to the fair tomorrow?" Elliot stood to get another piece of pizza. "*Ewww…* there's only veggie and Hawaiian left."

"We can't go tomorrow," Eli said. "Sam and I are baling hay. I have Connor McMurray lined up for Sunday to finish what we don't get done, so we can go then."

"What about Mom?" Lita asked. "Do you think she'll want to go?"

"You'll have to ask her that." Eli started combining the remaining pizza slices in one box. "Do you want to call her tonight?"

After a pause, Lita set down her fork with a bang. The sound reverberated through the kitchen like the ringing of an opening bell in a boxing match. "I'm not calling her. I don't even think she'll really come."

Jordan's concern about the impending visit from Nikki increased by the hour. From what Eli had said, Nikki was scheduled to arrive the day after tomorrow. She had no desire to meet Eli's ex-wife. Her plan was to be long gone before she arrived.

"Who's going to help me drive the tractor tomorrow?" Sam looked at Lita and Elliot. "Let's get that hay baled so we can have a fun day at the fair." He stood and set his plate in the sink.

"I'll help," Elliot said, following his uncle's lead. Once his dishes were put in the sink, he turned to Eli. "Can I go show Uncle Sammy the newborn calves?"

"Sure," Eli said.

"Can I go, too?" Lita asked. "I'm finished eating."

Eli nodded, and off she went.

"I just remembered something I left at my house." Heidi slipped on her sandals. "I'll be right back to help clean up."

After the screen door slammed shut for the third time, Jordan glanced across the table at Eli. "What just happened here?"

"I think that was my family's very awkward way of giving us some time alone." The smile he sent her heated her core.

Eli might not have the smooth grace of his brother, but he was pure rough and rugged male. Even the thin lines that bracketed his eyes and mouth enhanced his sexual appeal. He was a man who made his living working outdoors, and he made no excuses for who he was. With wide shoulders and a broad chest, he could be mistaken for a football player. But instead, at his heart, he was a musician. Those large hands, which carried such heavy loads, were also polished and precise when playing the guitar or touching her skin.

Jordan hated the thought of leaving him.

"Why would they want to give us time alone?" She couldn't look at his mouth without having a hot flash.

Eli set his folded hands on the table. "Isn't it obvious? They can tell how crazy I am about you."

She stood and went to gaze out the big picture window behind the table. The corn field stretched on as far as she could see. This place was so beautiful. So peaceful. And Eli, Heidi, Elliot, and Lita were a great family. But her time was almost up. Jordan Spencer, country star, couldn't hide here forever.

"I decided to leave a day early. I'm driving home tomorrow." Turning her head, she looked back at him.

Eli's shoulders lowered. "The kids will be disappointed. They wanted to take you to the fair on Sunday." He raised his gaze to meet hers.

Gold sparks shot across the distance, straight into her heart. How would she walk away from the best man she'd ever met? "I thought it would be best I wasn't here when their mom arrived, since she has the impression there's something going on between us."

"Don't worry about Nikki." Eli rounded the table and took her hand. "I want you to stay. Even for one more day. Let me take you to the fair. Nikki will have the kids." He ran a finger as light as corn silk down her arm, causing jolts of pleasure to shoot through her body.

"Eli." Her protest was hushed by Eli placing a finger over her lips.

"Don't worry. I remember every word you said to me that night in the field. You aren't interested in a relationship, and I respect that. But one day of fun together doesn't equal forever. Will you give me that, Ann? One day?"

The warmth inside her turned to cold guilt at the sound of him calling her Ann. She had lied to him, not only about her name but who she was.

But who really was she? The persona she'd created over the years, or the girl with the rich, country voice who loved to write music and sing? Hadn't she been more her true self with Eli than with any other man? He had seen a part of her soul that she normally kept locked up tight.

Jordan trusted him. And she had lied to him from the start. She really should leave tomorrow and let Eli get back to his normal life. Leading him on was only being cruel.

"I want to. I really do. But I've stayed too long already."

"You haven't stayed nearly long enough." He lifted her chin so their vision locked. "Is it safe to go home? I hate the idea of you going back to a dangerous situation."

Another lie. "My ex has moved on." Now that was the truth. Just that morning, she'd read an article online about Henry romancing a model in a London nightclub. "He seems to have lost interest in hurting me." Only the pain Henry like to inflict was psychological, not physical. He'd set out to ruin her reputation. And why? Jordan never really understood his motivation. During their relationship, he had treated her very well. Even went above and beyond to be romantic. In the end, he'd shown his true nature, just like she'd shown hers. Only deep down, Jordan was an insecure woman suffering from anxiety. Henry was simply a jerk.

Eli moved closed and heat sizzled between them. Did he feel the same strong pull of attraction she was fighting so hard against? Based on the look churning in his eyes, he did.

"I've only begun to get to know you." Eli wrapped her in his arms.

She laid her head on his muscular chest and felt his heart beat, slow and steady. "I promise to keep in touch. I just don't know how regular my communication will be. My schedule for the next month is very busy."

"You never told me what you do for a living. I know you're not a professional chef." Laughter vibrated through his chest.

"Funny." Jordan didn't know how to answer his question without telling another lie. She was considering her options when she glanced out the window to see Lita heading toward the house. Stepping out of Eli's embrace was physically painful, but necessary. The last thing she wanted to do was to give his children a false impression of their relationship, especially right before Nikki's arrival.

As she moved back to the sink, Eli sent her a questioning gaze. Then Lita burst in from the mud room, grinning from ear to ear.

"Ann, you have to come out to the barn," she said while trying to catch her breath. "Missy May is having her calf."

"Who's Missy May?" Jordan asked.

"One of Elliot's cows." Lita took Jordan's hand and spared a glance at her dad. "Sorry, Dad, did I interrupt something?"

Eli sighed. "Let's go. That is… if Ann wants to see a calf birth."

She wasn't sure if she did or not, but this was the perfect excuse to get out of answering Eli's personal questions. "Of course, I do," she said. "I might never have the chance again."

Eli's face tightened with her words.

And the sick feeling of disappointment started thickening inside her gut.

Chapter Nineteen

Eli didn't have time to sit around and sulk. Ann was leaving today and there was nothing he could do about it. He had no right to ask her to stay. And he definitely had no claim on her heart.

Ann had no idea how deep his feelings had grown. And Eli knew about roots and their need for nourishment in order for the plant to thrive. Once Ann was gone, his romantic feelings would starve, no longer basking in the heat of her sun.

With Sam doing the baling, Eli spent the morning in the milk house. Several cows had shown signs of becoming ill. He separated them from the rest of the herd and made a call to the vet. Doc Wilson promised to come out early tomorrow morning before Eli had to leave for the fair.

He still wasn't sure about Nikki's plans. After years of experience, he'd learned not to assume anything when she was involved. Unfortunately, Lita and Elliot had learned the same tough lesson.

Eli checked the time on the big clock in his office. Almost noon. Ann had assured him that she wouldn't take off until after lunch. He knew the kids were upset over her leaving. They'd both cried last night when she'd told them, which had caused Ann to tear up, too.

He was mad at himself. This whole situation could have been avoided if he'd been firmer about keeping her out of their lives.

At first, he'd been physically attracted to her. Then, their emotional connection grew. He'd fallen for her hard, and because of that, let his guard down.

Now all three of them were going to be licking their wounds later tonight. Ann would be gone. They may never hear from her again. Could he forget about her and move on? He had a gut feeling that wouldn't be so easy.

After shutting down his computer, Eli turned off the light to his office and stepped out into the barn. He inhaled deeply, enjoying the varied scents. Even the smell of the animals, which most people found gross, comforted him. The mooing of the cows, the scent of straw, and the feeling of tired muscles after a hard day's work all gave him a sense of purpose. Farming was in his blood, whether he liked it or not.

He could no more easily turn his back on his farm than he could his own children.

Eli got into his truck and turned up the radio for the short drive back home. When his father had built the upgraded milking facilities, he picked a site away from the family's home. He had hired help and grown his herd. Over the years, dairy farming had become a complicated business, with DNR, EPA and FDA regulations, drug testing, insurance, and a host of other tiny details.

Thankfully, Heidi had agreed to take on a majority of the farm management duties. He'd be lost without her.

A Nirvana song started to play, and he tapped his hands on the steering wheel. He'd met Dave Grohl once, after a concert. Eli had been starstruck, hardly able to put two words together. The guy was as cool in person as he was as a performer.

A smile crept on his face, remembering those crazy days in LA. He'd wanted a music career so badly the fire had almost consumed him. And Nikki had fed his fire with her dreams of fame.

That life wasn't meant to be. Did he miss that fast-paced freedom? Sure. But he'd never give up what he had now.

Eli parked his truck in the driveway and stepped out to join Ann in the front yard. She was standing between Elliot and Lita, with a football in her hands.

"I'm glad to see you're still here." He came to stand beside Ann.

She looked up and gave him one of her sunshine smiles. "Of course. I wouldn't leave without saying goodbye. Your kids talked me into a game of keep away."

"Not keep away," Elliot said. "I just want to play football, but Ann can't catch."

"I can, too." She stuck out her bottom lip in protest. "The ball's slippery."

Lita bent over to tie her shoe. "I bet Ann that if she can't catch one of Elliot's passes, then she has to stay one more day and go to the fair."

"And I never agreed to that."

"I wish you'd stay and come to the fair with us." Elliot took the football and spun the tip on his pointer finger. The ball made a few rotations before falling to the ground. "Ginger has the showmanship award and blue ribbon judging tomorrow. You need to see her win."

"I'm sure she'll win, honey, but I really need to head home. I've had so much fun here, but my work needs my attention now." Ann was doing a good job of avoiding Eli's gaze.

She was still such a mystery to him. Ann had never answered his question yesterday regarding her profession. She purposely avoided telling him too much information about herself. He didn't even know where she lived.

Eli realized that he might never see her again. He better make the most of the last minutes they had together. "How about we play a quick game of touch football? Boys against the girls?"

"No offense, Ann, but that wouldn't really be fair," Lita said.

Ann frowned. "Hey, I'm not that bad."

"Okay, I'll take Ann. You and Elliot can team up." Eli put his arm around Ann's shoulders and gave her a squeeze.

Lita's smile grew, showing off her white teeth. "Come on, Elliot. We need a strategy."

"No, we don't," Elliot said. "Those two old fogies don't stand a chance."

Eli raised his arm and flexed his bicep muscle. "Old fogy, huh? These young whippersnappers need a lesson in respecting their elders."

The game started. Eli threw a pass to Ann, which she fumbled. The ball bounced into Lita's hands and she ran back for a touchdown. After a little celebratory dance, Lita tossed Eli the ball.

He gave it to Ann. "How about you play quarterback. I'll run to the right. When I get close to the flagpole, throw me the ball."

She nodded and grasped the ball in both hands.

Just as he'd instructed, Ann didn't throw until he was in position. Eli was stunned when the ball landed spot on, into his outstretched arms. He ran to the gravel driveway, which served as their end zone.

Ann hollered and came running over to him. She jumped up, and he caught her as she wrapped her arms around his neck.

Eli spun her around, both of them laughing like a couple of little kids.

The real kids stood off to the side. Lita rolled her eyes but never lost the smile on her face.

A car horn broke through the revelry. Turning toward the road, Eli saw a white, midsize car pull into their driveway. His stomach dropped at the sight of the woman riding in the passenger seat.

Carefully, he set Ann's feet down on the ground, and he caught the questioning expression on her face—her eyebrows arched high over swirling gray pools.

The car came to a stop, and Nikki stepped out. She held Eli's gaze before turning her attention to Lita and Elliot.

Eli felt Ann step behind him.

The kids held their ground. Neither smiled at their mother.

"Hey, babies. Surprise." Nikki opened up her arms. When she got no response, she straightened her spine. Some of the charm faded from her smile. "Aren't you glad to see me?"

Lita spoke first. "You said you weren't getting here until tomorrow."

"Like I said, baby, I wanted to surprise you. I thought you'd be happy."

Elliot glanced over at Eli. Maybe Elliot was waiting for confirmation from Eli before he talked, or just needed reassurance from the one parent in his life who was always there. "I'm happy, Mom." Elliot took a tentative step in her direction. Then another. Before long, he was in Nikki's embrace.

"I've missed you so much. You've grown so big." She ruffled his hair. "You'll be as tall as your dad soon." Nikki's gaze flickered over to Eli.

His gut churned. What were Nikki's intentions? Why had she come early and not told him?

Nikki's sudden presence would send Ann running. He might not have the time to say the things he'd planned.

He'd resolved to lay it all out. Tell Ann that he'd fallen for her and he'd wait until she was ready for a relationship. He was not the type of man who sat back and let fate decide. But now, with Nikki here, he might lose his last chance.

***

Jordan needed to get out of there. Those sideways glances Eli's ex-wife tossed her way were not friendly. What if Nikki recognized her? Heidi had after their first full day together. And Nikki was in the music industry.

She noticed Lita still holding back, unwilling to embrace her mother. The mother who'd for the most part abandoned her.

Nikki was tall and thin, with long blonde hair that waterfalled around her face.

Eli's ex was beautiful, and Jordan felt a twinge of jealousy. Once upon a time, Nikki had lived here, with Eli and their two precious children. A life Jordan would have envied.

Jordan imagined herself in Nikki's position. She knew the kind of drive it took to break into the music industry. How much had Jordan given up building her own career?

But even without knowing the love of her own child, she couldn't image turning her back on her family. Around her, she looked at Lita, Elliot, and Eli, and decided Nikki was crazy to leave such wonderful, loving people.

"Did I interrupt your little game?" Nikki's gaze flitted from Lita to Eli, then over to Jordan.

"We were playing tag football." Elliot left his mom and went to stand by his dad.

The lines were drawn. Even Jordan could feel the tension building. Nikki was practically a stranger to her own children. The whole situation was incredibly sad.

A man got out of the car and came to hold Nikki's hand. "Hey, Eli." He tipped his ratty, black fedora.

"Rick." Eli's mouth was pressed together in a thin line.

Rick James looked every bit the rock star, even standing on a Wisconsin farm. He had a trim build, with long legs clothed in black, skinny jeans.

"Elliot and I need to be at the fair tomorrow." Lita's solemn face did not show emotion. She stood with her arms crossed over her body. "I know how much you hate going to the fair."

"Oh, baby, I'd love to see you show your animals. I promised I'd go with you. Remember?" Nikki took a step forward, wringing her hands.

Jordan took several steps backward, away from the action. Would anyone even notice if she snuck away?

"I care more if Ann comes." Lita lifted her little chin. "At least she knows what I'm showing."

Nikki's mouth opened for a brief moment then she snapped her lips shut and glared over at Jordan. "So, this is the Ann I've been hearing so much about." Taking a step to the side, she now had an unobstructed view of her rival. "You and Eli must have something real special going on here."

"I've already explained the situation to you," Eli said. "Don't start anything, Nikki."

"I'm going to Heidi's." Jordan gestured to the ranch house. Her presence was not helping the tense situation.

She was walking away when Lita ran up and wrapped her arms around Jordan's waist.

"Don't leave," she whispered. "Promise you won't leave yet."

Looking at Eli, she caught the warmth in his eyes, which shot straight into her heart. At that moment, in the middle of their emotional turmoil, she felt her body fill with love.

In her quest to become country music royalty, she'd allowed her life to become shallow and empty. With all the effort she'd spent on maintaining her appearance and building her brand, she hadn't lived a true life.

Jordan had been content living for fame. Now, she saw Eli's love for his children and wanted a family of her own. As little Lita's arms squeezed tightly around her, Jordan knew without a shadow of a doubt she'd move heaven and earth to keep them in her life. She loved them, with a strength that surprised her.

She bent down to speak quietly in Lita's ear. "I won't leave today. How about you spend some time with your mom. Let her take you to the fair. I promise to meet you there tomorrow in time to see you show your rabbits." Jordan tucked a piece of wavy blonde hair behind Lita's ear. "Sound like a plan?"

Lita glanced at her with round, blue eyes that were brimming with tears. "I hate my mom."

"Oh, honey. Don't say that. Right now, accept your mom for who she is and don't let hatred poison your heart. She's here for you."

"But she'll just leave, and who knows when I'll see her again," Lita said in a hushed voice.

"You'll always have your dad. He loves you more than the sun and moon." Jordan straightened and rubbed Lita's back. "I'll see you tomorrow. Pinky promise."

Lita's quivering mouth turned up in a small smile. She held hands with Jordan and they crossed pinky fingers.

As Jordan walked back to Heidi's house, she turned back to see Lita standing beside Nikki. Elliot was there, on her other side. Eli still stood firm, feet spread out wide, arms crossed.

The thought of attending a crowded county fair made Jordan's chest tighten and her throat constrict. Memories of her childhood came flooding back.

She'd do it for Lita and Elliot.

If she put on a baseball cap and sunglasses, hopefully she wouldn't be recognized. Maybe she'd break away every once in a while to do some deep breathing exercises and calm down her nerves. She could do this—because she loved them all.

But she'd have to steer clear of Nikki. That woman meant trouble. Jordan could feel it from the top of her head to the tips of her toes.

She was on Nikki's turf. Eli had been her husband. Lita and Elliot were her kids.

Jordan needed to watch her back.

Chapter Twenty

After some persuading, Lita and Elliot went with their mom. But only after Eli promised he'd bring Ann to the fair tomorrow.

Heidi, Sam, and Eli ate a quick dinner, and then Sam went back to bale hay out in the field. The weather report predicted a front coming through, bringing with it the threat of rain. All the hay needed to be baled before the first raindrop fell. He'd hired a high school kid to finish so both he and Sam could take tomorrow off.

Heidi sat at the computer in his home office, going over the monthly budget for the farm. She was a whiz with numbers, and her skills kept the farm in the black year after year. Some days, he didn't know how they'd make do. But they always did. Eli would never be a wealthy man, but for him, providing for his family was enough.

With a quiet house and, for once, nothing else to do, Eli put on his boots and made the short walk over to see Ann. She hadn't joined them for dinner, and he wondered if she was feeling ill. He wouldn't blame her after that scene with Nikki.

He was halfway to Heidi's when the sound of a guitar drifted through the air. When he saw Ann sitting on the front porch, playing, he stayed back in the shadows and listened.

The melody she played had a country music vibe. It sounded sad and hopeful at the same time. Was this song something she'd written? Ann was more musically gifted than she'd let on.

Eli stood frozen, unsure whether to approach her, stay hidden, or sneak away and leave her to her music. He didn't have to wait long before the choice was made for him.

Ann finished her song. "Hate to break it to you, Eli, but you'd make a terrible spy."

He laughed and joined her on the porch. "There go my dreams of joining the CIA."

She scooted over and patted the seat. "It's a beautiful night."

Sitting next to her on the swing, he put his arm around her and rested it on the back of the seat. "What were you playing just now?"

She shrugged. "Something I wrote recently. I can't seem to get the chorus right. There's something off about it, either the notes or the rhythm."

"Play it again."

Ann positioned the guitar on her lap and started the song from the beginning, humming the melody.

Eli knew music, and he knew the difference between someone who simply played guitar and someone who felt each chord with their soul. Ann was the latter. When she played, she became one with the instrument.

He remembered the feeling—letting go of everything except the music.

When she was finished, she looked up at him. "What do you think?"

"It's really good, but you're right. The chorus needs tweaking. Can I see the guitar?"

She handed it over to his outstretched hands.

Eli played the chorus. "Can you hum the melody?"

"I can do one better." She picked up an iPad. "I have a piano app on here. Let me play the song for you."

He listened to her play the first verse and chorus. The second time through, he accompanied her with the guitar. "How about you change these half notes to quarter notes? And change the A major chord at the beginning of the chorus to A minor." He played his idea for her.

"Yes." Ann nodded her head in time to the beat. "I'll have to play it with the lyrics, but I think that might work."

"Let me hear the lyrics."

Even with only the porch light to illuminate them, he could see a blush brighten her cheeks.

"I'm not ready to share those. Not yet." She scratched the tan skin of her thigh.

"And when you're ready, who do you share your songs with?" He shifted to face her. "Is songwriting a hobby for you, Ann, or something more?"

He was staring so deeply into her eyes that her kiss took him by surprise. But he got over the shock quickly and placed his hands on either side of her face. He touched her gently, like she was a shimmering butterfly ready to take flight.

Ann's sweet lips pressed against his. Eli loved the taste of her, as delicately fresh as a peach on a summer's day. His tongue touched hers and a jolt of pleasure burned through his veins.

He had enough sense left to pull back for a second to set the guitar on the floor. Now, there was nothing between them. He went back for more—more spark, more warmth, more Ann.

He slid his hand up the soft skin of her leg. Here and now, she was the center of his existence. His body felt light, almost like he was levitating.

She lifted her arms to wrap them around his neck, grounding him back to her. Ann's fingers ran through his hair, pulling ever so lightly at the curls resting on his nape. A low growl escaped from his lips and he pulled her closer, but not close enough. Never close enough. At least not while they sat outside on the porch.

Eli's fingertips trailed down her neck and he felt the rapid pulse of her carotid artery. He lingered at that spot, enjoying the strong rhythm of the blood flowing inside her, knowing it was his touch, his kiss that caused her heart to beat fast.

Lowering his hands, he traced them along her collarbone and down each side of her body, finally resting on her hips. His large hands seemed to engulf her small frame. Eli wanted more than ever to protect her from whatever, or whomever, had threatened to hurt her.

Ann's mouth smiled against his before nipping at his lower lip. She held it between her teeth, sucking in slightly before letting go. "How did you get so good at this?" Her voice sounded breathless.

The pulse pounding in his ears muffled her words. He bent over to kiss the indentation at the base of her neck, the sweet spot of soft flesh between her collarbones.

Eli had worked hard to respect her wish to keep their relationship as only friends. But tonight, kissing her under the emerging stars, he felt something shift inside his chest.

He'd fallen in love with her. As hard as he'd worked to never let that happen again after Nikki, he'd opened his heart once more. Ann held his heart in the palm of her small hand. Would she crush it the way Nikki had? He couldn't imagine Ann being so cruel.

He knew so little about her life. Which was strange, because he felt more connected to her than he'd ever felt with anyone. Maybe the feeling came from their shared love of music, something he'd set aside for too long, or the way she cared about his children. She would make a wonderful mother someday.

Whatever the reason, Eli wouldn't let her leave without a commitment to see each other again. Even if that meant that he was the one traveling to see her.

He had stepped onto a tightrope, balancing his own desire for Ann with protecting and caring for his family.

"I shouldn't have kissed you." Ann squeezed his hand. "But seeing you play guitar is so sexy."

"Why didn't you tell me sooner?" He kept a smile on his face, trying to hide his fear of losing her.

She looked at him with her beautiful, wide eyes. "Tomorrow... attending the fair will be hard for me. It will bring back very bad memories."

"You don't have to go. Lita and Elliot would understand." Eli stood, pulling her up with him.

She relaxed into his embrace. "I promised I'd be there. Although, having Nikki with them is all that really matters."

"You matter to them, too." He rested his chin on the top of her head. A few of her fine hairs blew up to tickle his nose. Eli brushed them down with the back of his hand.

"I don't want to let my own fear and anxiety stop me. I'd be disappointed in myself if I wasn't there for them after I made a promise."

"You are a strong woman, Ann. I respect that about you." Eli stroked her back.

She sighed and stepped away. "I should turn in for the night if we're going to spend the day at the fair."

Eli watched her take the guitar and walk toward the front door.

Before she stepped inside the house, she turned to him with a smile that glowed despite the darkness. "You make it hard for a lady to go to bed by herself. Good night, Eli. Sweet dreams."

As the door closed behind her, Eli thought the same could be said about her. After the kisses they'd shared, he would be tossing and turning in bed. And if he was lucky, sweet dreams would finally find him.

He walked through the grass, back to his house. Stopping, he tipped his head up to take in the night sky. Millions of stars sparkled above him, making him feel small.

How much would he give up for love? With Nikki, he'd stubbornly held onto the farm and his own desire to make things right with his deceased father. Was he about to make the same mistakes with Ann?

Eli wanted to kick himself. Even though he'd fallen in love with Ann, he didn't know enough about her to say they wanted the same things in life.

But the memory of their kiss still burned inside him.

Something that special was worth fighting for.

***

Jordan couldn't sleep. How could she when her mind kept going back to kissing Eli on the porch swing?

What had she been *thinking*? But seriously, what woman could resist the lure of a hunky man playing sensual music on a guitar? Eli was so hot when he went into musician mode. Farmer Eli warmed her up and made her glow. Guitar Eli set her world on fire.

She slipped on a pair of cut-off shorts and a T-shirt and tied up her shoes. She needed to get outside in the fresh air and think. After quietly leaving the house, as not to wake Heidi, she walked toward the farmhouse. The interior was dark. Eli must have gone to bed.

Tomorrow, she'd tell him everything. Then, he could decide if he wanted Jordan Spencer as much as he thought he wanted Ann Dufour.

Up ahead lay a corn field. Despite the darkness, Jordan found the narrow strip of grass that ran down the side. She strolled under the waxing moon and a sky full of stars. An owl hooted somewhere in the distance. The landscape was perfectly serene. If only she could put it all in a bottle and recapture this calm feeling whenever she was anxious.

Sliding the phone out of her back pocket, Jordan pulled up Phil's number. She dialed.

"Jordan," Phil said with urgency in his voice. "I'm glad you called. We need you back home. Now."

"Whoa. Slow down." This was unlike Phil. It took a lot to get him riled up. "What's going on?"

He sighed. "This whole mess with Henry. I don't know how much you've kept up to date on what's being said about you in the media, but it's not good. And because you're MIA, they're speculating up a storm."

"So, let them speculate. I'll be home Monday, and then we can clean up this mess."

"This can't wait until Monday," Phil said. "I'm getting calls from your music label, companies of products you endorse, and the producer of the awards show you're performing for next week. The reports are you OD'd on cocaine and are in rehab. I hate to do this to you, but you need to be seen in public to disprove what's being said. This scandal could permanently damage your career."

Fury burned inside her. Stupid Henry and his stupid lies. Of course, the public ate them all up like Thanksgiving dinner. "Please, Phil. I promised the Hintz kids I'd go to the fair tomorrow and watch them show their Four-H animals. I can't leave. Handle this for me for two more days."

"I've been working non-stop to put out the fires, but your PR team and I can only do so much." Phil paused. "People need to see you. To know you're all right. I think it's great you want to keep your promise to a couple kids, but your career is more important."

She trusted Phil. He'd been instrumental in building her fame. Jordan normally wouldn't think twice about following his advice. But this time, she'd follow her heart. What good were fame and a good public image if she disappointed the people she loved? "I understand that my absence is making the gossip worse. And I know you always have my best interests in mind. Here's the thing… I'm staying here until Monday."

Phil groaned.

"Just hear me out. I'll fly home Monday. Lacy and I are leaving for Vegas on Friday for the awards show. I want to keep a low profile until then." Her insides tingled with excitement. "Think about it, Phil. Once I step out on the red carpet, looking rested and refreshed, all the gossip and bad press will go away. I can do a few interviews and tell the world how I've used my time off to write my next album, called Jordan Ann."

When she stopped talking, she heard only silence from the other end of the call. "Phil? You still there?"

"Yeah, I'm here." Another pause. "I'm not going to tell you what to do. You've earned the right to make decisions about your own career, and to be perfectly honest, I'm glad you're standing up for what you want. I'll fill the rest of the team in on your plan. We'll do our best to keep things under control."

"Thanks, Phil." Her heart squeezed with love for her manager/stand-in father.

"You've really written an entire album while you've been there?" Phil asked.

"Almost. Ideas keep coming to me, and I keep writing them down. I know you'll love the direction I'm going."

"Jordan Ann. I like the title."

"Me, too." She smiled.

Once she ended the call, she sat cross-legged on the cool grass and pulled up Cole's number.

The phone rang several times before his groggy voice answered. "Hello."

"Cole, are you asleep?" Jordan couldn't believe it. Cole never went to bed before one a.m.

After a few seconds of mumbling, Cole cleared his throat. "What's the matter, Jordan?

"Nothing." She suddenly felt sheepish for calling him. Interrupting his trysts had never bothered her before, but this time he'd been actually sleeping. Uncharacteristically sleeping. "Forget it, Cole. I'm fine. Go back to bed."

"Stop. Let me put on some pants and step outside."

"I need to scrub that image from my brain." In truth, Jordan thought Cole had an amazing body, despite the fact she saw him more as a brother. She'd never let him know how attractive she found him, though. His ego was big enough.

She heard the sound of a door closing, and then a long car honk.

"I wanted to let you know that I'm leaving a day later than planned."

"You want to me come get you? I'm actually not very far away. Chicago, to be exact."

Slowly standing, Jordan wiped off blades of grass from the backside of her shorts. "No, I'll be fine. People don't seem to recognize me with short, brown hair and no makeup."

"Have you read the media reports? They're working themselves up into a frenzy trying to figure out what rehab facility you're hiding in."

Feeling chilled, Jordan decided to head back to Heidi's house. "Then they'll be very disappointed when I arrive on the red carpet next weekend looking more fabulous than ever."

"If the media finds out where you're staying, you will need me there to protect you."

They were not going to find her. Because if they did, Jordan and whomever she was with would be pushed into the eye of a media storm. She'd never want to do that to Eli and his family.

"Everything will be fine. Come to my house on Tuesday and we'll go through my upcoming schedule. Fair warning, you're going to be very busy for the foreseeable future."

"I wouldn't want it any other way. Sleep tight, sweetcakes. See you soon." Cole ended the call.

Jordan hugged her phone to her chest, wanting to keep the feeling of connection. As much as she hated to leave Eli and the farm, she knew her place was back in Nashville.

She missed Lacy, Cole, Phil, and Doreen. And even her pushy trainer, dietitian, and music producers. They were her people.

Lacy and Jordan shared a past. Cole, her surrogate big brother, put himself in danger time and again to protect her. Phil and Doreen loved her like a daughter.

But even wrapped in the love of her family, would she ever feel complete again without Eli, Lita, and Elliot in her life?

Chapter Twenty-One

Eli checked his rearview mirror, seeing Ann in the backseat of his truck. She looked cute, wearing the green John Deere hat he'd given her that morning, with a pair of aviator shades perched on top.

Tearing his gaze away from her and back on the road, his thoughts drifted to his daughter. Lita had been exceptionally hostile to Nikki yesterday. On the other hand, she'd reached out to Ann. He knew his ex well enough to know that the rejection wouldn't sit well. Add all the rumors swirling about his relationship with their guest. Eli needed to be ready for an explosion.

Behind him, he heard whispering. Then they started to giggle. He laughed himself when he heard Ann's hyena laugh.

Heidi and Ann had become fast friends. And for someone like Heidi who didn't socialize very often, a good girlfriend was exactly what she needed.

"What are you two ladies up to back there?" Sam turned in his front seat to face the rear of the truck. The scoundrel winked at Ann.

Eli's blood boiled. Couldn't his shameless flirt of a brother give it a rest for one day? But once Eli saw the lopsided grin on Sam's face, his temper cooled. Sam was only doing what a little brother did best—annoy their older brother.

"I can't wait to see how Lita and Elliot do today," Ann said. "Do you really think Lita will stop doing 4H after this year?"

Eli put on his blinker and turned into the fairground's parking lot. "I don't know. I want the choice to be hers. Once I was Lita's age, I started to resent being pushed into agriculture. The last thing I want is for her to follow in my footsteps."

"You didn't turn out so bad." Ann patted his shoulder.

After parking, Eli took a deep breath to steady his nerves. His stomach felt like it was home to a swarm of bees. He'd never been this nervous with a woman before. With his family tagging along, he shouldn't feel like he was on a date. But he wanted today, and tonight, to be perfect.

Ann lifted her sunglasses and set them on her face. "Where to first?"

Sure was a shame to cover up those pretty eyes.

The group of four made their way to the ticket stand. Eli paid for Ann, who protested but finally gave in. She'd delayed her trip home in order to come today for his children. Paying her admission was the least he could do.

The fairground was already busy. A group of kids darted past them, followed by their parents, who moved at a much slower pace.

"Let's go to the barn and see how Elliot's doing." Eli reached over to take Ann's hand.

She glanced from Eli's face down to their joined hands, and then back to his face. Her brows arched above the rim of her sunglasses.

He nodded. "Friends are allowed to hold hands."

He didn't care what anyone else thought, from the local busybodies to his ex-wife. He wanted the world to know Ann was with him. They might not have tomorrow, but they had today, and he wanted to make the most of his time with her.

Squeezing his hand, Ann smiled. "Yes, let's go find Elliot. I'm eager to see how he's holding up."

"Sam and I are going over to the Agriculture Building," Heidi said. "I heard a new farm equipment retailer will be there and I wanted to do some comparison shopping."

Sam's grim expression made it obvious the Ag Building was the last place on earth he wanted to be. But he shrugged and followed Heidi, while she began explaining the latest milking hose technology.

Eli walked hand in hand with Ann toward the cattle barn, and didn't miss the sideways glances of the people who knew him. They'd probably all heard the gossip. Elijah Hintz, a divorced father of two, who never dated any of the local girls, was now involved with the strange woman who'd crashed her car in front of his house.

He took a deep breath. If he was going to ask her out, he needed to do it now. Take advantage of the few rare minutes he had her to himself.

"Let me take you out to dinner tonight," Eli said. "Just you and me. For your last night in Wisconsin."

"What about the rest of the family?"

He planned to make sure they were all otherwise occupied. "The kids will be with Nikki at her parents'. And Sam and Heidi can take care of themselves." He reached over and slid her sunglasses down to the tip of her nose. Really was a shame to cover those gorgeous eyes.

She batted her long, black lashes. "Are you asking me out on a date?"

"Call it what you'd like. Just say yes."

Pushing her sunglasses back in place, she smiled. The dimple in the center of her chin deepened. "I'd call dinner alone with you a fabulous idea. I have some things I want to talk to you about."

"Great. There's a bar in Sterling that books live bands on the weekends. We could go there if bar food is okay. Otherwise, I'll make a reservation at a nicer restaurant."

"I love to hear live music. Let's go to the bar."

"Lester's Place it is." He gave her a quick peck on the cheek. By the end of the night, he wanted to officially move their relationship out of the friends category.

Two large buildings loomed ahead. Elliot's cows were housed in barn A. As they entered the barn, the pungent smell of cow poo greeted them.

Ann scrunched up her nose. "These cows sure have the life. Eat, poop, eat, poop. Maybe take a drink of water and pee."

"Most dairy cows that live on family farms are very well cared for." Eli strolled with Ann down one of the large aisles. "We raise them from birth and care for them. Our livelihoods are based on making sure they're happy and healthy."

He caught a glimpse of Elliot's cows, housed in separate pens at the end of the aisle.

Eli's good mood soured when Nikki appeared in the doorway ahead of him. She was dressed in a miniskirt and crop top. Always the rock star. Her husband, Rick, had on his signature black skinny jeans and fedora. The pair looked out of place at a Midwestern county fair.

Nikki caught his gaze and smirked. "Nice of you to bring your girlfriend." She glanced at Eli's hand that was still firmly entwined with Ann's. "Elliot ran off to get something, and Lita went with her friend Bailey."

"It's Hailey." Eli didn't disguise his irritation. Nikki seemed totally disinterested in what the kids were doing.

"I have to get out of this barn," Nikki said. "I forgot how bad cows stink. I still remember Eli coming home at the end of the day smelling as bad as these cows. He wasn't allowed to touch me until he showered." She leveled a sneering gaze at Ann. "You obviously find the smell attractive or you wouldn't be with Eli."

Curbing the need to lash back, Eli willed himself to remain calm. "Our stinky cows provide milk, which in turns provides for your children, and yourself, don't forget." He didn't want to bicker with her, not here. And not in front of Ann. Unfortunately, Nikki brought out the worst in him.

"If you would have stayed in the band, we would have been rich and famous. But I guess some people crave the simple life." Nikki hooked her arm through her husband's and turned to leave.

"I try to be civil with her...," Eli said to Ann once Nikki was gone.

"She enjoys pressing your buttons." Ann walked over to give Ginger, Elliot's Guernsey, a pat on the rump.

He stepped behind her and brushed her hair aside, exposing her neck. Her skin was creamy and smooth, creating a beautiful wave over the ridges of her spine. Eli exhaled a warm breath and he saw goose bumps rise on her skin in response.

Elliot's voice sounded in the distance, and he quickly moved away.

"Dad, you're here." A large smile radiated on Elliot's face. "Hi, Ann." He waved at her. "I can't find my grooming combs. I've looked everywhere."

"We set your box of grooming tools on your assigned shelf in the barn," Eli said. "Have you checked there?"

"Yes. Like a hundred times. They're gone." Elliot rocked back on his heels. His smile faded into a frown. "I have to take Ginger to be judged soon."

"Okay, buddy. We'll either find the grooming combs or see if we can borrow some." Eli lifted his gaze to Ann. "You mind waiting here while I go with Elliot?"

"Of course not." She slipped her hand out of Eli's and reached out to smooth out Elliot's hair. "You could use a comb yourself before you go in the ring with Ginger."

"We'll be right back." Eli sent her a smile before following Elliot's hurried steps.

***

So far so good. Jordan was surrounded by hundreds of people, and no one had recognized her. But then there was Nikki—the wildcard. Jordan couldn't underestimate what Nikki would do if she discovered the woman with her ex-husband was Jordan Spencer.

Nothing, and no one, would ruin Jordan's plan. She'd come clean with Eli tonight, on her own terms, before someone else did.

While she waited for Eli to come back, she took off her sunglasses to study Ginger the Guernsey. Jordan stepped closer and rubbed her hand along the cow's silky-smooth side. Ginger pivoted her neck to look at Jordan. The cow was incredibly cute. Her eyes were dark brown orbs, tipped with long, thick lashes. *How do I get eyelashes like that? Wait... am I jealous of a cow?*

She laughed to herself and gave the cow another soft pat before stepping back into the aisle.

"Looks like someone's found a friend." Nikki's cool voice sounded from behind her. "You and I need to have a talk. I sent Rick off to go listen to a local band. They're not very good, but what do you expect from a county fair?" She waved her hand in front of her nose. "How about we step outside? This smell is making me sick."

Jordan wanted to tell her to go take a flying leap into the pile of cow manure, but stopped her tongue. No use brewing bad blood. At least not yet, anyway.

Once she put her sunglasses back in place, she went with Nikki out into the fresh air. "What's so important that you're taking time away from your children to talk with me?"

Nikki raised one penciled eyebrow. "You're a feisty one. No wonder Eli likes you. He liked that quality in me at one time."

Jordan crossed her arms and pressed her lips together. She swore not to say another word unless pressured. The last thing she wanted to do was cause trouble for Eli. Plus, Lita and Elliot were her children. Nikki did have a right to be concerned about someone new in their lives.

"How is it my ex-husband has no idea who you are?" Nikki asked. "I mean, really? Eli was never one for keeping up on celebrities, but you are one of the biggest country music stars in the world. And he's obviously got my kids so sheltered, they don't know who you are either."

A sickening sensation churned in her gut. Jordan's throat tightened so she couldn't take a full breath. For the first time since Jordan had met her, Nikki's smile appeared genuine.

"I'm right, aren't I? Eli has no idea who you really are?" Nikki's face glowed.

Jordan involuntarily took a step away. She tried to take a deep breath, but the air couldn't move past the knot tightening inside her throat. "I don't know who you think I am. My name is Ann Dufour."

This time, Nikki raised both brows. "Oh, come on. The jig is up. I'm not as simple as the rest of these country bumpkins around here. I follow the music industry. I know who all the big players are, and you, Jordan, are at the top of the list." She clapped her hands. "I can't believe I'm talking to a multi-platinum artist."

"Keep your voice down," Jordan hissed. "Do you know the hysteria you'd cause if someone overheard you blabbing away?"

"Well, I'm sorry." Nikki lowered her voice. "This is so exciting."

Jordan didn't think so. "You figured out the mystery. Good for you, Scooby Doo."

"I want to know why you're here." Nikki grabbed Jordan's arm to stop her from walking away. "And why you changed your appearance? If I were you, I'd be at a five-star resort now, sipping champagne with a hunky man rubbing sunscreen on my back."

Jordan wouldn't explain that she'd had her fill of five-star resorts and the men that came along with them. She took Nikki by the elbow and led her off to a quiet, shaded spot, away from the growing crowds. "What do you want?" Might as well get all the cards on the table. She'd played this game plenty of times. They always wanted something.

Nikki pulled her arm out of Jordan's hold. "Of course you think I'd want something. Well, if you're gonna ask, here it is. Stay away from Eli and my kids. Leave right now and never see or speak to any of them again."

The sting of Nikki's words felt like a slap across the face. "Why?"

"Really? You have to ask?" Nikki hooked her fingers into the waistband loops of her tight miniskirt.

That skirt, combined with her high-heeled boots, left Jordan wondering how Nikki could walk.

"I've done nothing to hurt Eli, Lita, and Elliot," Jordan said. "And once Eli knows who I really am, it's his decision if I remain a part of their life. Not yours."

"I'm their mother." Nikki stepped backward and cocked her head. "How about I go tell Eli right now that the woman he has the hots for is another career-driven musician, just like his wonderful ex?"

"You underestimate who you're dealing with," Jordan hissed. She'd spent her life surrounded by sharks. She knew exactly how to handle people like Nikki James. "You think you're the first person to try and manipulate me? Everyone wants a connection to my record label, or an audition with my producer, or a meeting with my agent."

Nikki's blue eyes widened, appearing hungry. "Promise me an audition with your music producer and my lips are sealed." She crossed her pink manicured hand across her heart. "If I get signed with a big record label my career will finally take off. I could afford to come home more often to see my kids. I'd be a better mother."

Jordan forced herself not to roll her eyes. Undoubtedly, Lita's influence. Nikki had fallen for the bait. No surprise.

Was Nikki really that driven to succeed, despite all costs? Jordan had seen it time and again, artists giving up everything for a shot at fame. They'd lie, cheat, steal, and backstab in order to get what they wanted, and they didn't care who got hurt. Even if it was their own family.

"Don't get ahead of yourself," Jordan said. "My producer listening to your demo does not guarantee a record deal."

"No. I want a live audition for me and my band. That's more personal, you know. He can see me, along with hearing my voice." She fluffed out her long, blonde hair.

There was that impulse to roll her eyes again, and Jordan had to fight the urge and stop herself. "He'll do a live audition after he listens to your recording and only if he thinks you're worth his time."

Nikki's lips curled up in a hybrid of a snarl and a smile. "You are Jordan Spencer. Do I need to make an announcement, right here and now? You will get me that live audition or everyone, including your precious Eli, will find out who you are. And here's a tip, free of charge: Eli will not take kindly to being lied to. He's always been a stickler for the truth."

Jordan's chest squeezed until she struggled to breathe. Adrenaline pulsed through her body. Her anxiety threatened to take control. She fought the panic, willing her body to relax. "I will arrange a live audition, but only if you promise not to say a word to anyone, including your husband, that I'm Jordan Spencer."

"I have to tell Rick. At least let me tell him about our audition." Nikki bounced up and down on the soles of her high-heeled boots. "And how soon can we get it?"

Jordan breathed in slowly, and then breathed out. *Don't let her see how deeply she's rattled you.* "My producer will be in touch with you soon. He's very busy and will have to find a spot in his schedule to fit you in. And again, there is no guarantee he'll sign you. That's the deal. Take it or leave it."

"It's a deal," Nikki squealed. "This makes coming home so worth it. See ya around, Ann." She lifted her hand and gave Jordan a mock salute before walking away.

Jordan wanted to give the salute right back to her, only with one finger. But once again, maturity prevailed. Instead, she balled up her fists and looked around for something to punch.

Chapter Twenty-Two

When Eli came back to Ginger's pen, Ann was nowhere in sight. When she did come back, her full lips were pursed together in a tight line. She wasn't happy, and he wanted to know why.

While Elliot performed the final touch-ups on Ginger, Eli took Ann's hand and led her outside.

"What's wrong?" He placed a finger under her chin and lifted her face so she made eye contact.

"Nothing. I just went out for some fresh air. It's getting hot in the barn." Her mouth twitched with a brief smile.

He wasn't buying it. "Was it Nikki? I know she can be blunt, and she wasn't very welcoming to you earlier."

Ann shook her head. "No, I have no issue with Nikki. I'm fine… honestly." Ann placed the palm of her hand on his cheek. "You're sweet for caring."

They went back to join Elliot, who was slipping the harness onto Ginger.

"Who's a pretty girl?" Elliot patted the cow's head then guided her out of her stall, into the aisle.

"She's going to win blue," Eli said. "I can feel it." He was proud of his son, a boy who reminded Eli so much of his own dad. If only his dad were here now. Frank Hintz would have been so proud of his grandson.

Eli and Ann escorted Elliot and Ginger over to the show ring, and then got seated in the bleachers next to Sam and Heidi. He caught sight of Nikki and Rick striding in just as the judging began. She acted like she was the star of the show instead of the kids and their animals.

Lita entered the bleacher section from the other side, followed by Hailey and Layla. The trio sat on the bench in front of them.

Out of the corner of his eye, Eli noticed Sam visibly stiffen. His brother usually avoided his high school girlfriend on the rare occasions he came home.

When it was Elliot's turn, his face turned solemn as he led Ginger out to parade past the judges' table. Then he stopped and let the judges have a good look. After he'd been given a nod by the head judge, he walked off with Ginger.

Eli waited until Elliot looked over at him before giving him two thumbs up. A wide smile grew on Elliot's face.

After a long, nervous wait for the scores, Elliot was called up to accept his blue ribbon. Eli glanced over to where Nikki had been sitting, but he found their spot now empty.

A red rage burned deep in his chest. How could she have missed their son's special moment? Add it to the list of every other important event she'd been absent for.

"My rabbits are showing soon," Lita said. Her smile had faded. Her frosty blue eyes narrowed as she glanced at her mom's now empty bleacher. "I'm heading over to the small livestock barn. Don't be late." She grabbed Hailey's hand, and they took off running like rabbits themselves.

"I'll probably head over there too." Layla stood, and then flicked a glance at Sam.

Sam had his gaze focused on the peanut shells littered by his feet.

"I'll come with you." Heidi followed Layla down the bleacher steps.

"I need to find Nikki." Eli stood and stretched his legs. "She will *not* miss Lita's rabbit judging."

"Go talk to Nikki," Ann said. "I'm sure Sam will keep me company."

Her beautiful smile melted some of his anger.

"Nothing would make me happier." Sam grinned and slung his arm around Ann's shoulders. "Run along, Eli. And don't hurry back."

Ann laughed. "Don't worry. I'll make sure he behaves."

Eli ground his teeth and turned on his heel to go search out Nikki. His hunt didn't take long. He first found Rick, standing outside the women's restroom. Before too long, Nikki appeared. Her hips sashayed in time to the rhythm of the clicking of her high-heeled boots.

"Elliot won first place."

She clapped her hands. "Oh, that's wonderful."

"You would know that if you'd stuck around long enough to see him win." Eli's body grew warmer and warmer. His face felt flush.

Nikki glared at Eli. "I had to use the ladies' room. Excuse me. I didn't know I needed a hall pass from you to pee."

"You missed a big moment in our son's life." He lowered his voice, noticing people had stopped to watch them. "Lita noticed."

"Well, I'm sorry. I just got so hot in there, and they were taking so long. I thought I'd be back in time." Her lower lip swelled into a pout.

He was not buying her "poor Nikki" act. "Lita is showing her rabbits soon." He pointed at the white barn that housed the small livestock. "I suggest you get moving."

Now, Nikki bit her lower lip. "I can't. Rick and I are leaving." She waved her hands in front of his face. "Before you get all mad at me, just listen. The band got a huge opportunity. We're finally getting our big break."

"What do you mean you're *leaving*? You've been here for twenty-four hours." His simmering temper boiled to full-fledged anger.

"I'll talk to Lita and Elliot and explain everything. Don't worry."

"Don't worry." Eli's voice rose. He didn't care who overheard. "Leave now and they will never forgive you."

"Lita already hates me. And all Elliot ever talks about are his animals. They act like they don't even care that I'm here." Nikki crossed her arms over her chest.

"What do you expect? You haven't seen them in over a year. Every time you promise to visit, you back out. They're hurting, Nikki. Can't you see that?"

Eli knew the time would come when the kids would push Nikki out of their lives for good, just as she'd done to them.

Rick moved to stand beside his wife and held her hand. "Maybe we could stay one more night. We'll leave tomorrow."

Narrowing her eyes, Nikki turned to face Rick. "We have to go now. You know why."

"But we don't even have an appointment yet."

"We will and we need to be ready. The rest of the band is meeting us in Nashville tomorrow."

Rick shrugged and looked at Eli. "Sorry, man. Guess we're hitting the road."

"Can you swing by my parents' house to get the kids' suitcases?" Nikki asked as she pulled her cell from her purse.

Studying her, Eli's anger turned to sadness. They had loved each other. Made two beautiful children together. When he'd married her, he had meant his vow to stay with her forever. How had their relationship deteriorated to this?

"What appointment do you have in Nashville that's more important than your own children?" Eli pleaded.

"Our band, Hallowed Sun, is auditioning for a music producer. I can see it now... me signing a contract for tons of money. This is what I've been waiting for."

How had Nikki's band suddenly got an audition with a producer, in Nashville, of all places? "Why didn't you say something about this audition before?"

"Because I only arranged it this afternoon." Looping her arm inside her husband's, Nikki's face glowed. "I found a connection to the music industry. The real deal. And just think, when I finally make it big, I'll be able to come visit more often."

Make it big? Who was she kidding? Sure, Nikki had a decent voice, and the band was a little above average. But Eli didn't think they had the special spark needed to elevate their music into the national spotlight.

Looking at Nikki, he saw the fire of fame licking at her heels. Eli decided to surrender the fight. "Go find the kids and say goodbye. I'll make sure to get their stuff from your parents' house."

He stood frozen and watched Nikki walk toward the barn. How many times would he pick up the pieces of his children's broken hearts?

It seemed as if it would be at least once more.

***

Jordan's stomach churned with overwhelming nausea. The feeling wasn't from eating too much cotton candy and frozen custard. Or the nervous excitement of watching Lita as her rabbits won blue ribbons.

Her sickness was from knowing Lita and Elliot's hurt and anger over their mother's early departure was all her fault. Nikki had taken Jordan's promise of an audition and twisted it into something awful. She should have let Nikki blow her cover instead of continuing to hide behind her lie.

Poor Elliot now had tears streaking down his cheeks. Lita, on the other hand, was eerily silent.

Then there was Eli, whose expression was a cross between anger and sorrow.

"I need to talk to Nikki," Jordan whispered to Eli. "Do you know where she went?"

He placed his arm around her waist, pulling her close. "Don't waste your time. She's probably halfway to Milwaukee by now."

"I want to go home." Elliot swiped at his runny nose with his arm. "My tummy doesn't feel good."

"Okay, buddy," Eli said. "Let me figure out a way to get everyone home. I'll come back early tomorrow morning for the animals."

Layla approached with Hailey. "I can take Lita and Elliot and get their stuff, and then bring them back to your house." She glanced up at Sam.

Jordan couldn't help but notice the way Sam looked at Hailey. Did he wish that Layla's daughter was his own? Eli had told her about Layla's unplanned pregnancy, and Sam's broken heart over the baby not being his. She hoped that someday the two of them could leave regrets in the past and reconcile. Even Jordan, a relative stranger, could see there was still a spark between them.

"Thanks," Eli said to Layla. "That will be a big help."

Surely, Eli would now cancel their date. He'd want to be home with Lita and Elliot since they were so upset. She resigned herself to the fact that she might not have a private moment to tell Eli the truth. Not before she had to leave tomorrow.

As she followed Eli out to the parking lot toward his truck, her heart ached. She'd wanted her last day with him to be perfect. Instead, she'd set into motion a complete disaster.

"We're still on for tonight." He glanced quickly over at her. "I talked to Heidi. She's staying at my house with Lita and Elliot."

"Don't you want to be home with them, after everything that's happened today?" Those kids needed their dad, now more than ever. And Eli always put his family first.

"Lita and Elliot both instructed me not to break my date with you tonight. I know it sounds callous, but they're used to Nikki's behavior. No one was very surprised when she decided to head out." He took her hand and lifted her up into the truck.

She sighed at his touch. "I'm sorry."

"What do you have to be sorry for?" He gently turned her hand and brushed his lips over the underside of her wrist. "You are the one who stayed for them. You are the one who kept her promise."

There were so many reasons why she shouldn't have stayed. Her cell had been buzzing all day with calls she'd let go to voicemail. Phil, Lacy, and her PR team all sounding more panicked with each call. Maybe she should have listened to Phil and gone home to do damage control. Her public image was not going to improve as long as she remained tucked away in Wisconsin.

And on top of it all, Eli might hate her after he learned the truth. "I expected you would cancel."

"What I expect is for you to be sitting next to me again in this truck in a couple hours." He patted her hip before closing the truck door. After getting into the driver's seat, he twisted to face her. "Tonight is about you and me. As friends, or whatever category you decide. Nobody, especially Nikki, will ruin that for us." Eli turned the key in the ignition and was about to put the truck in drive.

Scooting over, she set her hand on his knee. Time for her to have some fun. She felt the muscles under her touch flex in response. Then, she heard his sharp inhale as she began moving higher. Jordan floated her fingers very lightly up his thigh and over his abdomen. She stroked a zigzag pattern across his strong chest, enjoying the sensation of control. Moving up the scruff of his neck and jaw, she finally pressed a finger against his lips. His breath came out quick and hot.

"Tonight is about you and me," Jordan said. "But now, we still have company."

As he swallowed, his Adam's apple bobbed up and down. "Sam and Heidi." His voice was low and rough.

She nodded her head. "It'd be very rude to leave your babysitters stranded at the fair."

Out of the corner of her eye, she saw Sam and Heidi approach the truck. Reluctantly, she moved away from Eli.

Tonight, she'd tell him everything. And when the dust settled, she hoped to find her heart still in one piece.

Chapter Twenty-Three

A hole-in-the-wall bar in Sterling, Wisconsin wasn't Eli's top choice for a first date, but anywhere with Ann was perfect.

Lester's Place had been the hot spot in the area for fifty years. Their food was decent. The bands they booked to play on the weekends were above average. Even the ambient glow of neon beer signs was kind of romantic.

Eli parked on the street and hopped out to run around and open the passenger-side door for Ann. She looked smoking hot in a denim miniskirt that showed off her amazing legs. When she hopped down, her brown and turquoise cowboy boots clapped on the pavement.

Very cute. And very sexy. He was in so much trouble.

Raindrops fell from the sky, hitting the ground with rhythmic plops. The air smelled of the coming storm. Good thing his hired helper had baled the rest of the hay today.

He took her hand and hustled with her to the covered entrance. "It doesn't look like much from the outside, but Lester's Place is a cool joint." Eli's skin warmed when she looped her arm around his and moved closer. "Although, I think tonight they have a country band playing."

Ann smiled up at him. "Country music is my favorite."

"Mom listened to country all the time growing up." He opened the door for her to go inside. "Whenever we were in the car, she'd always have the country station on." Memories of his mom washed over him, bringing the sting of tears. He'd listen to country music for hours if it meant being able to see his mom again. "When I was in high school, she became obsessed with this song. I think it was called 'Real Country.' No… 'Country Redemption,' that's it. She bought the CD. It had the singer on the cover. A slip of a teenage girl. Mom would play that song over and over again and sing along like she was performing onstage."

Ann's foot must have hit the step in the entry because she stumbled forward.

"Hey, I got you." Eli held her steady. He noticed her cheeks were flushed pink. "Are you feeling all right?"

"Yeah, I'm fine. Wasn't watching where I was going."

He guided her to an empty table toward the back. Private, and far enough from the stage that they'd be able to hear each other talk once the music started.

As she sat, Ann smoothed her hands over her miniskirt. How had he gotten her to agree to go out with him? She was breathtakingly beautiful. He was nothing but an average guy who ran a dairy farm.

A nervous flutter grew inside him. He'd be devastated if she told him, once again, that she wanted to leave things as friends. He was afraid of a future without her. No romance. No happily ever after. Ann would go back to her life and forget about him.

Eli studied everything about her face. What could he say to make her realize what a great thing they had together?

He wouldn't turn into a coward. Not after coming so far. Plus, Lita and Elliot would kill him if they found out that he didn't at least try. His children had grown to love Ann, just as he had. And something told him his parents would have adored her as well.

He cleared his mind of all doubts and fears.

Time to man up and fight for what you want.

***

Jordan took a sip of a drink called an Old Fashioned. Not bad, considering she wasn't a big fan of brandy. She set the tumbler on the table, and then took the little plastic sword and nibbled off one of the cherries. The sweet flavor of the fruit mixed with the tartness of the brandy made her taste buds do the happy dance.

"How's your burger?" Eli reached across the table with his napkin in hand and dabbed at the corner of her mouth. "It looks good on you."

"Thanks. I'm a messy eater, what can I say?" She laughed.

He looked absolutely gorgeous. Quite honestly the best-looking man she'd ever been with, and that was saying a lot, considering the men Jordan dated. Movie stars to a crown prince, none came close to Eli.

He'd shaved, and his wavy hair had been parted and brushed, changing his look from country farm boy to male model.

"These little nuggets of gooey cheese are the best." Jordan popped another fried cheese curd into her mouth. After the first crunch, she tasted the divine pleasure of warm cheddar.

"The cheese comes from a local dairy, which I sell milk to." Eli picked a cheese curd and wiggled his eyebrows. "I better have a few before you eat them all."

"Wisconsin really is the dairy state." The bar around her was filled with old-time decor. Seemed like Lester's Place hadn't seen a facelift since the nineteen-seventies. Earlier, when they'd first arrived, she'd noticed Lester's Supper Club situated across the street. Before today, she'd never heard of a Supper Club. To her Southern eyes, it looked like a regular restaurant. *Best keep that observation to yourself.*

"We have a million and a quarter dairy cows in the state. That's one cow for every five residents." Eli ate the last cheese curd.

Darn. She'd have to ask their waitress to bring more.

"That's a lot of cows." She paused and fiddled with her napkin. "I've made some inquiries into buying the Turner mansion," Jordan said. "Because it's held in a trust, the process won't be easy. Hopefully, they'll agree to let me restore it."

"I still don't understand why you'd want to own that dump, let alone restore it. But I like the idea if it means you'll be coming back to the area."

How could she explain the connection she felt to the property? At one time, she'd felt uncared for and abandoned. That's when Phil had been the one person who'd seen her as something more than a shy girl in a dirty dress. Someone worth loving.

Jordan glanced up to see their waitress approach.

"How's your food so far?" she asked with a large smile.

Jordan guessed the woman was in her mid-sixties and trying hard not to look it. "Everything's wonderful. My compliments to the chef."

The waitress, Luann, snorted. "The chef would be Big Bubba in the back. He might not be much to look at, but the man can fry up a mighty fine burger. Eli, next time you take this lovely lady on a date, bring her to the Supper Club. The prime rib will melt in your mouth,

I tell you. And the baked potatoes are as big as your face, topped with sour cream and chives."

"I'll keep that in mind." Eli peered over at Jordan. "If the lovely lady agrees to go out with me again."

"How could I say no?" She smiled at Luann. "That sounds delicious."

Luann put her hand on one of her round hips. "I've worked here for going on twenty-five years. I remember Frank and Kathleen would bring the kids in here for Friday Night Fish Fry. Eli here would always ask for an extra dish of tartar sauce and two straws."

"Why two straws?" Jordan glanced at Eli, puzzled.

"I used one to drink with." He grinned.

"And the other for spitballs," Luann interjected. "The little rascal had the best shot I've ever seen. Hit old man Hermanson right between the eyeballs once."

"Yeah, and then I got my butt whacked when I got home." Eli rubbed his hand over his backside.

"We got the band coming on in about fifteen minutes," Luann said. "They're from down south. Ohio, I think. I heard them warming up earlier. They sound pretty good."

Jordan tried not to laugh at Ohio being described as "down south." "How do you attract live bands from out of state?" The small town of Sterling, Wisconsin was not exactly a mecca for music.

"Old Lester has some connections. A good band draws a good crowd. You'll see. This place will be packed by nine." As Luann turned to leave, she smiled down at Jordan. "You've got the prettiest accent, honey. I'll be watching to make sure our Eli here treats you good tonight." With a wink, she left to check on another table.

"Spitballs, huh." Jordan laughed at the thought of little Eli, with his mop of curly hair, shooting spitballs at unsuspecting diners.

"My folks finally banned straws at our table. We all had to drink directly from our cups. But I'd swing by the waitress station on my way to the bathroom and pocket a few. Let's just say my dad used his belt for more than holding up his pants."

"Why doesn't it surprise me you were a naughty little boy?"

He reached across the table and placed his hand over hers. "Maybe I still am."

Heat surged through her body. What a wickedly attractive man. She had so many ways to answer him but decided to stick to the safe path.

He might change his tune after he discovered he'd taken Jordan Spencer on a date.

"Will you dance with me when the band starts?"

A flash of lightning shone through the windows at the front of the bar. Several seconds later, deep thunder rattled the glassware inside. The weatherman had gotten it right for once. They'd predicted a sunny day with thunderstorms rolling in around dinner time.

One corner of Eli's mouth rose in a crooked smirk. "I haven't danced in a long time. I don't want to embarrass you." He pointed to the scuffed-up dance floor.

"I know you're hiding some smooth moves under that innocent, Midwestern facade. Didn't you learn how to shake your booty when you lived in LA?"

He actually blushed. How cute. "I only lived in LA for a short time, and not once did I shake my booty, as you so eloquently put it." Taking her arm, he pulled her toward him, until their faces were only inches apart. "But I'd consider an exchange. You play me the song you've been working on, with the lyrics, and I'll dance with you."

There was no way she'd sing that song for him. The lyrics were too personal. They were about Eli. Now was not the right time. Maybe there would never be a right time. The song might go down as an anthem to unrequited love.

Jordan planned to play "Eli's Song" for Phil once she returned home. Her new album would be pure country music. No more techno beats and electronic voice manipulation. Jordan wanted to sing the way she did when she first began; when she'd recorded "Country Redemption," the song that had connected with Eli's mom.

"I told you that song isn't ready. Not even for you." *Especially not for you.*

The warmth of his breath floated over her face. Jordan tipped her gaze down to see his delicious lips, so close to her own.

They were in public. At a bar. Memories of camera flashes made her pull away. What if she was recognized? She couldn't handle the onslaught. Not here. Not now.

"I want to hear what you've created, even if it's not perfect yet." Eli brushed back a lock of hair that had fallen over her cheek. His touch seared her skin.

With every touch, with every look, he weakened her defenses. The need to open up to him became unbearable. Bitter fear kept her confession locked away. The two were at war inside her head and her heart. She was so afraid of losing him. But if she continued to lie, she'd never have the true love she desperately wanted.

"I'll even line dance." He tipped his head toward the stage, where the band played the first notes of their opening song. "For you. Promise you'll sing me your song."

Darn. She really wanted to dance with him. It might be her one and only chance.

Two songs on the dance floor and then you sit him down and tell him. No more procrastinating.

"Fine." She sighed. "Line dancing for a song. You drive a hard bargain."

Eli leaned back on his chair wearing a cocky smile. He linked his hands behind his head, causing his biceps to flex. They stretched the short sleeves of his gray T-shirt.

Nothing like a gun show to send her heart racing. And what a magnificent set of muscles they were. Her breath grew shallow at the thought of his strength wrapped around her. Protecting her from the world.

The band finished their first song. "What's goin' on, Sterling, Wisconsin?" The lead singer, a tall cowboy wearing a beat-up Stetson, shouted out to the growing crowd. "We are Asleep in the Saddle and we're going to get this joint moving with some great music."

A cheer went up from the group gathered on the dance floor.

To her surprise, Jordan had heard of this band before. Phil had shown some interest in them and had asked her to listen to their recording. She remembered Phil liking their music but hating the band's name.

They began their next song, a decent cover of "Friends in Low Places" by Garth Brooks.

"How can you not like country?" Jordan shouted to Eli over the loud music.

His face was screwed up like he was in pain. "I wouldn't necessarily call this noise music."

"Oh, look. They've started the Cowboy Cha-Cha." She pointed to the assembly on the dance floor. She hadn't line danced in a long time. Real dancing. Not the gyrating they did in the techno clubs.

She watched as the dancers stood in a line in front of the stage, stepping and turning in formation. Swinging their hips to the beat. Hoots of laughter rang throughout the bar.

The lights around the dance floor had dimmed, and the area was now lit by strands of white twinkle lights hung across the ceiling and around the stage. The scene looked magical, and Jordan couldn't wait to join the fun.

"I changed my mind about line dancing." Eli crossed his arms over his chest. "There is no way I can keep up with that."

"Sure you can." She stood and went to pull Eli up on his feet. "Trust me. You'll have fun."

"I highly doubt it," he grumbled, but followed her anyway, dragging his feet all the way to the dance floor.

Jordan joined at the end of the line and Eli positioned himself next to her. She grabbed his hand to keep him from sneaking away.

"Watch and follow along. The Cowboy Cha-Cha is easy to pick up." She stepped forward with her left foot and rocked, cha-cha-cha, then stepped back with her right, cha-cha-cha. Turning around, she rocked back, cha-cha-cha.

She pointed to his feet, which had not moved. "Come on, Eli. Imitate what I do. See, step forward and rock. Step back and rock. Turn and rock. Turn again to face the front."

After a few cycles, Eli picked up the basic moves. His hips moved like he'd worked as an exotic dancer.

Jordan lost her place in the dance more than once. Eli's body swaying next to her was way too distracting.

Once the song ended, he swung his arm around her waist and kissed her cheek.

The band began to play "Boot Scootin' Boogie," and someone decided the next dance should be the Electric Slide.

"I know this one." Eli grinned. "The Electric Slide and the Chicken Dance are required dances at every wedding reception in Wisconsin."

They stayed out on the dance floor through the next three songs. Finally, Jordan insisted they go back to their table to get a drink.

She pursed her lips. "How Eli got his groove back. The story of a farmer who discovered a hidden talent for shaking his booty." She took a long drink out of her cup of ice water. The cool, refreshing moisture soothed her parched throat. Dancing was hard work. And dancing with Eli—that was a fun way to burn off several hundred calories.

"I guess country music isn't so bad. Must be growing on me."

His wide grin left her with a desire to lean over the table and kiss him until they were both breathless. But first, she needed to say what she'd been rehearsing.

She ran over her speech one last time in her head—

My name is really Jordan Spencer. I'm a country music singer. A very famous singer.

The night I crashed into your ditch, I had just finished the last concert of my tour. My life was spinning out of control. I took a break to focus on finding myself again.

I understand you feel betrayed. I did mislead you, but only to protect my real identity. I needed a safe, quiet place to emotionally heal, and I couldn't do that being stalked by paparazzi.

Eli, I've fallen in love with both you and your children. I want more than anything to stay in your lives.

She raised her gaze to see Eli looking back at her. His smile had faded. "Where'd you go just now? Everything all right?"

Jordan slowly inhaled and concentrated on the feeling of her lungs expanding. She could do this. All she had to do was start with the first sentence.

Pursing her lips together, she fortified her nerves. But before she could speak, the band began playing a slow ballad.

"May I have this dance?" Eli extended his hand across the table.

She exhaled her held breath. "Yes. I would love to slow dance with you."

He took her hand and guided her onto the dance floor, and then into his arms. Jordan's body molded snugly against him. Her hands rested on his wide shoulders, and she felt the pack of hard muscles underneath the fabric of his shirt.

Maybe this was the right moment to tell him the truth. He was holding her close. She had his rapt attention. All she had to do was whisper what was in her heart.

***

Eli wrapped his arms around her waist, resting his hands on her lower back. He loved the feel of her body, which had filled out a little during her time at the farm. Everything about her was perfect, from her beautiful face to the swell of her hips, to her long, tan legs.

"People are watching us," she whispered in his ear.

They seemed to be the center of attention. Heads turned, and bodies shifted in their seats, in order for people to get a good look at them. He didn't care. Let them talk. The only thing Eli wanted to focus on was Ann. Right now, she was the center of his world.

"I have a confession to make," he said with nerves strumming in his chest.

"You do?" Ann peered up at him and her eyebrows arched. "So do I."

Eli bent over and touched his nose to hers. "I've fallen for you. Hard. You told me you're not ready for a relationship, and I respect that. But I will wait until you are. I need you in my life." He kissed one cheek, and then the other. "I need you."

Their bodies swayed in time to the beat of the music.

She leaned into his embrace. "I've fallen for you, too, Eli. I can't imagine saying goodbye tomorrow and never seeing you again."

"After the fall harvest is done, we'll get together. I'll take a trip to visit you. That is, if you tell me where you live." He felt Ann shiver in his embrace.

"Once you hear my confession, your feelings may change." Her head rested on his chest. "You may not want to see me again."

"I highly doubt it." Tightening his hold on her, Eli wanted to reassure her that he wasn't going anywhere. He knew the pain of being abandoned. He'd never do that to someone he cared about.

The song ended, replaced with one with a fast-paced melody.

"You mind if I use the ladies' room? Then, we need to sit down and have a talk."

He nodded, and she almost ran toward the back of the bar and disappeared into the women's restroom. Had he freaked her out by telling her how deep his feelings had become? Ann might be climbing out the bathroom window right now to avoid hurting him.

Eli walked over to the bar and get another drink. He ordered a beer on tap for himself and an Old Fashioned for Ann.

His fingers had just wrapped around the handle of the beer mug when a man entered the bar. The guy was tall. At least six and a half feet. And as wide as the front end of a tractor. There was a mean-looking scar running down one cheek from the outer corner of his eye to his jaw line. The lower portion of his face was covered in dark stubble. He reminded him of Rambo. No, he reminded him of the photo of the guy who'd called Ann's cell the night of their picnic. The mean-looking man with the same last name as Ann.

The guy strode over to the bar and waved over the gray-haired bartender. "Good evening. I'm looking for Eli Hintz. I heard he might be here."

Eli set down his drink and approached with wary caution. "I'm Eli. What do you need?"

The bartender stepped away but kept a side-eye view of the two men.

"I need to speak to your date." As he spoke, the muscles in the guy's wide neck bulged. His scowl grew. He glanced around the bar.

Luckily, Ann was still in the bathroom.

"What do you want with her?" Eli wouldn't be intimidated, or at least not show it. This meathead wasn't getting anywhere near Ann.

"My name," he said in a slow drawl, "is Cole Dufour. What I need to speak to her about is none of your business."

A red rage colored the air. This man was Ann's ex-husband. He glanced down at Cole's hand. Empty ring finger. The last thing Eli wanted to consider was that she was still married to the brute. But she'd told him she had a confession, and that it could change the way he felt about her.

"So, you're Cole." Eli took a step toward the man. "You're the person she's hiding from."

"Look." Cole leaned forward. "I'm not looking for trouble. I need to speak with your date."

"Leave now. I won't let you hurt her."

Cole's lips twitched with what appeared to be a smile. "Hurt her? Do you know who I am?"

"Yes, I do. Now leave before I call the sheriff."

"And what, ask them to arrest me for walking into a bar? If that was illegal, most of the residents of Wisconsin would be sitting in jail." Cole crossed his meaty arms. "Now go be a good boy and tell Jordan that Cole's here."

"Who's Jordan?"

Cole laughed. "Well, shoot. How was I supposed to know the little minx hadn't told you the truth yet?"

"The truth?" Eli took a long drink of beer for courage. "Let me show you the door." He put as much force into his words as he could muster. In reality, the thought of getting into a physical altercation with this muscle man made his stomach sick.

"You're kidding, right? You think you can make me leave?" He flexed his biceps, alternatively from left to right, to prove his point.

A point not missed on Eli. The bartender approached them. "Any trouble over here, gentlemen?"

"No." Eli didn't take his gaze off Cole. "We don't have what Mr. Dufour is looking for."

"Look, man," Cole growled, moving inside Eli's personal space. He grabbed Eli's arm and squeezed. "Go tell your girlfriend that Cole's here to see her. And hurry up. Okay?"

"I won't let you near her." Not backing down, Eli rolled his shoulders back and balled his fists. He was fast on his feet. He could take this guy.

"Don't do it, brother." Cole breathed out a long sigh and shook his head.

Eli cocked back his arm and swung. At the moment his fist connected with Cole's incredibly hard jawbone, he heard a woman's scream.

"Eli, stop," Ann shouted from somewhere in the distance.

But it was too late.

Chapter Twenty-Four

The scene was total bedlam. Jordan had rushed forward in hopes of stopping the first punch. Cole was used to taking a beating for her, but this time, he was fighting back. Why *now*? Why with *Eli*?

Jordan hovered at the edge of the fist fight, waiting for an opening to intercede. A crowd had gathered, most cheering Eli on. Some, mostly women, *oohed* and *ahhed* every time Cole swung his arm.

Enough of this juvenile behavior. "Cole, cut it out," she hollered. "Eli, stop." Both continued like she hadn't uttered a word.

Finally, Eli turned toward her and made eye contact. His lower lip was puffy and bleeding. During the momentary distraction, Cole swept Eli's legs out from underneath him and drove his body to the ground.

A few other men had decided to join in. Maybe in an attempt to help Eli. Or maybe using the fight as an excuse to punch and throw things. As a chair flew past her head, Jordan jumped back.

Oh, for crying out loud. This was a playground brawl.

Cole's lips were turned up in a grin. And Eli's clenched jaw did not disguise a hint of a smile. Both men's eyes gleamed. *The ingrates were actually enjoying this.*

While Cole struggled to put Eli in a headlock, he glanced up at Jordan. "The media knows you're here. They're going to be here any minute." He used his free hand to pull out a set of car keys. "These are for the silver Chevy parked out front. Go, before the paparazzi turns this place into a zoo."

"I'm pretty sure you've done that already." She ground her foot on Cole's outstretched hand.

He bellowed out a curse, but she didn't care. Then Cole yelled even louder, and higher, when Eli bent his leg backward and kicked Cole in between the legs.

"Ann, call the police," Eli managed to huff out once he got free from Cole's grasp.

"Just stop fighting. Cole is my friend." She saw something pass by her face in just enough time to duck. Good thing her fitness trainer had insisted she take boxing lessons.

She took a step back and bumped into the growing crowd. The band had stopped playing. Everyone's gaze was glued to the rumble at the end of the bar.

"How did they find out?" Jordan shouted above the noise. Between glass breaking, tables crashing, and the shouts of spectators, she could hardly hear herself think.

"Someone reported you were staying in Sterling, Wisconsin." Cole blocked an oncoming punch with the palm of his hand. "I tried calling you but kept getting voicemail. So, I drove up here, hoping to get to you before the media did."

Cole had started a fight for a distraction. The idea hit her like one of the punches being thrown.

In the chaos, Jordan had lost track of Eli. After a brief scan of the group of brawling men, she saw a flash of his face. She rushed to him, not caring for her own safety. "Eli, I need to leave... now." When she touched his arm, he stiffened. "Don't hit me, you fool. Stop fighting. Cole is here to help."

He swiped at the blood dripping off his chin. "Are you going with him?"

How could she explain? Before she could speak, Cole approached and took her by the arm. "Sweetcakes, get out of here. Don't let them find you."

Eli's gaze narrowed in on Jordan. "Isn't this the guy you've been hiding from?"

"I've called the police, you bunch of idiots," the bartender yelled at the crowd. "No one leaves until they arrive."

"I'm hiding from the paparazzi, Eli. If they find me here, in the middle of a bar fight, our pictures will be on every media Internet site by tomorrow morning." She took hold of his hand. "I'm sorry. I lied to you about who I am." Her words came out in a jumbled rush. "But, please, trust me that it's best I sneak out of here."

Eli's gaze traveled from Jordan to Cole and back to Jordan. "Who are you?"

The front door to the bar opened and a woman holding a camera stepped inside. She was dripping wet and visually swept the room.

Jordan ducked behind Cole, an ingrained reaction, and saw Eli's eyes flash with pain.

"Crawl over to the swinging door. It leads into the kitchen." Cole pointed toward the route. "Then head out the back door. Get in my car and drive. Call Lacy. There's a private plane at the Milwaukee airport for your flight home." He shifted closer to Eli, effectively blocking the photographer's view of both Jordan and the kitchen door.

"I'm not leaving like this." She needed time to tell Eli everything. When she glanced at him, her heart broke. This was not how she imagined their date would end.

The front door blew open again. This time, the new arrival was a uniformed sheriff's deputy. He sauntered over to the bartender, who in turn, pointed to Cole and Eli.

"Just go." Eli crossed his arms. He wouldn't even look at her.

"I need to explain."

His back faced her when he spoke. "I think the time for explanations has passed. Listen to your husband and sneak out."

"But Cole's not my husband."

Cole kicked behind him and struck her shin. A not-so-subtle hint.

"*Oww*. I'm going," she said. "But while you're in that jail cell with Eli, tell him the truth."

"Always covering your ass," Cole mumbled.

Jordan glanced at Eli one last time before crawling on all fours like the devil was on her tail. She grabbed her purse, which was still lying on their table.

The kitchen was empty. The staff must have all cleared out to watch the fight. Running toward the back door, she slipped on a puddle of water on the floor by the sink. Her legs shot out from under her and she landed hard on her rear.

Tears stung her eyes. As she stood, she rubbed her butt and hobbled to the door.

Outside, standing on the back steps in the pouring rain, Jordan debated if she should return to Eli.

But she imagined the fallout. The paparazzi would go crazy. They'd follow Eli to his farm, and then start harassing the rest of the family.

Leaving was the only way to protect them.

In the safety of Cole's car, she began to cry. Sobs racked her body. Why did fame have such a high cost? All she wanted to do was write music and sing.

Her breath came out in short, shallow bursts. Bright stars floated in front of her vision. She wanted—no, needed—to throw up. What she was experiencing was a classic Jordan anxiety attack. Her brain told her so. She commanded herself to take stock of her surroundings. A voice in her head, Lacy's voice, told her to quiet her breathing and relax, one muscle at a time.

Jordan struggled to regain control. After she noticed several cars stop in front of the bar and people holding cameras run inside, she realized it was time to go.

Turning the key to the ignition with one hand, she used the other to wipe away the tears filling her eyes. In the backseat sat her suitcases and guitar case. Cole must have stopped by the farm first, looking for her.

Remembering the hurt on Eli's face, she started crying again. He'd fought Cole in order to protect her. And this was how she repaid him.

Tonight should have been the start of something wonderful. Instead, Eli might end up in jail.

Jordan's hands shook as they rested on the steering wheel. How could she run away and leave the man she loved?

Her time with him had been a dream. A wonderful fantasy that had come crashing down under the weight of reality. This mess only served as a reminder that she did not get happy endings.

***

Old Lester Hofstetter, the owner and frequent bartender of Lester's Place, had known Eli a long time. So as Eli sat on a barstool, holding a package of frozen vegetables to his cheek, he wasn't too offended at the flurry of names the ancient guy called him. Eli did feel like an idiot, and a knucklehead—and sure, even a moron. Nothing Lester, or anyone else, said would make him feel worse than he already did.

Cole motioned for Lester to step aside. Lester wasn't directing any anger Cole's way since Eli had been the one to throw the first punch. Plus, Cole's biceps were the size of an Amazon python, which surely helped smooth over Lester's mood toward him.

Two waitresses moved around the bar, sweeping up broken glass. Eli had offered to help, but since he was the cause of the mess, he'd been told to sit down and stay out of the way.

Eli remained where he was, sulking, and watched Cole and Lester talk. After a few minutes, they shook hands, and Lester actually smiled.

"Eli, I won't be bringing up any charges against you, even though you deserve it. Deserve a good ass whipping, too, but I'm getting too old for that sort of thing." Lester waved to one of the ladies still working behind the bar. She promptly brought over a full bottle of beer. He took a sip and sighed. "Your new friend, Cole, made me a mighty fine offer. Instead of just fixing the damages, I'll be able to totally remodel the place."

Eli looked over at Cole and cocked one brow.

Cole just smiled in return and sat on the barstool next to him.

"You two boys play nice. I'm going home for the night. Haven't seen that much excitement around this place since Monty Yale punched Harv Brewer in 1975. Now that was a real fight. Everyone picked sides and got the whole joint brawling. See this scar?" He pointed to a white mark on his eyebrow. "Got it for trying to break it up."

Eli was sure the old guy would tell tonight's tale from now until he was lying on his deathbed.

Taking his beer, Lester walked to the back and disappeared into what looked like an office.

One of the waitresses set two tumblers on the bar in front of Eli and Cole. "Here, boys. Looks like you could use a drink."

Whiskey on ice. Eli took a long drink, burning the back of his throat. Warmth settled in his belly. He glanced over at Cole, who was finishing off his drink, too. "You work for her?" Eli couldn't say her name. Not her real name. The pain was still too raw.

"Jordan, you mean?" Cole nodded his head. He traced the rim of the tumbler with his finger. "I've been her bodyguard for five years. She has a team when she travels, but I'm the only one who's always around."

"Except for the past two weeks, when she was hiding out at my farm." Eli set his glass on the worn wood bar top, jingling the ice cubes inside.

"Don't judge her too hard, man. You don't know what it's like."

"I would if she'd told me the truth."

Cole turned his tall, wide body to face Eli. "Do an Internet search of her name—Jordan Spencer. It's great reading, trust me. The girl can't blow her nose without someone writing a story, speculating that she's snorting cocaine. Or if she's a little bloated, they write that she got knocked up."

Eli hunched his shoulders. His body hurt all over. Even his eyelids were sore. "You two seem very close. Why didn't you just take off with her?" Eli hadn't missed the way Ann, or Jordan, had gone to Cole for protection. He'd been jealous, still was. Cole was a muscular, good-looking guy. Not that he was a judge of male attractiveness.

"Listen, man." Cole slid his glass toward the waitress and winked. An unspoken request for a refill. "Jordan pays me to be her bodyguard, but I'm her friend for free. We've been through a lot together. I've seen her heart broken more times than you can imagine. I'm not the type of guy who can give her what she's looking for, and she has too much respect for our professional relationship to let hanky-panky get in the way."

"And what type of man is she looking for?" Eli ventured a guess. "Famous, handsome, and loaded?" He asked with sarcasm. *Everything I'm not.*

Cole winced as he opened and closed his bruised fist. "Jordan's dating history is full of drama. That's one of the reasons the media loves following her every move. For a while, it was fun to read what crazy stuff they'd write up. Jordan Spencer caught out at a Tokyo nightclub with the crown prince of Belgium. Did Jordan Spencer cause the breakup of another Hollywood marriage?" A dark shadow passed over his face. "But then things went from funny to hurtful. And the people she called her friends loved to spread gossip. What Jordan needs, what she's been searching for, is a man who really loves her."

Eli swallowed hard. He had thought he loved her. But Ann was a mirage. He'd fallen in love with a woman who didn't exist. Slowly standing, he placed his hands on the bar rail to steady himself. He cringed at the thought of trying to explain this to his kids.

"Since I'm not going to jail, I'll head out." He reached out to shake Cole's hand and tried not to flinch at the vise-like handshake.

"If you care about her, give her a chance to explain. Don't be a jerk like the rest of them." Turning to face the waitress who stood on the other side of the bar, Cole's frown morphed into a smile.

As Eli exited into the pouring rain, his emotions fought their own battle. Anger pounded his heart. Grief drenched him like the rain. His hurt pride begged him to push Ann, or Jordan, out of his mind forever. He wanted to hit something. He wanted someone to hit him. Hadn't he had enough of that in the bar with Cole?

Obviously, he needed more than a little bar fight to cleanse his system.

What he wanted to do and what he *needed* to do were two separate things. Eli needed to go home and explain to Lita and Elliot why their friend Ann was gone and most likely never coming back.

Ann Dufour was Jordan Spencer, multimillionaire and country music superstar. She was famous and well connected and wouldn't have time for a farm family in central Wisconsin. Hadn't she told him exactly that the night in the corn field?

While he'd been ready to put his heart on the line, she'd been working up the nerve to let him down gently.

He was such a *fool*. To think that after all this time, he'd thought he found a woman to share his life with.

He'd sworn after Nikki that he would devote himself to raising his children. They were the most important things in his life. Now, on the same day their mother left them, once again, he'd have to go home and add to their pain.

Chapter Twenty-Five

Jordan's hairstylist ran his fingers through her hair. "Tsk, tsk. Honey, I'm never letting you near a pair of scissors again. And this color. I will never recover from the fact you put box hair coloring on your head."

Nothing could have prepared Enrique for the sight of her self-cut, self-colored hair. The poor man had gone into hysterics.

While Enrique fussed with her hair, Jordan stared straight ahead into the lighted mirror. She was in a luxurious suite in Las Vegas, preparing for the award show tonight.

In six hours, she'd walk the red carpet. But her mind was thousands of miles away, on a dairy farm in Wisconsin.

Good thing she had Lacy, who kept her on track and on schedule.

"I have your dresses." Lacy entered the bedroom rolling a garment rack. She unzipped one of the bags. "The seamstress assured me the dress would fit perfectly." Removing the gown, she laid it on the bed and began her inspection. She checked over every bead and sequin, making sure they were sewn on tight.

"Makeup will be here at five," Lacy said. "Limo at seven. The venue is only two miles away, but I predict a backup at the red carpet drop-off, so plan on arriving around seven-thirty. By the time you get past all the media and reporters, you'll have just enough time to get to your seat before the show starts."

"I'm not giving any interviews." Jordan wanted her appearance to be drama free. They said pictures were worth a thousand words. And she was sure the photos taken of her tonight, looking healthy and happy, would do more to stop the speculation than any interview. Although, she'd have to fake the happiness part.

"You have to at least stop and talk to Missy Rowe from *Country Today*. I'm sorry but I already committed you."

Jordan sighed. "Wave a wand and make this all disappear. The pressure is too much."

"Hey." Enrique took a break from putting foil in her hair to wag a finger in her face. "Don't wish me away, honey. At least not until after I fix your hair."

She couldn't help but laugh. "My hair looked perfectly fine. Didn't it, Lacy?"

Lacy turned to face them. "Don't bring me into this."

"This was your idea." She waved her hands, accidentally hitting Enrique.

"Hands folded on your lap," he reprimanded.

Sitting down on the edge of the bed, Lacy smiled. "It did work pretty well. People didn't recognize you."

"Heidi did, and so did Nikki. Plus, someone called the media and let them know where I was."

"It was Nikki, and I don't know why you let her keep the audition." Lacy scowled.

"We don't know that for sure. Anyone at the fair on Sunday could have recognized me. I gave Nikki my word and I couldn't break it without proof."

"How did her band's audition go?" Lacy asked.

"Garrett called me yesterday, after they were done." Jordan was fairly sure Nikki was the one who'd told the media—and probably got a nice reward for the information. "He said they had a good sound. He liked Nikki's voice and said she had good pitch and was vocally strong. But there was nothing special about them. In order to be noticed in today's market, a band needs to bring something different."

"Serves her right to go home disappointed." Lacy stood, came over, and gave Jordan a kiss on the cheek. "I have some people to call. I'll be back once Enrique's done, and then you can try on both dresses, and we'll check for fit."

As her stylist continued to work, Jordan closed her eyes and summoned up the memory of Eli's face. She missed him so much. Missed Lita and Elliot, too. Since that fateful night in Sterling, she'd only talked with Eli one time. Their conversation had been short and to the point. Eli had made it clear that if he couldn't trust her, he didn't want her in his family's life.

Jordan's faint hopes had been crushed by Eli's final words. *"I don't want another person floating into my children's life whenever she can fit it into her schedule. Goodbye, Jordan."*

Tears burned her eyes at the memory.

Enrique patted her shoulders. "Girl, open your eyes and look at your fabulous self."

Jordan did as commanded, daring to peer at her reflection in the mirror. Her hair was still chin length—there was not enough time to fix that, but the cut was layered. Enrique had done an ombre color treatment, going from a caramel blonde up at the roots to a rich brown at the tips. "It's beautiful." She fingered her hair, enjoying the silky smoothness. "Whatever I'm paying you, it's not nearly enough."

"Oh, don't you worry. Lacy makes sure I'm paid what I'm worth." Enrique set the can of hairspray on the vanity. "You are going to knock 'em dead when you shimmy out of that limo."

Jordan's stomach churned thinking about tonight. First, she'd have to make it through the red-carpet gauntlet. Then sit and smile while her peers in the music industry presented and performed. Finally, she'd step onstage and sing, before presenting the Country Music Album of the Year award.

Yesterday, when she'd gone to the venue for rehearsals, she'd sprinted off stage halfway through her song and threw up her lunch in the bathroom trashcan. She didn't want to cope with the stress anymore. Not alone.

She now knew what real love felt like. Before Eli, she hadn't known what she was missing. Now, Jordan's heart was a hollow shell inside her aching chest.

"Eli, I need you."

When she pulled up his number, his picture popped up on her screen. Her heart burned for him. A simple farmer, living in Wisconsin. He put Hollywood men to shame.

Jordan touched the call button. As she listened to the first few rings, her heart lodged in her throat. Would he answer this time?

Nope. She soon heard his familiar voicemail message. For a few seconds, she felt his presence wash over her. A warm, soothing comfort.

"Hey, Eli. It's Jordan." She took a deep breath. "I'm in Vegas, getting ready for a show tonight. I wish you were here with me or I was with you on the farm. I miss you so much." Jordan sniffled. "I hope you keep playing the guitar. You're very talented. Music was the only thing that ever spoke to my soul, until I met you. Anyway, I promise not to call you again. I can take a hint. Please tell Lita and Elliot I say goodbye. It breaks my heart that I never had a chance before I left." She paused. "Goodbye, Eli."

Gathering her willpower, she ended the call. Jordan sank onto the king-sized bed, all alone, and cried.

***

Eli listened to her voicemail, and then fought the urge to listen again. He'd probably played it ten times already. Her silky Southern accent gave him chills, in the very best way.

But he couldn't forgive her for lying. She'd not only lied to him, but his kids. He wouldn't be in a relationship with a woman he couldn't trust. Protecting Lita and Elliot was more important than his own desires.

Eli had turned on the TV when Heidi and Lita charged into the family room. Heidi snatched the remote out of his hand and changed the channel.

"Hey, the game's starting." Eli made a grab for the remote but failed.

Heidi held it against her chest. "The Country Music Awards are starting soon. Look, they're showing the stars walking the red carpet."

"Then go over to your house and watch."

"I promised Lita that we'd watch together."

Lita plopped down on the sofa and smiled.

"Then you can both go over to Heidi's house and watch your awards show," Eli said. "If you forgot, this is my house and my TV, and I want to watch the baseball game."

"You need to watch with us." Lita raised the footrest on the reclining sofa. "It's important."

"I'm not sitting here and watching overpaid and under-talented celebrities give each other pats on the back." Eli stood to leave. Let them watch their show. He'd go out to the barn and check on the calves.

Suddenly, a flash of pink on the TV screen caught his attention. Around him, everything faded. His vision narrowed in on one woman. Eli slowly sank back down onto his chair. There, in the middle of his television screen, was Jordan.

She looked like royalty in a soft pink ball gown. Her hair was different, and the makeup she wore made her face glow. Her gorgeous eyes, the focal point of her features, were large and bewitching.

Eli let out a long breath at the sight of her. His body reacted with the force of a hurricane. He had the feeling Heidi and Lita were watching him, but he couldn't tear his gaze away from the most beautiful woman he'd ever seen. A woman he was still madly in love with.

As rows of cameras flashed, Jordan waved and smiled. She walked alone. No date. Or at least not one he could see.

A woman stepped toward Jordan, holding out a microphone. "Jordan Spencer. It's so good to see you."

"Hi, Missy. What a great night to honor country music." Jordan's smile was dazzling, but it didn't reach her eyes. She appeared stiff. Her face taut.

"Yes, and I'm looking forward to your performance tonight." Missy, the reporter, raised her microphone to Jordan.

"Well, let's hope I don't disappoint." Jordan laughed.

"You took a short break after your last concert tour. There was a lot of speculation about where you were. I'm happy to see you're happy and healthy. Midwestern farm life must have treated you well."

"Farm life is great. I've never felt so deeply satisfied." Jordan turned her gaze from Missy to the camera.

Eli held his breath. It seemed like she was looking right at him.

A smile softened her face. "I discovered a few things about myself. The biggest being that as much as I love singing and performing, there's more to life… like love and family. I've been in the music industry since I was fourteen years old. That's half of my life. It's time to start reevaluating my priorities."

"Are you hinting at retirement?" Missy gasped.

"Oh, no. I actually wrote a lot during my hiatus. I'm starting on a new album soon. What I'm talking about is finding balance in my life."

After a few more pleasantries, Jordan waved and walked off camera.

"Doesn't she look beautiful, Dad?" Lita asked, with a wistful expression. "Just like Cinderella."

"Yeah." He could barely manage one word.

"You okay, Eli? Your face looks a little flushed." Heidi's smirk grew. "Jordan's performing a little later. Still want to turn the channel back to the game?"

"No." His pulse pounded like a kick drum behind his ears.

Lita giggled. "I wonder what she'll wear when she sings. Hopefully something sexy."

"What?" Eli whipped his head to look at his little girl. "You're too young to know anything about that." His face grew warm at the memory of Jordan's sexy legs.

Rolling her eyes, Lita turned back to the TV.

The show started. Country music stars, comedians, and other celebrities took turns handing out awards and performing. It was the most boring thing Eli had ever seen, and that included sitting through a nineteen-inning baseball game last year.

The only thing that held his attention were glimpses of Jordan. She was sitting in the front row, between two other women, which meant she did not have a date.

He couldn't get over how different she looked, but yet, he still saw the woman he'd laughed with, talked to, and kissed. Who was she really? Jordan, dressed in thousands of dollars of clothing and jewelry, with hair and makeup done to perfection? Or Ann, a woman who seemed happy wearing cut-off shorts and a T-shirt while bottle-feeding a calf?

Could she be both? Was she everything he needed?

He must have been daydreaming when a sharp elbow jabbed him in the ribs.

"Dad, look. She's getting ready to sing." Lita scooted off the sofa and knelt down in front of the TV.

"Move a little to the left," Eli said. He'd endured the entire show for this moment.

Elliot had appeared at some point. He sat on the floor next to Lita, looking at the TV with wide eyes.

Jordan stepped out onto the stage wearing a short, black dress. The shoes she wore made her legs look a mile long. *Wow.* And to think, he'd kissed those red lips. And he'd kissed the bejeweled hand that now held a microphone. The hand of a queen. How could he ever be worthy of her?

An uncharacteristic hush fell over Eli's living room.

On stage, Jordan tapped her foot to the first few bars of melody. Then, she opened her mouth to sing.

Eli felt like he'd been hit by a cattle prod. The hairs on the back of his neck and arms rose, causing him to shiver. He recognized her singing voice from the times he'd heard her, but this time, she didn't hold back. Her voice was strong and pure, hitting every note with confidence. She had a wide range, and didn't strain to reach any of the high or low notes, but belted them out with ease.

He wasn't just impressed with the quality of her singing. Her stage presence was mesmerizing. She made him feel like she was singing only for him.

Was she thinking about him right now, while singing lyrics about a broken heart? What were the chances, when she was surrounded by all that glitz and glamour?

When she finished with an impossibly high note, the audience in the theater, along with his family at home, broke into applause. Jordan's smile was stunning. Center stage was where she belonged. She was clearly in her element.

A man came out to join her and he handed her an envelope. Jealousy surged in Eli's veins. He was probably a fellow country music star, and a decent-looking one at that. Eli wondered if Jordan had ever dated him. From what he'd read online about her, she had dated a lot of famous men.

Jordan opened the envelope and announced the winner of Album of the Year. She stepped back to allow the winners to have their moment to shine. But Eli couldn't take his gaze off Jordan, even as she tried to hide in the back.

Before he knew it, the show was done, and Heidi turned off the TV.

"How about you give her a call, Eli."

"Yeah. Call her, Dad. Tell her we watched her tonight." Lita jumped up and came over to sit on his lap. "Please."

"And tell her Bridgette is going to have her baby soon," Elliot said. "Jordan loved snuggling with the newborn calves."

Eli tried to block them all out. Why couldn't the rest of his family be more like Sam instead of a bunch of busybodies? The night after the bar fight, Sam had taken him out for a beer. After one comment from Sam about both of them being better off without women, the brothers had talked sports the rest of the time.

"We've had this discussion before. Jordan's not a part of our lives anymore." Eli wrapped his arms around Lita.

She, in turn, pushed off of his chest. "Give me a break. You're just being a big, ole chicken."

Elliot started making clucking sounds.

"That's enough," Eli said, starting to get flustered. "Time for bed."

After some moaning and complaining, Lita and Elliot went upstairs.

Heidi gave Eli a kiss on the cheek. "You fell in love with her not because of her famous name or her money. You love her for the woman she is. Don't turn your back on her."

Heidi went home, which left Eli sitting alone, wondering if they were right. Was he staying away from Jordan to protect his family, or was he just plain scared?

Chapter Twenty-Six

"Let's go over the song order one last time." Lacy sat at the island in Jordan's huge kitchen, swiping her finger across the screen of her tablet. "Are you sure you want to include so many of your new songs?"

"Definitely. This concert is a fresh start." Jordan's plans had taken shape. Through Cole's research, she'd located the estate manager for the Turner mansion and paid cash for the property. He'd also located a cousin of Willy Turner named Beatrice, who resided in Georgia. Last week, Jordan traveled to her home to pick up some old family photographs that featured the Wisconsin Turner mansion, wanting to use them as reference for her remodel.

Over sweet tea and cake, Jordan had been shocked to learn Rosemary's disappearance had been staged by Mr. and Mrs. Turner. They'd arranged for one of the maids to travel with Rosemary to a psychiatric hospital in New York. Due to the stigma of mental illness at the time, her hospitalization and treatment were kept secret. Six months after Rosemary left for New York, the rest of her family followed.

Cousin Beatrice, a beautiful, silver-haired woman in her eighties, told stories of family gatherings held in Georgia, which Rosemary attended. She remembered Rosemary as a bright young woman who'd eventually married and moved out of the country. From what Jordan learned, the girl who'd disappeared so many years ago had found a good, safe life.

A goal Jordan shared. Soon, she'd begin the remodeling project that would bring her back to Eli, Lita, Elliot, and Heidi. She'd take back her life, one piece at a time, and find balance in pursuing dreams that didn't revolve around her music career.

During her time in Wisconsin she'd found her voice again. Not only in writing songs, but in standing up for herself. Jordan was taking control of her career again. She would record the songs she wanted. Her tours would be scaled down, losing the fancy theatrics. People paid money to hear and see her sing, and that's what she planned on giving them.

Jordan filled up her glass with ice then pressed the button for water. The loud boom of the back door opening made her jump and she almost lost her grip on her full glass of ice water. "Cole. What the heck."

He filled the doorway with his massive body, his arms splayed out and sweat dripping down his face. The man looked absolutely disgusting. "Who wants to volunteer and give me a hug."

"Stay away from me," Jordan shouted as he started to walk her way. "I just took a shower and I won't appreciate being covered in your stinky sweat."

"Oh, come on. I just finished a killer workout. Where's the love?" He smiled and turned to Lacy. "Come give daddy some sugar."

She giggled. Lacy, her always-business sister, actually giggled.

Then, she jumped off her stool and backed away. "No, Cole Dufour. Don't you come anywhere near me." Lacy bolted around the kitchen island.

Like a slab of marble would protect her from Cole. Jordan knew her bodyguard pretty well, and when he wanted something, nothing stood in his way. And today, it seemed the sweaty beast wanted Lacy.

Cole moved too fast. He swept Lacy up in his arms, while she let out a mix of giggles and screams.

Jordan just stood there. At some point, she managed to pick her jaw up off the floor. When would these two drop the act and just admit that they were crazy for each other?

She cleared her throat. "Excuse me. Hate to break up the fun, but Lacy and I have things to do. Important things."

"You still doing the concert in Milwaukee?" Cole leaned with his elbow on the countertop.

He wasn't the least bit out of breath. Lacy, on the other hand, was breathing so hard, Jordan feared she'd pass out.

"Yes. In two weeks. Lacy will e-mail you an itinerary once the schedule's set." Jordan put on her best game face. She didn't want to answer the question she knew was coming next.

"Eli going to be there?" Cole smirked, and then winked at Lacy.

Jordan turned her gaze to her bare feet so neither could see the pain and uncertainty in her eyes. "I'm not sure."

She thought of Eli, and how he fit into her plan. Every change she made in her life she did for herself. But her love for Eli served as her motivation. He'd helped her see her own value—and that was a gift money could not buy.

"But you're going to invite him, right? That's the plan?" Cole sat on a barstool opposite her.

The plan had sounded good at the time. Now, Jordan was having doubts. "He'll probably not come."

After the last voicemail she'd left for him, she'd stopped reaching out to Eli. How could she convince him to give her another chance when he wouldn't answer her calls? At least he hadn't talked to the media. That was a first for an ex. But Eli wasn't really an ex-boyfriend, was he?

No. He was so much more.

"We will get Eli to that concert, even if Cole and I have to go up to Wisconsin and drag him there." Lacy patted Jordan on the back.

"Sounds like fun," Cole said. "I still owe the guy for my bruised jaw."

"Didn't you see what you did to his face?" Jordan glared at Cole with narrow eyes. "You stay away from him."

"I have to admit, that fight really wasn't my best work." Crossing his muscular arms over his chest, Cole tipped his chin toward Lacy. "Next time I step into the ring, I'll bring you two along. Then you can see how it's really done."

Lacy's dreamy smile earned her an elbow in the ribs from Jordan.

"We are not attending a cage match," Jordan said. "I have a reputation to protect."

"Ah, come on Jordan," Lacy said. "It might be fun. Plus, I remember you telling me that you weren't making choices based on what other people thought of you."

Who was this woman and what had she done with her sister? "First." Jordan ticked off one finger. "Seeing two grown men beat each other to a pulp is not fun. Second, going to a cage match is not a life choice."

As Cole made his way back outside, his deep laughter echoed through the kitchen. After a quick glance at Cole's retreating form, Lacy picked up her tablet and walked into the family room.

Jordan sighed and shook her head at just how ridiculous this infatuation was making her sister. *Hopeless.*

Left alone, she glanced around the kitchen and, not for the first time since coming back from the farm, noticed its lack of character. Even the outdated one in Eli's farmhouse was more appealing than her own. But what her home lacked couldn't be bought or designed.

Jordan imagined Lita and Elliot sitting at the counter, working on homework while she and Eli cooked dinner together, standing in front of the eight-burner stove top. A dream that constantly filled her mind.

A knock on the back door brought her back to reality. She looked up to see Phil enter the kitchen. The sight of his familiar lined face and silver hair lifted her spirits.

"Hey, there." Phil gave her a hug. "Wanted to swing by and talk to you before I left town for vacation."

Jordan pointed to the kitchen table, and they both sat. "You want to stay for dinner? I'm making stuffed shells and marinara sauce. I found a recipe online that looked easy enough."

"Thanks, but as anxious as I am to sample your new cooking skills, Doreen and I need to catch a flight." Phil didn't hide the fact he was studying her. "How are you doing? You have this air of calm that I've never seen before. And I like that pretty smile on your face."

"It's nice to be happy… mostly happy." She shifted in her seat. A beam of sunlight shone through the window and warmed one side of her face. "I feel like I'm doing the right thing with regaining control of my career. I'm excited again."

"That's good. I've told you all along that you are in the driver's seat. We worked together to build you up to where you are today. These last few years I've notice a change in you, and your anxiety had me concerned. I care about you, kid."

"I know." And she did.

"I wanted you to be the first to know—I'm retiring." He paused. "Doreen and I have talked long and hard, and I think it's the right time. You've made a positive transition in your career. I have the utmost confidence in you."

"I didn't think you'd ever retire." Jordan was surprised, but the news didn't totally take her off guard. Phil had just celebrated his sixtieth birthday. He'd reached an age where people wanted to relax and enjoy life. "I'm happy for you and Doreen. You deserve it."

Phil blushed. "I didn't deserve *you*. I was simply a lucky fool who had enough sense to recognize a diamond when he saw one."

"I owe you a debt I can never repay." Jordan reached across the table to take his hand.

"You have repaid me, a thousand times over. I love you, Jordan. I want to see you settled down with a good man. A baby in your arms. Happy."

"Someday," she whispered.

"I know you too well. You still love that farmer in Wisconsin. So why are you sitting around here moping? Go after him." Phil slapped his palm on the table.

Jordan winced. "If I were an ordinary girl, then maybe. But I can't ask someone to take on the challenges of my life, not if they don't want to. Or don't want me."

As Phil stood, the legs of the kitchen chair scraped against the tile. He came over and gave her a kiss on the cheek. "Sounds to me like what you need is an extraordinary love."

***

All Eli needed was a few minutes of peace and quiet to think. But, from the escalating volume of the voices surrounding him, he didn't think he'd be getting it anytime soon.

"I got a new dress and shoes." Lita punctuated her statement with a stamp of her bare foot. "You're ruining my life."

"The fact that you got a new dress to attend a concert I never said you could go to is not my fault." Eli stood in the center of the family room, surrounded by angry faces—with the exception of Sam, who just looked perturbed.

"Then why did I come all the way up here?" Sam asked from his perch on the arm of the sofa. He turned his gaze to Heidi, who stood on the opposite side of the room. "You told me Eli needed my help so he could go to Jordan's concert in Milwaukee."

"I didn't anticipate he'd be this stubborn." Heidi glared at Eli through narrowed eyes.

"We're talking about Eli here," Sam said. "He was a week late because he was too stubborn to be born."

Now they were just playing dirty. "I'm not being stubborn. I never said we were going to begin with." Eli stared at Heidi, who'd instigated this whole mess.

As Heidi, Lita, Elliot, and Sam all began to talk over one another, the noise level rose once again. Lita had tears shining in her eyes. Elliot's usually solemn face had turned a vivid shade of red. Attending Jordan's concert tonight meant a lot to them. So why couldn't he make himself say yes?

His unresolved feelings for the star of the concert, for one. How could he see her again, not knowing if his heart was ready? And then there was the fact that a real relationship between them would be impossible to manage. With Eli tied to the farm and Jordan busy in Nashville and traveling around the world, how would they spend enough time together for the sparks to grow into a fire that would last forever?

"I'll never forgive you if you don't let us go," Lita shouted. "Jordan wants to see us. She talked with Aunt Heidi for a long time to make sure we could all come. And you're going to ruin everything." She spun on her feet and ran out of the room. The sounds of footsteps pounding up the stairs were followed by the slamming of her bedroom door.

Eli sank into his leather recliner and put his head in his hands. Even in the face of all this anger, he couldn't say yes.

"Why don't you stay home, Dad? Let Lita and me go with Aunt Heidi." Elliot rested a hand on Eli's shoulder.

"I'll go with them," Sam said. "When we were together at the fair, I felt a connection. Maybe we can have some private time backstage after the show."

"Sam," Eli barked out. "Don't push me right now."

Sam laughed. "But it's so much fun. If anyone needs me, I'll be in the machine shed to see if I can get that combine working." He left the room with Elliot in tow.

If there was one thing Elliot loved as much as animals, it was fixing things.

"Why did you put me in this position?" Eli asked Heidi, who was now the only other person left in the room. "How am I going to say no without them hating me for the rest of their lives?"

"Easy. You say yes." Heidi sat on the chair next to him. "Eli, I helped plan this because I love you and I want to see you smile again."

Eli grunted. "So far, your plan is not working. Do you see a smile on this face?" He pointed to his mouth, which was turned down in a frown.

"What's holding you back?" Heidi asked.

"From smiling?"

She snorted. "No, from seeing Jordan again?"

Eli wasn't much of a talker to begin with. And chatting about his broken heart with his kid sister wasn't something he'd ever considered doing in the past. But now, he needed to get the heavy weight off his chest. "I can't see her again. Jordan Spencer is not Ann. She and I live in two different worlds."

"Jordan *is* Ann. You are one of the few people who saw the real person inside the celebrity shell. The only reason she worked through me to arrange tonight is because you wouldn't call her back."

"It would never work between us," Eli said with finality. "I can't see her again. I don't want the kids thinking Jordan will stay a part of their lives. It's not realistic."

"Why not?"

"Because I don't know her. Not really. I fell in love with Ann. I don't know who Jordan is."

"They are the same person." Her voice held an edge of temper. "Give her a chance to show you." Heidi stood and walked over to the window. She put her hand on the window frame and looked outside.

Eli came to stand by her side. He took in the view—acres of corn fields, a large red barn, four tall silos, and a handful of heifers grazing in their enclosure. "This is my life. It's the kids' life. You understand better than most the time and energy it takes to run this farm. I don't have the luxury to date a woman like Jordan. I don't have the luxury to date, period."

Turning her gaze to Eli, Heidi's eyes burned bright. "Then sell it. Don't make the same mistake twice. Don't pick your duty to the family farm over what's best for you. Mom and Dad would have wanted you to follow your heart. They always did."

The image of his parents brought a tear to his eye. He missed them so much.

"Is the farm where your heart is?" Heidi pressed.

"None of that matters. I have a duty—"

"The only duty you have is to yourself and your children." She reached out to take his hand. "Sam and I have talked, and you have our blessing to sell, if that's what you want."

Eli couldn't speak. He was too stunned. Heidi, the one who loved the family farm the most, was giving him permission to sell it off.

"Just think about it," Heidi said. "And think about tonight. The limo will be here at five. We'll eat dinner before the concert. Jordan is a special woman. Don't let this opportunity pass you by."

***

Jordan stood on the side of the stage, secretly watching the people enter the theater before taking their seats. Tonight's concert was considerably smaller than her usual productions. She'd wanted it that way. Back when she'd planned tonight, she thought a more personal venue would serve as a catalyst to reconnect with Eli.

Now, all she wanted was to make it through the show without breaking down.

Heidi had texted an hour ago, saying Eli was not coming. He'd given his permission for her to bring Lita and Elliot along, but he was staying behind.

Her heart had sunk when she'd read the text. With his decision, he'd made his feelings about her clear. He was no longer fearful of her hurting his children, but Eli had closed his own heart.

When the time came to start the concert, Jordan shook off all the negative energy surrounding her. She was a performer, after all, and she would not disappoint her fans, no matter how broken she was on the inside.

Without an introduction or fanfare, she walked onto the stage. The small crowd clapped. A few whistled. One person yelled out how much they loved Jordan.

Each step brought her closer to the front of the stage and closer to the seats of her special guests. Next to Heidi sat an empty chair. The one meant for Eli.

Lita and Elliot waved up at her, and Jordan's smile to them was genuine. She'd missed those kids so much. Thankfully, Eli didn't have the heart to ban them from her life. Even he knew how deeply she cared for his children.

Jordan sang every song in the opening set with as much passion as she could muster. When it came time for Eli's song, her chest compressed with emotion. After she'd found out Eli wasn't coming, she'd instructed her band to skip it. No use making tonight harder than it already was.

As soon as the concert ended, Jordan left the stage visibly shaking. Not two minutes later, Elliot and Lita came running up to her. They both threw their arms around her waist.

"I've missed you so much," Lita said with a sniffle. "Aunt Heidi can't braid my hair like you can."

Heidi, standing behind them, grinned. "You could always ask your dad to do your hair."

Jordan laughed and gave each kid a kiss on the head. Surrounded by Eli's family, she missed him even more. "How about we move to my dressing room? We'll be more comfortable in there."

Elliot took hold of her hand. "Are we still going to have a party at your hotel? I left my suitcase in the long car that drove us here."

"It's called a limo." Lita rolled her eyes. "Do we get to ride in it again on the way home?"

No one could roll their eyes like Lita.

"You bet. And I have a huge hotel suite booked for the night. As soon as I've changed and finished up here, we'll head over."

Lita and Elliot ran up ahead to the room with Jordan's name posted on the door. Linking arms, Jordan walked slowly next to Heidi.

"I'm sorry about Eli," Heidi said. "I tried."

"You're not allowed to apologize. This entire situation is my own fault. I should have been truthful to him from the start."

Heidi halted and turned to face her. "Don't give up on him. Okay? I hate to say this, but I think the whole concert thing scared him off. What he needs to get through his thick head is that you are the same person he got to know on the farm." Pointing to Jordan's dress, she smiled. "You look amazing tonight, but my brother's heart is stuck on a girl who wears cut-off jean shorts and sandals."

Of course. How could she have been so mistaken? Jordan was so used to people going gaga over her singer persona, she'd forgotten her relationship to Eli was different. She'd never even considered he might be intimidated by her in this environment.

"So, now what?" she asked Heidi.

"Now, we go to your big hotel suite and order pizza. Then eat and talk until we can't keep our eyes open. I can't tell you how excited Lita and Elliot are about this whole thing."

Through the open doorway, she saw Lita searching through her rack of dresses. Finding one she must have liked, Lita lifted the hanger and held the dress up to her body. Then she did a little twirl in front of the full-length mirror.

"This is my final concert for a while. I'm taking a year hiatus. The Turner mansion project will be my main focus during that time. I plan on being up in your neck of the woods a lot." Jordan stepped into her dressing room with Heidi following. After a long talk with Phil and Lacy, she'd made the decision to put all her energy into her new project. She wanted to personally oversee the remodel, every step of the way. The house deserved her full attention.

She also needed to find the right staff to run the business once the remodel was complete. After long meetings with her architects, the plans to transform the house into an eight-room bed and breakfast were coming to life. Along with lodging, they planned to create a space large enough to host events. Her dream of watching a wedding held on the grounds would one day come true.

Heidi went over to Elliot who was spinning in Jordan's makeup chair and put a stilling hand on his shoulder. "I'm happy you'll be close by. And I'm happy you found a project that speaks to your heart."

After sliding on a pair of Jordan's high-heeled shoes, Lita wobbled over to stand beside her. She hooked one around Jordan's waist.

Tears welled up in Jordan's eyes as she peered over Lita's head at Heidi. "So am I."

Chapter Twenty-Seven

Two weeks had passed since Jordan's concert, and every night Eli had to listen to a recap as they sat around the dinner table.

And tonight was not different.

"We each got a huge bed all to ourselves," Elliot said in between bites of fish. "And Jordan didn't even yell at Lita and me when we jumped on the beds."

"She caught us and didn't yell at us at all," Lita said, looking lost in a fond memory. "And then she got up on the bed and started jumping with us."

"I whacked her good with a pillow. But don't worry, Dad, she got me back."

Heidi just looked at him from across the table, an amused smile on her face. Since the concert, his sister had been strangely mute on the subject of Jordan. Which had him worried. He knew from experience Heidi didn't give up that easily.

"How about you finish your dinner before the sun goes down," Eli said to his kids. "I'd like both of you to check the feed supply for the chickens and clean out their water dishes yet tonight."

"Okay." Lita began to hum.

He recognized the melody as one of Jordan's songs. Missing her was hard enough, but the constant reminders stabbed his heart. Caution had left him emotionally battered and bruised, the exact opposite of his goal.

Once the kids had finished eating, they ran outside to the chicken coop. Heidi stayed behind to help him clean up.

"Jordan is visiting the Turner mansion this weekend." Heidi rested her hip against the counter. "She's meeting with the architectural team and the general contractor. She wanted to know if it was all right if I brought Lita and Elliot over on Saturday."

Jordan's renovation project was taking place only a few miles from his house. Either he was being presented with a great opportunity or another chance to pile on the heartache. "Did she ask about me?" The question was a gamble. Did he really want to know the answer?

"Your name only came up because she wanted your permission to see the kids." She tilted her head. "Otherwise, we don't talk about you."

That was a surprise. "Why not?"

"Ha. Do you think we have nothing else to talk about besides how devastatingly handsome you are?" She lifted the faucet handle and began rinsing off their dinner plates.

His face heated. "That's not what I meant."

"I know." Heidi's dimpled smile was filled with teasing. "But honestly, she's not going to chase after you. If you want her, you'll have to make a move."

"Oh." He slumped into a chair.

Drying her hands on a towel, Heidi walked toward him. She laid a folded piece of paper on the table, patted him on the back, and returned to the sink. "I found this in the hotel room we stayed in with Jordan. It might have been wrong of me to take it, but I thought you could use some inspiration."

Once he heard the screen door close, he knew he was alone. With gentle hands, he opened the note. The inside was filled with Jordan's script, along with handwritten musical notations. After studying the melody she'd laid out, he recognized it was the song she'd played that evening on the porch. The one he'd helped her with.

He read the lyrics, and his heart shuttered to a stop. No wonder she hadn't wanted to share them. Not with him. Reading them over again, he felt his chest expand and come back to life. Her words exactly mirrored his own feelings.

As he jumped up, his chair fell over with a bang. How would he make things right with her? Maybe his kids, who loved Jordan with abandon, would guide him in the right direction.

While on his way over to the chicken coop, he noticed Elliot sprinting into the barn. Eli followed him inside, ready to reprimand him for neglecting his chores. But when he found his son curled up in the straw next to a newly born calf, his displeasure was replaced with overwhelming tenderness.

Eli opened the door to the pen, went inside, and took a seat beside Elliot. He ran his hand over the smooth, ivory coat of the calf. "Why aren't you helping Lita?"

"She said she didn't mind doing it herself because I wanted to check on Buttons." Elliot stroked the calf's head. "Dad, why don't you like Jordan anymore?"

"It's not that I don't like her." Eli sighed. How to explain the affairs of the heart to a nine-year-old boy?

"Then why don't you want to see her?" His wide, golden eyes peered up in question.

"I guess that I'm afraid of us becoming too attached to Jordan. Her job as a singer keeps her very busy, just like your mom."

"Jordan's not like Mom. Whenever I want to show Jordan something, she stops what she's doing to come. She listens to me, even when I talk about disgusting stuff, like how cows have four stomachs, and cleaning manure off of your boots."

The differences were as clear a contrast as night to day. Where Nikki couldn't be bothered with Lita and Elliot, even during the few times she was with them, Jordan's focus had always been first and foremost on them. She made them feel important.

Eli remembered the dinner when she'd listened to Elliot with rapt attention when he'd explained the life cycle of flies. And she'd chatted with Lita about clothes, makeup, and hair. Stuff he'd thought was silly girl talk. But now, looking at it through the eyes of his children, he understood how meaningful those moments were.

He'd assumed that because Jordan had a career in the music industry, she'd be as shallow and self-centered as Nikki. But hadn't she proven him wrong, time after time?

"I wish I would have gone with you guys to her concert. I sure missed out on a lot of fun."

Elliot's curly head of hair bounced as he nodded. "Yeah, but don't worry. She'll have plenty more."

He surrendered to the truth. Lita and Elliot, and Heidi all trusted Jordan. They loved her, not because she was a rich celebrity, but because she was a wonderful person.

Wasn't it time to drop the stubborn act and put his own heart on the line?

Elliot threw his arms around Eli's neck. "I love you, Dad."

"Love you, too, buddy."

***

Eli couldn't stop his nervous jitters. "Are you coming?" he yelled at Heidi, who was in her bedroom changing her outfit for the tenth time.

"Stop pressuring me, Eli. I can't make a decision with you barking at me every few minutes."

He wanted to pull out his hair.

Heidi finally appeared out of her bedroom, wearing the dress she'd started with. "This whole thing could have been avoided if you would have come to Jordan's concert with us."

Yeah, he already knew that. No need to keep pounding the fact that he was a stubborn fool over his head like a baseball bat. "All you're going to do is get her outside. I don't know why you felt the need to get all dressed up."

"Obviously, you know nothing about women." She grabbed her purse and headed out the door. "Are you coming?"

Grumbling, he followed his sister outside. To be fair, this whole thing was his plan. Heidi was only doing her part, as any meddling sister would do.

Fifteen minutes later, she drove off with Lita and Elliot. They were headed over to meet Jordan at the Turner mansion. He, on the other hand, was sneaking over while Jordan was kept distracted. While he climbed onto the ATV, he prayed she hadn't already hardened her heart to him.

When he arrived, he parked behind a large out building, grabbed his guitar from the back, and strode around to the front yard. His chest grew tighter with every step.

He sucked in a deep breath, and then let it out again. His heart pounded in his chest, louder with each passing second. Finally, after an excruciating wait, the front door cracked open.

Jordan stepped onto the porch, and his spinning world shuddered to a stop. She looked so beautiful. Why in the world did he think he was worthy of her love?

He waved her forward with a shaking hand. *Now or never, man. Don't screw this up.*

***

After a tour of the Turner mansion with Heidi and her architect, Jordan's mind spun with ideas, spurred on by the unlimited potential the house offered. So, when Heidi told her to go outside, she never expected to see Eli standing beside the sweeping branches of a weeping willow. What was he doing here? He was holding a guitar, and staring at her with so much heat, she thought she might melt into a puddle before she reached him.

What a good-looking man, dressed in nice jeans that hugged the lower half of his body. *Was he wearing a Jordan Spencer concert T-shirt?* He was. That made her laugh.

She turned around to see the front door was now closed. Heidi, Lita, and Elliot were nowhere to be found. It was just Eli and Jordan. They must have had this all planned. Interesting.

"Hey," Eli said as she approached. "Have a seat." He pointed to a white chair about five feet to his left.

Jordan did as she was instructed. "I didn't know there was a concert scheduled for today." She glanced around. "Not a very big turnout."

He smirked. "Good, because you're the only audience I want." Clearing his throat, he lifted his guitar. "I fell in love with Ann Dufour. Since I found out who you really are, I've struggled with putting those two people together."

She straightened in her chair. "You have every right to be upset with me. I lied to you."

"Hush. It's my turn to talk."

"Bossy man." Jordan pulled an imaginary zipper across her lips. In return, his sexy smile nearly made her faint.

"I've come to think of you as Jordan Ann. And I'd like the opportunity to get to know the whole you. Every single thing that's a part of you." He strummed a chord on the guitar. "I hope to be worthy of that right."

Jordan went to stand, but Eli motioned for her to sit back down. "I'm not finished yet." His calloused hands moved across the strings of the guitar, playing a melody she was very familiar with—"Eli's Song." Then, he started to sing.

How did he have the lyrics?

Heidi.

Imagining his hands strumming over her body, she closed her eyes and listened to the sound of his amazing voice.

"Love is a funny thing
Always moving with stops and starts
From the moment I met you
I knew you'd steal my heart
Those gray eyes melted my defenses
Your gentle hands knew just where to touch
I have no choice but to follow this through
Nothing's sweeter than loving you

An ordinary boy meets a not-so ordinary girl
Their dreams spin together in a web of gold
They talk, they laugh, they wish on above
But when the fire burns too hot, leaving only ashes to hold
The only thing that'll see us through, baby, is our extraordinary
love

You are my heart and soul
You are the one I've waited for
When I was lost you found me
You saved me from the dark
With every touch you brightened my world
A heat I want more and more
I had no choice but to start a war
My life is nothing without you

An ordinary boy meets a not-so ordinary girl
Their dreams spin together in a web of gold
They talk, they laugh, they wish on above
But when the fire burns too hot, leaving only ashes to hold
The only thing that'll see us through, baby, is our extraordinary
love."

Eli wiped tears from his eyes as he set down his guitar. "Hope you don't mind that I tweaked the lyrics. I love you, Jordan Ann. I can't spend another day without you."

"Can I talk now?" Her voice was choked with her own tears.

He nodded before kneeling before her. Grasping his large hands, she gazed into his eyes. Water droplets tipped his long eyelashes.

"You, Lita, and Elliot are more important to me than anything in the world." She brushed her fingers through his wavy hair. "I love you all. Our song has just begun."

Eli stood and pulled her up with him. He held her close, kissing one cheek, and then the other. Finally, he let his lips linger over her ear. "Welcome home."

Chapter Twenty-Eight

Nine months later

Jordan opened the door to the double-wide mobile home she'd lived in for the past eight months. Fresh, cool air blew across her face. She'd never get tired of seeing the Turner mansion each morning. Living on site had been a wise choice. One that had been entirely her own.

After a month of media flurry, they had moved on to more juicy stories. Jordan's quiet life now was not headline worthy.

Heidi had offered to let Jordan live at her place, but she'd politely declined. She liked her little trailer, which was a huge departure from her sprawling house outside of Nashville. Through this experience, she'd discovered the things she didn't need in her life.

And the things she couldn't live without.

One of those things was walking toward her at that moment.

Eli bounded up the three cement steps and wrapped her up in his arms. "Have I told you lately that I love you?"

"Yes. I think you stole that line from a song." She giggled in response to his nips along her neck. "Come on. I want to show you the dining room. They finished restoring the stained-glass window yesterday."

He followed her inside the big house through the back door. Eli had supported her dream, even if he couldn't fathom spending so much money on a house that was derelict and rotting away. But, since she was spending her own money, and she had plenty of it, Eli stood back and let her do her thing.

Every day, the progress excited her. But too soon, she was needed back in Tennessee. She had a new album to record. Her team was preparing for her next concert tour and planning her promo schedule. The crazy train would start up again, and she was ready to climb aboard. As much as she'd enjoyed managing her house project, she was anxious to get back to her music. This time, though, she wouldn't let the industry control her life.

When they entered the dining room, Eli went straight over to the large stained-glass window that dominated the south side of the room. "They did a great job." He traced over a section of indigo glass with his finger.

This room, along with the entire house, kept as much original construction as possible, which was mixed with new plaster walls and freshly milled wood. She found the combination of smells inspiring.

Jordan spun him around, wanting his full attention, and her fingers danced up his torso and across his hard chest. "There's something I'd like to discuss with you, now that we finally have a minute alone."

Eli sucked in his breath. His arms tightened around her. "I have some things I'd like to discuss, too." He drew her into a deep kiss, moving his lip over hers with demanding urgency.

Jordan felt the earth tilt under her feet. She grabbed on to Eli's biceps for balance. The feel of his muscles under her hands only increased the spinning sensation. Every time she kissed him, she experienced this thrill ride. He did amazing things to her brain. And to her body.

She needed to catch her breath, so she disentangled her lips from his. "When I said discuss, I really meant discuss."

He frowned. "Oh. That's not what I meant."

"I know." She stepped back, away from the heat radiating off his body. "It's about Phil. Or Phil's retirement."

"Didn't he give you names of associates for you to meet with?" Eli studied the crystal chandelier hanging above their heads. "You keeping that?"

"Probably." She needed to turn his attention back to her.

Over the past months, she'd noticed Eli was easily distracted by shiny things. Kind of like a cat.

"I already met with Phil's recommendations, and I just didn't connect with any of them. I need someone who I can trust, wholeheartedly. I don't want a yes man."

"Then hire a woman." Eli shrugged. "You still have time to find someone you click with."

Jordan stepped forward and placed the palms of her hands over Eli's heart. "I don't need more time. I've found the perfect person for the job. That is, if he wants it."

Eli tipped his head in question.

"I'm talking about you, Eli. You know enough about the music industry to start, and Phil would mentor you. I'm an established artist, so you'd basically be keeping the wheel spinning for me, so to speak." She pleaded with her eyes and stuck out her lower lip. "I'd pay you what I pay Phil. You can hire more help for the farm. Think about it, Eli. You'd make a perfect manager."

He stepped back. Not a good sign. Letting out a deep breath, he turned to face the stained-glass window, looking away from her. "It's a nice offer, but I had another title in mind." Turning toward her, he held out his hand. Resting on top his large, rough palm was an opened jewelry box. Something sparkled inside the blue velvet. "I was hoping for husband."

The world around Jordan started to spin again. The rainbow of colors highlighting the walls shimmered and danced.

Eli dropped before her, resting on one knee. "Jordan Ann Spencer. I love you. I want to spend my life at your side, in whatever capacity you need. And you should know that this proposal received the seal of approval from both Lita and Elliot."

She fell to her knees and planted a kiss on his lips. "Yes. Nothing would make me happier."

He stood first, and then took her hand to help her onto her feet.

"Before we celebrate, I want to tell you I'm thinking of selling the farm."

"Why? You don't have to sell in order for us to be together." She stroked Eli's stubble-covered cheek. "Let's talk before you make a final decision."

"The papers have been drawn up." He grinned. "Heidi wants to buy me out."

"What?" She wasn't sure she heard him right. Heidi? Run the dairy farm by herself?

"My sister is a very smart businesswoman. She's made some profitable investments with her savings and has enough to buy me outright. I'll pay off Nikki's share and be free of that obligation. Heidi has some good ideas for the farm. Ways to diversify and expand. She'll hire help where needed. And I'll be free to move, if that's what we decide is best for our family."

Jordan's heart was close to bursting with joy. "I guess this means I'll be a stepmom, as well as a wife."

His kiss was warm and gentle. "They asked me if they could call you Mom. I told them you'd have to accept my proposal first. And then, you'd have to agree to the title. If you don't want them calling you Mom, we can think of something else. Your Royal Highness, perhaps?"

Laughing, she rested against him. "I have no interest in becoming royalty."

Singer. Songwriter. Celebrity. Business owner.

Growing up unloved and abused, she'd never imagined laying claim to any of those titles. Now, looking at Eli, her future, the love of her life, she'd add wife and mother to that list.

"They'll call me Mom, starting today." Jordan's gaze traveled around the newly remodeled dining room, finally resting on Eli's handsome, smiling face. "And they'll always know that no matter where they are, or where they live, as long as we're together, they'll always be home."

ABOUT THE AUTHOR

Laurie Winter is a warrior of the heart. Inspired by her dreams, she creates authentic characters who overcome the odds and find true love. She keeps her life balanced with yoga and running. When not pounding the pavement or the keyboard, she enjoys time with her extended family who are scattered between Wisconsin and Michigan. Laurie has three kids and one fantastic husband, all who inspire her to chase her dreams.

Connect with Laurie –
lauriewinter.com
facebook.com/LaurieWinterAuthor
twitter.com/lauriew_author
instagram.com/lauriewinter_author

www.BOROUGHSPUBLISHINGGROUP.com

If you enjoyed this book, please write a review. Our authors appreciate the feedback, and it helps future readers find books they love. We welcome your comments and invite you to send them to info@boroughspublishinggroup.com. Follow us on Facebook, Twitter and Instagram, and be sure to sign up for our newsletter for surprises and new releases from your favorite authors.

Are you an aspiring writer? Check out www.boroughspublishinggroup.com/submit and see if we can help you make your dreams come true.

www.ingramcontent.com/pod-product-compliance
Lightning Source LLC
Chambersburg PA
CBHW030134180626
46812CB00002B/690